FIVE WAYS

TO

FALL OUT

OF

Love

**Books by Emily Martin
available from Inkyard Press**

Five Ways to Fall Out of Love

FIVE WAYS TO FALL OUT OF Love

Emily Martin

inkyard PRESS

ISBN-13: 978-1-335-14795-0

Five Ways to Fall Out of Love

This edition published by arrangement with Harlequin Books S.A.

For questions and comments about the quality of this book, please contact us at CustomerService@Harlequin.com.

Inkyard Press
22 Adelaide St. West, 40th Floor
Toronto, Ontario M5H 4E3, Canada
www.InkyardPress.com

Printed in U.S.A.

Recycling programs for this product may not exist in your area.

To my BFFs, Katie and Olivia

ONE:

Ghosted

WEBSTER – JUNIOR YEAR

1

I'M DEFINITELY NOT getting stood up.

Webster and I got our wires crossed, that's all. He forgot we were supposed to head over to Reese's house together before the dance, thought we were meeting at the school instead. He's probably waiting in the gymnasium right now, unaware his phone doesn't get any signal in there (which is why he hasn't responded to any of my texts), and so he's starting to wonder if *I'm* standing *him* up.

I wear a path in the living room carpet, back and forth in front of the micro-suede couch where my mother sits.

She tosses her *People* magazine onto the coffee table and reaches for her phone. "Why don't I call Carol and see if she knows where Webster is?"

"You cannot call my date's mother, that's…" *Humiliating.* I press my palm against the wrinkle on the front of my satin skirt and resume pacing.

"Hang on, stop there," she says when I'm in front of the fireplace. She lifts her phone higher. "Now smile."

"Mom."

She takes a few photos, her gaze locked on the screen instead of me.

I tug my hand through my hair, remembering too late that it's pinned back and coated with approximately half a can of hairspray. I extricate my fingers carefully to minimize the damage. "Do I really look like I want to remember this moment?"

"Sorry, honey. I promised your dad I'd get some pictures of you all dressed up."

The fact that my father is away on business remains the only bright spot of the evening. One less witness to my failed attempt at a first date. Plus, if they were both here, my parents would inevitably find something to fight about—me, probably—and honestly, I don't think my nerves could take that tonight.

"Maybe I should give him a few more minutes," I say, even though we've been waiting for over an hour. Reese and the rest of our group already left for the dance.

Come to think of it, Webster's car hasn't been in his driveway all afternoon. What if something happened to him?

I picture him getting ready, knotting his tie when he realizes—he forgot my corsage. And since he can't show up at my door empty-handed, he grabs his keys.

The whole way to the florist, he's distracted by thoughts of us on the dance floor. My arms around his neck and his hands on my waist, holding me close. He can smell my perfume, the same citrusy scent I wore all summer, and he's remembering how well we fit together, like that time we spent all day in the sun and fell asleep lying on the hammock in his backyard, and he's so wrapped up in the memory he doesn't notice the light has turned red—

In a movie, that's how it would happen. A terrible accident, Webster lying in a hospital bed somewhere, bruised and broken. And then I'd get a call from his mother, telling me he's awake, that he's asking for me.

In reality, the next time my phone buzzes, it's Reese's name on the screen. I'm still picturing Webster in a full-body cast as I read her message: He's here. I'm so sorry.

My mom is watching me, waiting to hear what it says.

"It's from Reese," I tell her. I stare at the message a beat longer before adding, "It was a miscommunication. Like I thought."

I lock the screen and grip my phone tight. The *I'm so sorry* included in her message makes it pretty clear Reese doesn't think this is a misunderstanding. But it has to be. And if it isn't…if Webster is blowing me off, he better have a damn good explanation.

"So I'm just going to head over to the school, meet up with everyone there."

"Oh. All right. Well, make sure you get a picture of you and Webster together."

Right. I need to get a grip. Get my purse.

I shove my phone and keys into the navy satin clutch I borrowed from Mom. She takes one more picture of me standing by the stairs, then ushers me out the door.

"Have a great time tonight, sweetie. And text me if you need anything, okay?"

I nod and shuffle to my car. A blister has bloomed on the

back of my heel. These shoes are killing me—I shouldn't have put them on so early. But it's fine. Once I get to the dance and talk to Webster, everything will be fine.

This is what I tell myself as I drive through our subdivision toward school, the silence like cotton stuffed in my ears. My turn signal too loud as I pull onto the main road. Finally I reach the student lot and pull into the first parking spot I find, and then practically launch out of the car.

As I walk to the gym entrance, the yellow lights overhead turn my dress a sickly green color. My shadow stretches out beside me, sticking to my ankles with every step, as though trying to drag me back to my car. I pick up my pace, the crisp October air biting at my bare arms as I hurry toward the double doors.

My hand shakes as I show my school ID to check in. I spot Reese and her sister Becca standing behind the small army of teachers here to chaperone. Becca is wearing jeans and a camera around her neck—she's taking pictures for yearbook tonight. Suddenly I wish I had a better reason for being here, a camera to hide behind. As I head over to them, I flex my fingers, fidget with the straps of my dress.

As soon as I'm close, Becca casts me an awkward sort of smile that tells me she—like everyone else, probably—knows exactly how my night started. She lifts her camera. "Duty calls. I'll see you guys in there."

Reese puts on her fake cheerleader smile, the one she wears when she asks everyone in the stands to give her a *B-R-O-N-C-O-S, Goooo Broncos!* "Yeah, see you in a minute."

I grip my clutch between both hands and step around Reese, beelining for the gym doors. "Actually, I'm ready now."

"Aubrey, hang on—"

Reese follows me into the gymnasium, which looks exactly like it does during every terrible PE class, except the normal greenish hue of the fluorescents has been replaced with a multicolored light flashing from the DJ's booth, and some streamers and balloons have been stuck to the walls like Band-Aids.

We weave through kids dancing in clusters. It doesn't take long to spot Webster across the gym, standing in a loose circle of friends near the DJ. It instantly becomes clear he has not been in a terrible car wreck. Which…I have mixed feelings about.

Reese grabs my wrist. She nods toward her boyfriend and the rest of our group standing a few yards away. "Forget him. Come dance with us, we can still have fun."

I get that she's probably feeling some second-degree embarrassment right now, and that she wants to make it disappear, but obviously I can't just dance my cares away. I can't ignore him when he's standing *right there*, when I still have no clue why he wanted to hurt me.

I shake my head and tug out of her grasp. She immediately starts to pull at one eyebrow, a nervous habit she's been trying to kick for as long as I've known her. Carried by adrenaline, I start over to Webster, and it isn't until I'm too close—close enough for him to see me coming—that I notice the hard set to his jaw. I falter, but only for a second, because there's no turning back now.

"Can I talk to you?" I ask when I reach him.

He lifts his eyebrows like he's surprised, like my urgent tone is coming out of nowhere. "Sure."

My shoulders curl forward like the edges of paper lit on fire. He follows me past the wooden bleachers and the banners listing the school's track and field records, through the open doors and into the hall. Away from the dance floor, the air is less humid and the music softens to a dull pulse. Webster crosses his arms and suddenly all six feet of him seem to hover over me. Even in heels, I feel short compared to him.

"Are you…" My voice is unsteady. I swallow hard. "You came here alone?"

Webster's answering smile is bladed.

"But." I shift my weight, fold my arms even though Mom would be pissed off that I'm covering up the dress we paid so much for. I'm waiting for him to clarify. To tell me he drove alone but he isn't *here* alone, because those two things are different. I'm waiting for him to ask me to dance, except it's abundantly clear that's not going to happen. "We said we'd come together."

Webster's jaw twitches. "Yeah. Well. I decided I'd rather come with my friends."

My whole face has that stiff, swollen feeling that comes before a good cry. I still don't understand what's even happening right now—I've mentally retraced my steps, but I can't figure out where I stumbled, what could have changed between the last time we spoke and now to make him look at me like I just kicked a dog, like I disgust him. Like we were never friends in the first place. "Why are you doing this?"

He shakes his head at the ceiling, as if he can't believe he's having this conversation. Which makes two of us.

I rock forward and touch his arm just below the elbow. "Webster…please, just—"

"Stop." He pulls out of reach. "Can we be done with this now?"

I flinch and step back. My ankle wobbles.

For a second, Webster's expression is softer, almost pained. And in that moment I allow myself to believe he'll take it all back, offer a real explanation, apologize. Instead he straightens. Steers his gaze over the top of my head, like he's already half forgotten I exist. Like he's forgotten about everything we shared with each other over the summer.

By late August, it seemed impossible only two months had passed since Webster and his newly divorced mother moved in across the street. Two months since I'd worked up the courage to introduce myself, armed with a pan of brownies and the made-up excuse my own mother had sent me over. Because by August, I felt like I'd known Webster forever.

Finally I look away from him as well, glancing instead at the door to the gym, and then the basketball hoop anchored to the ceiling inside. But that just reminds me of summer, too, all those afternoons Webster spent teaching me to shoot free throws in his driveway. Before school started, and before my fears Webster would join the basketball team and achieve instant popularity became reality. Back when I was the only person Webster knew in our slice of suburban wasteland, when he was still nervous about being the new kid and I was still the last person he spoke to before bed most nights. Back when it was just us.

"I thought we were friends," I say. When I asked him to this dance and he said yes, I thought…I thought we could be more than friends. "Why do you suddenly hate me?"

Webster huffs a humorless laugh. I notice for the first time that all the freckles he acquired along his nose this past summer have faded. He holds my gaze, a look on his face like the answer should be obvious. "You make it easy."

I bite the inside of my lip, hard. Anything to help me ignore the sharp sting in my eyes.

"But hey, have a *great* night, Aubrey." He steps toward the gym entrance, then turns to face me once more. "I'm sure you can find someone else to share a pity dance with."

With that, he's gone, beelining back to his group of friends. Through the open door I can see all of them laughing, some behind closed hands while others literally double over in hysterics, clapping Webster on the shoulder once he's back within reach. He's smiling, laughing along with them.

I bolt down the hallway. My heel catches on the waxed floor, and I stumble but keep moving. I duck into the closest bathroom and shut myself in the last stall, the one with cigarette burns on the white plastic toilet seat. I lean against the cool wall. My fingers trace the spot where the paint is scrubbed away, the spot where last year someone wrote, *Veronica King is a slut.*

It's no wonder Webster fits in so well here—our school is full of assholes.

"Aubrey?" Reese's feet appear on the other side of the metal door. "Are you okay?"

My throat squeezes; I can't answer. Instead I rip off a few squares of the world's thinnest toilet paper. It's rough against my lips, shredding as I scrub off my lipstick. All night I didn't eat anything because I was afraid of messing up my stupid makeup.

"If you don't open the door, I'm crawling under."

I toss the stained paper into the toilet and watch the water seep through, soften the pink shade like a watercolor.

Reese sighs and the next moment she drops to her stomach and army crawls under the door, which effectively breaks me out of my trance.

"Oh my god." I laugh, and it sounds watery. "You're such a creep."

"I know, right?" Reese climbs to her feet and dusts off the front of her dress. She's slow to lift her gaze to meet mine again, and when she does, it's with a wince, her gaze flickering around my face like she's looking for a wound to treat.

Pressure builds behind my eyes again, and this time I can't hold in the tears. "He said it was easy to hate me."

"*What?* I'm so sorry, babe," she says as she pulls me into a hug.

I sniff over her shoulder. No point trying to hold it together now. Reese can read me better than anyone, which is why she didn't believe me the other day when I tried to pretend I'd only asked Webster to this dance to make my mother happy. Reese knows how much I like him. How much this hurts. "I don't know what I did."

"Nothing." Reese leans back. "Seriously, he's an asshole, end of story."

If that's true, I want an epilogue. I deserve to know why Webster is acting this way, why he'd rather come to a school dance *alone* than as my date. I keep replaying our conversation, trying to find some hidden meaning behind his words, but nothing he said makes any sense.

Reese rips off some more toilet paper and blots my face.

The tissue comes away black from my mascara. "I'm a mess," I say. "I have to get out of here."

"I'll go with you."

"You can't leave." I sniffle again, wipe my nose on the back of my hand. "You're on the homecoming court."

She hesitates. Reese hates nothing more than feeling like she's missing out. We both know she doesn't want to bail.

"Then you should stay, too! Screw Webster." Already those words sound like a mantra. "Don't let him ruin your night."

A few girls walk in, a scuffle of heels against the tile floor, and I shrink back against the wall. "It was ruined hours ago. I just want to go home."

I want to disappear. So after one more hug and a promise to call Reese in the morning, I slip out of the stall and do my best to be invisible. Outside, I chase my shadow across the parking lot and start ripping bobby pins out of my hair. Slowly my updo comes undone. A small mountain of pins collects in my palm as stiff, unnatural curls fall down my neck. My scalp is screaming. My hair feels tacky and unclean and *how are there still so many bobby pins attached to my head???*

I reach my car and slide into the driver's seat, chuck the bobby pins into the cup holder. My hands are trembling again as I put the key into the ignition and check my rearview mirror—and that's when I see it. Webster's car, parked directly behind mine.

I turn my engine off. Shift in my seat and glare at his car through my rear window. Webster shouldn't get away with treating me this way. Because it's not as though Webster just ruined tonight. It's not like tomorrow I'll be able to move on, forget this ever happened. People are going to talk about it at school. Everyone will know Webster only said yes to me as some kind of *Carrie*-esque prank. He and all his jock friends will laugh every time they pass me in the halls.

And seeing as I'm never speaking to him again, I'll probably never get a real explanation.

I throw open my door and pop the trunk, dig a pair of needle-nose pliers out of the extensive roadside emergency kit my dad gave me the moment I got my driver's license. And then I walk over to crouch between Webster's car and the SUV parked beside it.

I almost text Reese for backup, despite the fact this definitely isn't a two-person job, but she's probably just gotten back onto the dance floor, and even if she *was* willing to be my accomplice, she'd want to do this later, when we've had enough time to plan every little detail, like what outfit would make us blend in most with our surroundings, and what alibi would be the most airtight. But if I wait I won't do it, because *I am not this person.*

Except all four valve stem caps are currently in my palm, and the needle-nose pliers are fitting into the stem just like my dad taught me, and the tire is making a *whooshing* sound, and I can see it start to deflate. So…I guess this is exactly who I am now.

After it's done I drive home on autopilot, past the mall and a few of the newer subdivisions full of identical McMansions. When I pull onto my street, my gaze catches on Webster's driveway. I slow to a stop between our houses. The floodlight above the garage illuminates his basketball hoop.

He's everywhere I look.

I won't be able to avoid him. Not for the next two years. But I can make sure of one thing:

Webster Casey will never, ever hurt me again.

TWO:
The Walking Wounded

MOM AND DAD – SENIOR YEAR

2

I THINK WE can all agree New Year's Eve is an overhyped holiday. The notion that this one night is somehow symbolic of the next twelve months is absolutely ridiculous.

And yet.

I'd be a bit more optimistic about my future if I wasn't about to crash Webster Casey's party.

This whole thing was Reese's idea. I was perfectly content with our original plan to eat popcorn for dinner and lounge in our pajamas and mock all the people freezing their asses off in places like Times Square. But Reese is still in the hearts-for-eyes phase of her newest relationship. As soon as the boyfriend texted to invite us (but really just her) to Webster's and the words *midnight kiss* came out of her mouth, I knew our girls' night was a lost cause.

And since Reese could sell a hot dog to a vegan, I regret

to admit it took her less than twenty minutes to talk me into tagging along.

See, in the version of tonight she painted, coming here was a giant *eff you* to Webster, proof that I am completely over what he did to me junior year. But now that I'm standing on his front porch, I find myself simultaneously sweating through my clothes and shivering. Though that's also partly because, at Reese's urging, I skipped snow boots in favor of stilettos, paired with my favorite high-waisted jeans to make my legs appear significantly longer than they actually are.

"Okay, you look miserable," Reese says with her finger poised over the doorbell. Her hand drops to her side. "We can bail if you want. Just say the word."

The thing is, Webster has always had the upper hand. He was never able to pin the tire incident on me, but he's found so many small ways to make my life miserable since then. Constantly slamming my locker door closed when I'm still using it, or the time he "accidentally" dropped his basketball on my lunch tray. It's been over a year and I still leave for school fifteen minutes earlier than I need to, just so I won't run into him.

But as I look at the driveway where we spent hours shooting hoops that first summer, it doesn't feel like so long ago that Webster was grilling me about the social scene at school, about how the cafeteria food was and whether the majority of kids wore backpacks.

It doesn't seem so long ago that Webster trusted me with his biggest secret.

"It's going to be weird, not knowing anyone at school," he said one day while we were sitting in the shade of his backyard.

I picked up a helicopter leaf from the maple overhead and twirled it around by the stem. I tossed it in the air and watched it spin back down to my lap. "Well, you'll really like Reese. Everyone does." Reese had been gone practically the entire summer, first on vacation with her family, and then at cheer camp. I'd told her all about Webster already, but it was so weird that my two best friends hadn't met yet. I was dying to introduce them. "And you've got me."

"True. But…" His jaw worked for a moment before he spoke again. "The thing is, we haven't actually known each other that long, and there are things—it doesn't get easier, even if you know you can trust someone, because every time it's like starting over, you know?"

"Um…not exactly." I shifted to face him. "Sorry, you kind of lost me…"

He licked his lips and looked down at the ever-present basketball in his hands. Back up at me. "I'm bisexual."

"Oh." *Yes, good, give the most inadequate response possible.* But the thing was, no one had ever come out to me before. I only knew one openly gay kid—Phil Marlow—who was a grade below us and had been out since before high school, so everyone was just kind of *aware.* But I didn't know what would be the right thing to say. I didn't want to come off like it changed the way I felt about him, but I also didn't want to sound like I was brushing past it when it was clearly a big deal for him to tell me. I swallowed and put on a shy smile and finally managed to add, "Okay."

He scratched his temple, then raked his hand through his shaggy hair. "Yeah. So. That's a thing no one here knows about me. And I don't think… I'm not ready to go through it all again. To be out at school. So will you keep it between us?"

"Of course," I said quickly. "I won't say anything to anyone, I promise. And…thank you. For telling me."

Now I shift my gaze to his car, to the Pride bumper sticker he put on after coming out at school at the beginning of senior year. A lot has changed since we were juniors, for both of us. And Reese was right, I shouldn't allow Webster—or the past—to have this power over me anymore. "No, it's fine. I'm good."

"Are you sure?"

I reach around her to hit the doorbell in response.

"Listen, Kevin said there are a bunch of people here," she says, talking fast. "So chances are you won't even have to interact with Web. Plus, it's not like we have far to go if the party ends up sucking."

Inside the pocket of my coat I start fiddling with my Chap-Stick, nudging the cap off with my thumb and then pushing it back down until I feel the satisfying *click*.

Mrs. Casey opens the door. "Hi, girls, come on in!" She steps to the side to let us pass. "The kids are all downstairs. And, Aubrey, I think your mom is in the living room if you want to say hello."

We shrug off our coats, and I scan the rooms full of boozy adults for my parents. A bunch of people are clustered around the dining room table where the food is set up, but in a sea of balding heads, my father's is nowhere to be found. Through the sliding glass door in the kitchen, I spot another group of men outside smoking cigars. Dad hates the smell of tobacco in all forms, but he's a sucker for anything he thinks men are supposed to enjoy, so I'd be willing to bet he's out there drinking scotch and discussing his golf game.

Reese points her chin to a spot over my shoulder. "Behold your future."

December 31 has always brought out the worst in my mom, same as when she decides to go on one of her diets and spends the whole day before bingeing on ice cream. As if tomorrow she'll miraculously wake up as the person she's always wanted to be, so what's the harm in making a few terrible choices tonight?

I know better. I know you can't just wish for something to change and expect it to happen. Change requires actual work—a concept lost entirely on the woman currently belting out an old Prince song with her champagne flute raised overhead.

"I'm going to assume that was in reference to getting our hands on some alcohol, and not a broader commentary on my genetic makeup."

Reese bites down on her grin and kindly refrains from pointing out I inherited my mother's nose and that we both stopped growing at five foot four. "Of course it was."

She threads her arm through mine and steers me toward the door off the kitchen that leads to Webster's basement. I let her pull me along because, despite the very real concern that I will in fact turn out like my mother—who is now urging those around her to sing along—I'm sick of being the only sober person in sight.

We descend into the finished basement, and I check to make sure my nose isn't running after coming in from outside. My stomach doesn't feel right. I'm coming down with something—the flu, probably. Plus, my parents rarely leave the house together anymore, so I should really go back and enjoy the peace and quiet while it lasts. But before I can offer up an excuse and bail, we reach the bottom step.

The first thing I notice is a bed set up in one corner of the basement. Navy comforter, plaid sheets, drunken classmates clamoring for a spot on the end closest to the TV. A ton of people are packed into this tiny area, but unfortunately Reese was wrong when she claimed it would be easy to avoid Webster. He's standing right next to Reese's boyfriend, and both of them beeline over the second she locks eyes.

"Aubrey." Webster slings his arm around my shoulders and squeezes my neck a little too tight. He's drunk. And as big an asshole as ever. "Good of you to take a night off from polishing your rock collection to join us."

My skin tingles in the spots he's touching. I shrug his hand off me, but he keeps on grinning like he just unearthed a photo album filled with old pictures of me, all braces and the unfortunate cowlick I tried to pass off as bangs until I met Reese and she talked some sense into me.

I automatically finger comb the front of my hair—which I made the grave error of chopping into a short bob at the end of last summer. It looked great for about two weeks, and I've been waiting for it to get long enough to fit into a ponytail again ever since.

"Already moved into your mom's basement, I see. Should be really cozy down here by the time you're thirty-five."

He sucks his teeth in mock regret. "Yeah. Guess you'll have to find another use for that telescope now that our bedrooms aren't facing each other."

"And how does Webster define *creeper*?" I ask. "With a self-portrait, perhaps?"

"*Okay*, let's all play nice." As a cheerleader, Reese seems to feel a moral obligation to keep spirits high in situations like this. But as she is well aware, Webster is about as likely to *play nice* as a grizzly bear.

"Why don't we get you ladies something to drink?" Kevin asks. And aside from the obvious fact that she's finally found someone as enthusiastic about watching random documentaries and attending trivia nights as she is, I'm starting to see why Reese likes him so much. He's got great ideas.

He leads us away from Webster, around the stairs and past a folding table to a little bar area packed with sports memorabilia. The bar top is scattered with the usual flimsy decorations—cheap cardboard glasses shaped into numbers and plastic noisemakers that will just end up in the trash tomorrow—and the drink selection is limited to bourbon and a vanilla-flavored vodka presumably smuggled in by someone with a fake ID or an older sibling.

I've met Webster's mom numerous times, and while she's a nice woman who doesn't come off as particularly oblivious, she does seem to have her head in the sand when it comes to Webster. Then again, so do the majority of my classmates. I look forward to the day he's no longer a basketball star and the realization dawns that he actually has nothing else going for him. But until then, as our resident golden boy, he gets away with murder.

Though I'm not particularly mad about it as I pick up the bottle of bourbon and pour a healthy dose into my cup. I mix it with some Coke and sip my drink while Reese makes hers, and then we start to mingle. And by mingle, I mean I follow Reese around while she does her social butterfly thing, greeting every single person we pass. She has this innate ability to make conversation with literally anyone. It's partly her personality, and partly because Reese's interests are ridiculously varied—her bedside table is always piled high with library books covering everything from philosophy to fashion design, and she's changed her mind about what she wants to major in next year at least a dozen times.

Most of the guys she's dated have been popular, or at least popular-adjacent, but I have to hand it to Kevin—he's the first one who can keep up with her, both in terms of her subject-hopping and her inclination to say hello to everyone she sees.

She waves at another cheerleader, Sam Palmer, and her boyfriend, Mike Chen. Sam's sweet, and one of the few cheerleaders who actually acknowledges my presence whenever I'm shadowing Reese like this. Her boyfriend seems like kind of a douche, but to be fair, I've never actually talked to him. And I guess he must not be all bad, since the two of them have been together since they were fifteen, which—side note—is incomprehensible to me.

"Hey, Dan!" Reese nudges my rib cage while Kevin does a complicated handshake with Dan Epstein. "You guys know each other, right?" she asks as she looks at me.

"Um…" If seeing him throw up in fourth grade gym class and then picturing that every time I'm in the same room with him counts as knowing each other…sure.

"Yeah, I've seen you around," he offers.

"Did you know Dan plays point guard?" Reese asks with a suggestive lilt.

"No, but…good for you, Dan."

"Yeah, thanks." He promptly turns to his buddy, making it clear he doesn't find me any more interesting than I find him.

We end up standing near the table, which is being used to play flip cup. I stash my coat under the table and scan the basement again. The countdown in Times Square is playing on the big screen by Webster's bed, and I try to catch Reese's attention with a smirk, but she's wrapped up in what Kevin is saying and doesn't notice.

To her credit, Reese never actually ditches me for the guy she's dating. She makes every attempt to loop me into the discussion over the next half hour. It's just, there's only so much I can contribute to a conversation that revolves around basketball (a sport I know next to nothing about) and an essay assigned before break in AP French (a class I don't take).

I turn back to the TV and note the time. Another hour until midnight. I'm not convinced I'll last that long.

But going home now would just mean watching some movie I've already seen a million times, and then tomorrow Reese will call and tell me what a great time she had and probably lecture me about how people would really love me if I just put myself out there a little more.

All the guys standing on our side of the table let out a collective yell and start jumping around, sounding entirely too pleased with themselves, considering the object of their game is literally to drink fast and flip a cup over. It causes a tidal wave, a ripple of bodies pushing back until someone gets shoved into me—and spills his entire drink down the front of my shirt in the process.

I gasp and lift my hands like a shield, though of course it's

too late to do anything except die a slow death while everyone around me makes *ooh* sounds under their breath. I can't
tell if these noises are born out of sympathy or because they're
laughing at me. The guy jumps into action, hands flutter-
ing as he searches his pockets for…I'm not sure what, exactly. Presumably a tissue, which wouldn't do a hell of a lot
of good at this point.

"Oh, god. I'm so sorry. Here, let me—" He thrusts his
empty cup at me, which bounces off the back of my hand. I
try to catch it and end up sloshing the contents of my own
cup onto my arm. He freezes, eyes wide.

I lick my lips and blink up at him. "Seriously?"

He stands with his mouth open like a fish, and behind
him, I catch a glimpse of Webster—an unmistakable glint
of amusement in his eye. Pressure builds in my throat and I
lift my gaze to the ceiling and blow out a big breath. Screw
this. Screw New Year's and screw Webster Casey most of all.

"I'm out." I hand my cup to Reese and go to get my stuff.
I'm on my hands and knees, digging through the pile of coats
under the table, when someone crouches beside me.

"Hey." I turn to see the spiller gripping a stack of New-
Year's-Eve-themed cocktail napkins. "I'm so sorry about before."

I finally find my coat and push to my feet. The spiller follows suit and holds the napkins out to me. I don't really want
them at this point, but I take the pile because it seems more
awkward not to. His hands dive into the front pockets of his
jeans.

"It's fine." I blot my shirt with one of the napkins, try to
squeeze the moisture out.

"Are you leaving?"

"Yes," I say at the same time Reese sidles up to me and blurts, "No way!"

She flashes him a smile. "Well, Aubrey was considering leaving, but I think if we work together we can convince her to stay."

I'd ask what the hell she's doing, but I'm all too familiar with the routine at this point. Every time Reese starts a new relationship, she decides I need someone to date, too. So she gets super aggressive in her matchmaking pursuits, despite how many times I've told her I don't want a boyfriend.

Reese is cursed with a romantic streak, and she seems to think I'll change my mind if I meet the right guy. She thinks I'm ridiculous for ruling out the possibility of falling in love, for believing love doesn't actually lead to happiness—at least, not forever. But it's not like I pulled this theory out of thin air. Living with my parents has provided all the evidence I need to back it up.

"That would be fantastic actually, because I'm told I make a great second impression." He sticks out his hand again. "I'm Holland, by the way."

I'm still not sure why he wants to prolong this interaction, but I stop fiddling with my wet shirt and wipe my palm on my hip, which is about the only dry spot of clothing I have left, then shake his hand. "Aubrey."

Reese takes the napkins from me and gestures to the bar. "I'm just going to get us some fresh drinks. Back in a flash."

I try to grab Reese's arm, but she slips away. I huff and offer Holland a flat smile. "Look, no hard feelings or anything, but my friend was a bit overly optimistic just then. I really do have to take off."

He squints at me, a smile tugging at the corners of his mouth. "That's too bad. This has the potential to be a pretty epic meet-cute, don't you think?"

I swallow a comment about how I'm pretty sure it doesn't count as a meet-cute if you're immediately irritated by the other person.

Reese reappears holding two cups. She hands one to me and the other to Holland, then takes my coat and spins away again, ignoring me when I call after her.

Holland holds his cup up. "Cheers."

I shake my head before ultimately caving and tapping my cup against his. I take a sip and eye him over the rim. I'm 99 percent sure I've never seen this kid before. And while I'm nowhere near as popular as Reese, I do think I'd at least recognize him if he went to our school. Especially since he's not terrible looking. He has cropped dark hair and blue eyes with a ring of golden brown around the pupil. He's also ridiculously tall. I'm tempted to ask his height, but then I decide I don't care. "So, Spiller. Is there a reason I've never seen you around before?"

He gestures for me to come in close, like it's a secret. "Since we're already such good friends, I guess I can tell you... I go to West Rochester. I play basketball over there, so I'm trying to keep a low profile."

"Ohh," I say dramatically. Clearly I'm supposed to care that our teams are rivals, but we're halfway through senior year and I'm fresh out of school spirit. "So in other words, you couldn't find anyone from your own school to hang out with?"

"Ouch." He clutches his heart, but a smile takes his face hostage, cuts parentheses into his cheeks and crinkles the edges of his eyes. "That hurts, Aubrey. Especially since I've been working up my nerve all night to come talk to you."

"Is that right?"

"Yeah, I was hoping for a smoother introduction."

"What were you going to lead off with?"

He gives an easy shrug. "Probably a picture of my dog."

I sip my drink and lift one eyebrow. "Well, let's see it, then."

He pulls his phone out of his pocket and shows me the wallpaper. It's a picture of an adorable pit bull with a pink rhinestone collar.

"What a good girl!" It rushes out without my consent. But this dog, though. I need her in my life.

"See, I knew that would have worked." He grins and tilts the phone back toward himself. "She is good. Her name's Lucy. I'm fostering her for the next few months, getting her healthy enough to be adopted. Though I'm kind of hoping my parents will fall for her and want to keep her."

"Wait," I say, making myself sound super impressed. "You play basketball *and* you foster puppies? Swoon."

"This is what I've been trying to tell you. I'm kind of a catch, Aubrey."

I take another drink. "Clearly."

He laughs and shakes his head, all self-deprecating. "I do love animals, though. I'm actually thinking about becoming a vet."

I nearly choke on my next sip. "Wait, really?"

My smile must be weird, because his expression suddenly turns self-conscious. "Yeah. Why?"

"No, just...that's what I want to do, too."

This gets a reaction—his whole face lights up. "Wow. Who knew we'd have so much in common, am I right?"

To curb his excessive enthusiasm, I pretend to be interested in something across the room. But he keeps watching me, his mouth turned up in a pleased little smile. I roll my eyes and shift my gaze back to him. And I can't explain it, this sudden urge to find another common interest.

I notice the design on his T-shirt. "Are you a Janelle Monáe fan?"

"Huh?"

I point to the logo on his chest.

"Oh. Um. Actually, this isn't my shirt."

"Why are you wearing someone else's shirt?"

He scratches the back of his neck... "I don't want to tell you."

I cock my head. "I think you know you have to now."

His ears turn bright pink. He looks at the ceiling and smiles like he's bracing for something. "I knocked over a glass of pop at dinner."

My jaw shifts, barely containing my smile. "I'm sorry, aren't basketball players supposed to be good with their hands?"

His blush migrates down his neck. "*Anyway*, my cousin loaned me this shirt." He nods over my shoulder, to the far end of the table. Where Webster is standing. Because of course he is.

My thumb indents the side of my red plastic cup. "Webster Casey is your cousin?"

"Yeah."

"Did he tell you to do all this?"

"Do what?"

My eyes narrow, and I wait for Holland to crack. But he looks completely puzzled. My paranoia is getting the best of me. "Never mind. So…you're a Casey, then?"

He grins wide enough to hollow out dimples in his cheeks again. "Technically I'm a Sawyer? Suddenly that feels like an important distinction."

"I see."

His lips press together, and his eyes narrow in an amused way. "Are you at all interested in sharing your last name?"

I take another drink before answering. "Cash."

"As in…I'm supposed to pay you for it?"

"No, as in Johnny Cash? That's my last name."

"Aubrey Cash. Nice. Any chance I'll get a middle name, too?"

"No."

"You're right, we should save some of the good stuff for next time." A few people try to get around us, and he gestures for me to follow him to a less crowded spot. We end up leaning against the wall by the bar. "So, Aubrey TBD Cash, it's getting close to midnight. I think we should play a game."

"If it involves drinking whenever someone says 'ball drop,' I'm not playing."

"I was thinking more like coming up with resolutions for each other? I'll go first. As an example, you could resolve to attend more school functions. Like basketball games. Especially when Grove Hill is playing West Rochester."

"Under consideration." I press the rim of my cup against

my mouth, then straighten. "Okay. Your first resolution is to actually listen to Janelle Monáe."

He laughs. "That's fair. And if you like them, I'm sure they're awesome."

We go back and forth like this for a while—Holland daring me to live dangerously and order the meat loaf next time I'm at a diner we discover we both like, while I strongly encourage him to consider the rice pudding for dessert.

Then the energy in the room changes, everyone gathering closer to the TV. The clock at the bar reads 11:59. It's Holland's turn.

He stares down at his cup, which has been empty for a while. He's stalling. "You could always resolve to kiss someone at midnight," he says, and his eyes lift back up to meet mine.

A shyness has taken over his features, and he can barely hold my gaze. My heart rate kicks up. I swallow and glance around the room. "That guy over there is in my English class…"

"Sorry, that resolution was sort of vague. I actually had someone in mind already? Tall guy. Winning smile."

"Spills a lot?"

"That's the one."

The countdown starts. Suddenly my head fills with all the other resolutions I've made lately. To get straight As. To get into college, then vet school. Find a new place to call home so I won't have to come back to my parents' house unless I actually want to. All the work I've already put toward making a change.

I didn't see Holland coming tonight. And I don't know if he fits into anything I have planned. But if nothing else, I'm grateful to him for reminding me it's okay to be spontaneous every now and then. And in this moment, I want him to kiss me.

My voice comes out small. "Okay."

The shouts and all the music around us dim to white noise. My pulse is in my ears as Holland steps closer, slides one hand onto the curve of my waist. I'm looking at our feet, because I can't remember the last time I stood this close to a guy. And then my gaze slides up to his chest, his throat. I meet his eye briefly before turning my attention to his mouth. Holland smiles.

"Happy New Year, Aubrey."

His hand lifts to gently cup my jaw. My fingers find his shirt, tighten around the fabric, and I lift onto my toes as his lips meet mine.

Turns out Reese was right. Midnight kisses can be sort of great.

Suddenly this whole night feels fated, and already I'm thinking about seeing Holland again, getting worked up over this…*spark* between us, something that isn't even real yet.

A pinprick of hope, a tiny thrill of excitement over a make-believe future—it's enough to ruin everything.

We pull apart, and Holland smiles at me. I don't smile back. Instead I say it was nice to meet him. I say, *Have a happy new year*. And then I walk away.

3

"I CAN'T BELIEVE you didn't get his number."

I cradle the phone against my shoulder and carry a basket of clean clothes into my bedroom. Reese has been interrogating me all break about Holland, and keeps circling back to this same point.

"I should've known you'd chicken out. I should've just given him your number myself. I mean, you guys totally hit it off! I assumed you'd at least go on a second date."

"That wasn't a first date. It was a random, meaningless encounter."

"But there was chemistry!"

"Need I remind you he's Webster Casey's cousin?"

"So?"

I dump the basket of clothes onto my bed and start folding a shirt. "*So*, that's not a gene pool I need to get involved in."

"But the kiss was good, right?"

I shake the wrinkles out of another shirt. "I mean. It wasn't terrible."

Truth? I didn't actually know kisses could even be that good. Not that I have much to compare it to, aside from a few make-out sessions with random guys Reese tried to set me up with, but it definitely exceeded expectations. My Cinderella moment—freaking out and running home after the clock struck midnight—wasn't about the kiss. It was about everything that comes after a kiss.

Reese groans. "He seemed so sweet, too. And the way you met was crazy romantic."

"He certainly seemed to think so. Hey, maybe you should date him."

Because I don't see the point. We're talking about a guy who lives thirty minutes away. Which means I'd probably only be able to see him on weekends, and that's when we're not already busy doing our own thing. And only until we leave for college in the fall. Why would I start a relationship that already has a clear expiration date?

"I'm just saying, you guys seemed great together."

The good news is, Reese's disappointment will last only until she meets my next Perfect Match. She's always telling me the right person is just around the corner, so certain soul mates are real and everyone gets one. Her unwavering optimism is actually impressive, considering she's been dumped more times than anyone I know. Which, frankly, is a compelling argument for singledom in and of itself, because Reese is the actual best person alive, not to mention model-pretty, so if *she* can't make a relationship work, then what is the point of trying?

My dad climbs the stairs, yelling the whole way up. "I'm not stupid, Irene. I already looked. I'm telling you we don't have any left."

"And I'm telling you there is a new bottle in the hall closet," Mom yells back.

He throws open the door to the linen closet and mutters something under his breath. After a moment of searching he huffs and pivots toward the stairs again. "It isn't here!"

Mom stomps up the stairs then and I cover the bottom of my phone.

"I told you, behind the nail polish remover, white bottle, green label." She immediately plucks a bottle from the bottom shelf and thrusts it into his hands triumphantly. "I swear to god, John. If you bothered to listen to a single word I say—"

I kick my bedroom door closed. Take a deep breath.

Fights like this used to feel cute. Back when they laughed about them afterward. Before they ended in name-calling and passive-aggressive comments made days later.

Before I knew how broken my parents' marriage really is.

Maybe I should have realized sooner, but it didn't fully sink in until this past fall. The night I was supposed to sleep over at Reese's but wound up getting sick and coming home early. The night I walked in to find my mom cozied up on the couch with some guy named *David* who allegedly worked with her even though I'd literally never heard his name come up before.

It wasn't like I could prove she was lying. Briefly I considered jotting down the license plate number to the BMW he'd parked outside, but then I realized I had no idea what to do with a license plate number. My life is not a TV show;

I'm not a child prodigy turned private investigator with con-nections at the local sheriff's office.

So I let it go. And when she asked me not to say anything to my dad, said he was already upset with how many hours she'd been working and this would only make it worse, I agreed. Because technically I hadn't seen them do anything, so maybe it really was a platonic work thing. And because she was right—telling my dad would only make things worse. They fought so much already, I wasn't even sure what *worse* would look like, but I really didn't want to find out.

I figured it was partly my dad's fault, anyway. If he was home a little more often, maybe it never would have hap-pened.

I put the phone to my ear again. "Can we please just drop the Holland thing?"

"You know, there is someone who would be able to give you his number."

"Reese."

"It's not that big a deal! You could just ask him at school tomorrow."

Talk about a Hail Mary. Reese has to know that there is absolutely no way I'd turn to Webster about this.

As if anticipating my response, Reese adds, "Want me to ask for you?"

"No! Reese, I swear to god if you mention this to him…" The only thing worse than asking Webster for help with my romantic life would be having a friend do it for me. Just think-ing about it makes me want to curl up and die.

"You seriously want to drop this? Forget about the whole thing?"

Another door slams across the hall.

"That would be great."

"Even though I just found him on Instagram and his feed is *so freaking cute*?"

"Reese! Oh my god, do not follow him."

"Fine." She shoots the word at me like a weapon. Takes a long, loud breath. I can practically see her shaking her head in exasperation, and I brace for her to launch into one of her semiregular speeches about how I need to stop being so cynical and *open my heart*.

To my relief, she lets it go and refocuses on how happy she is that break is almost over and her older sister, Rachel, is going back to college. Being the middle child, Reese's sibling rivalry runs deep. I gladly commiserate as she tells me about their last fight over who got to use the family car, and keep folding my laundry. The word *practical* could be used to sum up my wardrobe—though Reese would probably be inclined to use a word like *homogenous* or *boring*. But what can I say? I like basics. I wear my favorite jeans until they get holes, and when I find a shirt I like, I'll buy it in three colors. It just makes life easier, and I have far fewer fashion crises than Reese.

When I pull the black T-shirt I was wearing on New Year's Eve from the pile, I pause.

Maybe Reese has a point. I barely know the guy, but we did seem to have a lot in common. And he was cute. And sort of funny. And technically not a Casey. I suppose there's a chance Holland and I could be good together. The thing is, it doesn't matter.

Because I'm not a cynic, I'm a scientist. And if there's one thing I've learned from observing my parents—and from what happened with Webster—it's that the whole concept of *true love* is inherently flawed.

I may have been naive enough in the past to believe feeling a connection with someone would keep them from hurting me. But I learn from my mistakes. And I'm not about to repeat the same experiment and expect different results.

On my way to school the next morning, I tell myself it's completely reasonable to still be thinking about Holland, given that Reese texted me about him *again* this morning with the link to his Instagram account—which is, as advertised, adorable. But so what if he's been on my mind a lot? It's only because I didn't have anything better to do over winter break. By this afternoon, I bet I'll forget all about him.

It starts to drizzle while I'm driving, an icy, relentless mist that should be snow but isn't, because I woke up early to style my hair this morning, and we live in a cruel world. And also because Michigan winters are the worst.

Head ducked against the chill, I hurry inside the building and move with the current of bodies heading toward the main staircase. I peel off to stop by my locker right before the first warning bell rings.

Most of my schedule is the same as last semester, so I coast through the first couple hours, teachers picking up where we left off before break. Third period is my only new elective, an easy-A course called Life Skills. The class meets in a room with high tables, sort of like the science labs, except they have ovens built-in under the counter. I pick a table toward the front and pull out a new notebook. And because I am the biggest nerd on the planet, I get a little rush cracking the spine and running my hand over the crisp blank page.

I don't look up again until someone slides onto the stool next to mine.

No.

Webster hoists his backpack onto the counter and starts rifling through it without so much as a glance in my direction.

"Uh…" I shake my head.

"Oh. Hi." He says it like he just noticed me sitting here.

"Hi." I look over my shoulder. A few chairs are still empty in the back, and for a moment I consider getting up and switching seats. But I got here first. "What are you doing?"

He pulls out a bag of potato chips. "I was looking for these. Want some?"

…"No."

Suddenly every instance of Webster slamming my locker shut during passing time or shooting me one of his cocky little smirks rushes to the front of my mind. All those times we tried to get at each other, gain the upper hand, because neither of us could believe we'd ever been friends in the first place. Though now that I think about it, Webster hasn't done anything like that recently. He lost interest in our chess match after last year. He stopped playing the game, started ignoring me instead. Still, this has to be another move. I just have to figure out how to block it.

I turn forward again. Run a hand over my no-longer-straight hair. At least I'm not the only one who looks like they got caught in a water balloon fight this morning—even Webster looks a little worse for wear. Out of the corner of my eye, I notice the shoulders of his hoodie are still damp.

Good. I hope he's uncomfortable for hours. The second our eyes meet I drop my gaze back to my notebook.

Webster lowers his bag to rest by his feet and leans his elbow on the counter, twists so his long legs are angled toward me. He eats his chips one at a time. Even with his mouth closed, the crunch is obnoxiously loud. A couple minutes are left before the bell will ring. Is he seriously going to stay here?

All around us, students are chattering with their neighbors, catching up after the break and complimenting each other on the new bags/sweaters/earrings they got for Christmas, and I try to focus on that noise, try to eavesdrop on the girls behind me, but all I hear is Webster chewing those goddamn potato chips. He's clearly trying to get under my skin.

A part of me actually wonders if Reese put Webster up to this. I can tell she isn't planning to drop the Holland thing anytime soon. And it seems like Webster isn't planning to leave me alone until I say something, either, and just because I ask for a number doesn't mean I have to actually use it, so fine, FINE, I'll do it.

I set my pen down and turn to face him. "I got to know your cousin a bit the other night."

He crumples up the empty chip bag and cocks his head. "Is that what the kids are calling it these days?"

My whole body lights up, heat kissing my collarbones and snaking up my neck. "He seems like a nice guy. Smart, too. You sure you're related?"

"Zing."

It's possible insulting Webster isn't the best way to get what I want. I swallow hard, straighten to perfect posture. I smile sweetly. "I was just wondering—"

"If he mentioned you?" He looks at me for a long moment, the same combativeness in his dark eyes as that night last fall. Then, a twitch at the corner of his mouth. "I'm sure it was a real memorable moment you two shared."

A laugh presses behind the words, like I'm just so ridiculous. So silly and stupid for implying there was even a remote possibility his cousin might have asked about me.

"Never mind," I mumble.

My gaze fixes on my notebook again. I write the date at the top of the page, then fiddle with my pen, pressing the tip into the pad of my finger so I have something to focus on besides Webster's smug face. I half expect him to get up and change seats, now that he's proven he can still get the better of me. But he stays right where he is, and a moment later the teacher walks in and leans against the counter at the front of the class.

"Welcome, everyone, to Life Skills! For those who don't know me, I'm Miss Holloway. In this class I'll do my best to teach you guys about adulting. This will include an overview of baking techniques so you can feed yourselves when you move out of your parents' house, a short accounting segment where you'll learn to avoid bank overdraft fees, and the bit you're all looking forward to, reproductive health and child development! We'll cover birth control methods and you and your partner will care for a slightly unsettling animatronic doll for two weeks. So! Say hello to the person next to you, because they will be your partner for the rest of the semester."

Everyone else seems to have paired off with someone they actually like, because no one protests.

"Also, if you have any food allergies, please raise your hand."

While she takes notes on who is allergic to nuts or dairy or gluten, those of us who weren't considering the possibility of being stuck with the person next to us for an entire semester contemplate transferring out of the class. Or at least I do. I glance at Webster, and he shoots me a wink.

Okay. No. This isn't going to work.

Miss Holloway hops off the counter and paces around it to pick up a stack of papers. She passes them out and explains that we'll be starting with a simple brownie recipe. "You'll find all the ingredients you need in the back cupboard. Please refrain from eating the raw batter. I'll be walking around to check on everyone's progress." She stops back at the front of the room when all the recipe handouts are distributed. We all look at her. She cocks an eyebrow. "Well? What are you guys waiting for?"

The room fills with the shrill sound of a dozen or so metal seats getting pushed back against the tile floors. Before I have a chance to react, Webster snatches our handout and shuffles over to the supply cabinet.

Everyone crowds around the closet at the same time, and it takes about twenty seconds for someone to drop an egg on the floor. Miss Holloway sighs and walks back to make sure they clean it up properly and every other student doesn't walk through it.

Webster returns a moment later with his arms full—a bar of baking chocolate, cocoa powder, a half carton of eggs, butter, and two canisters, one marked flour and one sugar. He sets it all down gently on the counter, then looks at me. "Let's get this going, shall we?"

Why is this my life? Why—out of the twenty-something

kids in this class—am I paired with the one person I try so hard to avoid? Webster obviously gets a kick out of messing with me, but even after enduring months of his jackassery last year, this is just…a level of commitment I did not expect. Sure, he has one up on me now, but we're also stuck with each other. There's no winner here.

And I can't believe I actually caved like that. I should never have mentioned Holland. All it did was give him even more ammunition on me. Though admittedly, now I kind of want to get in touch with Holland just to spite Webster.

Maybe I'll follow him on Instagram after all. Or go to one of his basketball games.

Webster is watching me with an expectant look. I grab the recipe from in front of him and turn the oven on to preheat. "We have to melt the chocolate in a bain-marie."

"Right. What is that?"

I take a saucepan to the faucet and fill it with an inch of water, then put it on the range down the counter from us. "Dump the chocolate into that glass bowl and then when the water starts to boil, put the bowl on top of it."

Webster moves at a snail's pace. Once he's finally finished with that step, he sits back and watches me measure out the rest of the ingredients. It's clear he's going to do the bare minimum, which was probably why he sat next to me in the first place. He knows I won't let us fail, that I'll do all the work and he'll barely have to lift a finger.

"So I guess you needed the easy A," I say as I reach for the carton of eggs. "That's why you signed up for this class, right?"

Webster recovers so quickly, I might have missed his wince

entirely if I weren't paying such close attention. I feel a tiny sting of regret over taking the low road. But it's outweighed by the thrill of hitting my mark.

"Well, that," he says. "Plus I have a pretty epic sweet tooth."

I'm smacked with the memory of him that first summer, chasing an ice-cream truck through the neighborhood because I said I was craving a Bomb Pop.

I pick up an egg and turn it over in my palm, examining the smooth white shell. Then I crack it against the lip of the bowl, pitch the broken pieces into the trash. "And you thought, what, that I'd take pity on you? Cover for you so you could keep playing basketball and going to parties and generally peaking in high school?"

I grab the bowl and a wooden spoon and start stirring everything together.

Webster's eyes narrow. "You might want to save some of that pity for yourself. Might need it the next time you're home alone on a Friday night watching reruns of *The Great British Bake Off.*"

I swear, Webster loves nothing more than reminding me we're on different rungs of the social ladder. But it's a little unnerving how accurately he just described my weekend plans.

I pour the batter into a greased baking dish and pop it into the oven. We wait in frigid silence. I contemplate asking Miss Holloway for the bathroom pass, just to get a few minutes away from Webster.

Instead I turn to him and say, "There's still time, you know."

Webster glances at me, confusion etched on his brow. "For what?"

"The drop/add deadline isn't until next week. If you want to transfer out of this class."

I'm not sure how to interpret the set to his jaw. "Actually, I think I'm going to like this class."

"Well, sure. What's not to like? I'm doing all the work."

Because as much as it sucks that I can't count on him to help out with our assignments, I can't bring myself to get a bad grade just to prove a point. Besides, I'm the one who should never have signed up for this class. Maybe I *have* been watching too many episodes of *The Great British Bake Off* for my own good. I should have taken another science credit.

Though, to be fair, baking *is* a science. That's why I love it. There are so many variables to consider—the temperature of the oven, the technique used for mixing ingredients, and the baking time all play important roles. You have to understand the way salt interacts with yeast, and which type of flour will yield the desired result. It's not easy to get a recipe just right.

Webster's only response is another smirk. He scrolls through his phone to kill time, and I'm hyperaware of every movement he makes, guarded in case he decides to come at me with another insult. I hate this—I need to train myself to ignore him the way he ignores me whenever it's convenient for him.

But Webster's attention has shifted to the table behind ours, where Ted Turner, one of the guys on Webster's basketball team, is loudly running his mouth about a junior girl he supposedly hooked up with.

"Hey, Ted." Webster leans back in his chair and rests his elbow on their workstation. Ted nods to Webster, an arrogant smile still dangling from his lips. Webster matches the smile for a beat, then abruptly turns his expression stony. "You sound like an asshole. Knock it off or I'll make sure every girl in this school knows to steer clear of you."

I raise an eyebrow, waiting to see whether this is going to turn into a fight, or at the very least a continued demonstration of toxic masculinity at work, but to my surprise Ted slumps a bit lower in his chair and mumbles, "Sorry, man." And that's the end of it.

I stare at Webster for a full thirty seconds after that, wondering if he even knows the girl Ted was talking about. But I decide it doesn't really matter. The point is he stood up for her, intervened when most guys wouldn't have, and that's... exactly the kind of thing I used to like about Webster. The kind of thing I might have expected from the version of him I knew that first summer—from the kid who frequently wore a T-shirt that read *We should all be feminists*. But not so much *this* version of Webster, the one who obviously only sat here to annoy me. Though I suppose it's fair to say his nice-guy attitude extends to everyone except me.

The smell of brownies starts to fill the room, stiflingly sweet. We pull ours out to find they're somehow burnt around the edges, even though they were in for the minimum baking time. I fan them with a spare cookie sheet and, as soon as they're cool enough, I cut them into perfect squares and cover my share in plastic wrap. I make a mental note to bring a few empty Tupperware containers to school for days like this. But since these brownies will probably end up as one giant mass at the bottom of my backpack anyway, I shove them in and reach for my notebook. Webster grabs it out of my hands and flips to a blank page.

"Excuse me."

"Almost forgot." He writes something down and slides it back to me. "Holland wanted you to have that."

I look down at the phone number he's jotted in his barely legible scroll. My eyes flick back up to his. He tosses me my pen, then turns on his heel and floats out of the room like the douchecanoe that he is.

4

REESE AND I don't have any classes together this semester, which means lunch is the only time I get to see her at school. We've shared the same little table along the wall with windows since freshman year, and as usual she makes it there before me, since she packs her own food.

"This semester already sucks," she says as soon as I set my tray down and slouch into the seat across from hers. "I thought most of my teachers would let seniors coast, but I already have *another* essay for AP French, plus a paper to write for lit, and I have cheer practice until four today, which is so stupid because we've been doing the same routines since football season—I think we know them by now." She steals one of my fries. "And I have cramps. So yeah. How's your day going?"

"Wow. Better than yours, apparently."

Reese looks down at her salad and sighs before spearing a piece of lettuce. She's forever trying to convince me salads can taste as good as French fries. And granted, the ones she puts together do have a bit more oomph to them than the sad-looking (and tasting) iceberg blends my mother always makes. But I still don't like salad, plus every time I eat lettuce it gets stuck in my teeth, and I'm pretty sure no one but Reese would tell me it's there, so I generally abstain.

I reach into my bag and pull out the brownies. "Will chocolate help?"

"Always." She immediately unwraps the cling film and picks off a corner. "Oh man, so good."

"Except for the part where they're somehow burned on the edges yet raw in the middle?"

She shrugs. "I like them."

"I made them in Life Skills. You'll never guess who I got partnered with."

"Who?" Her voice is bright, excited, like I'm about to tell her there's a sexy new kid she didn't know about until just now.

I shove a fry into my mouth. "Webster freaking Casey."

Her chewing slows, a surreptitious smile forming. "How'd that go?"

"He sat right next to me. Like, he *chose* that seat when there were several others available. Why would he do that?" Reese opens her mouth to respond, but I'm already on a roll. "To screw with me, that's why. And you know he's not going to pull his weight, so I'm going to have to carry our grade all semester, including the two weeks we're required to take care of a fake baby, which—I can't even think about that right now. He's just the *worst*."

Reese dips her head and tries to hide behind a sheet of

blond hair that is somehow still perfectly sleek and not at all frizzy despite the weather and the fact Reese has gym class second period. But I know her face too well.

"It's not funny!" I insist.

"I wasn't laughing!" Her brown eyes go wide and innocent. She bats mascara-coated lashes, makes what I call her Cartoon Princess Face. "Did you at least ask him about Holland?"

"Sort of."

"So, no."

"I did ask, and then after putting me through an entire hour of his pain-in-the-ass antics, he grabs my notebook and allegedly writes down Holland's number."

"Wait, what? You got his number?"

"Allegedly," I repeat.

Reese squints at me. "I don't know what that means in this context."

"Well, he wrote down *a* number, but I'm not entirely convinced it belongs to his cousin."

"Who else's would it be?"

"I don't know. Like, a strip club's? Or the library? Somewhere he knows I would never go, or that he wants to make fun of me for going to all the time. Oh my god, what if it's his? What if he's catfishing me?"

Though when I used to have Webster's number saved in my phone, I remember it having a Chicago area code. But that was over a year ago. He could have changed it by now.

"Are you honestly that paranoid?"

"The correct question would be whether Webster is that much of a vindictive asshole. And I think we both know the answer is yes."

Reese rolls her eyes but pulls out her own phone. "One way to find out."

"Are you calling him?" I sound more than a little panicked. She shoots me a look like I should know better, but when Reese gets her mind set on something...her boundaries are not always what I would consider reasonable. Plus, this isn't the first time Reese has dated someone in Webster's circle. And she's nice to everybody, including him. So despite her vowing to hate him forever on my behalf, I'm always a little afraid they'll become actual friends.

She taps out a text and, fifteen seconds later, Kevin slides into the seat next to hers and pecks her cheek. "Hey, babe."

"Oh, good, let's involve more people."

Kevin and I had English lit together last year, and based on the Shakespearean performance he gave for extra credit, I get the sense he's not easily embarrassed. I, on the other hand, feel like I've already torn through a lifetime's worth of humiliating moments and would really prefer to avoid any unnecessary witnesses to future indignities.

But Reese ignores me and smiles at Kevin. "Hey. Do you have Webster Casey's number?"

Kevin casts a curious glance in my direction. "Yeah... Why?"

"Ongoing investigation."

He frowns like he's equal parts confused and amused, and pulls his phone out of his pocket. He scrolls through for a minute, then holds it out to her. She looks at it, then back at my notebook.

"Different number," Reese concludes and hands Kevin's phone back.

"Okay, well, that still doesn't prove it's Holland's."

"You are ridiculous. Just text him!"

Kevin leans forward. "So are these brownies up for grabs?"

I push them closer to him. "Even if it *is* Holland's number, how desperate does it look to text him right away?"

"Zero percent desperate. He already made the first move!" Reese turns to Kevin. "If you gave someone your number, you'd want them to text right away, wouldn't you?"

Kevin eyes her like it's a trick question. "Who am I giving my number to?"

"No, just, hypothetically."

"Well…when I gave you my number, I hoped you'd call. So…yes?" He lifts his brows in a hopeful way, then shifts his gaze to me, as if waiting for confirmation he gave the right answer.

"See?" Reese says, as though this exercise proved anything besides Kevin's devotion to her.

"Yeah…no."

Reese scowls and Kevin leans back in his seat. "Are my services no longer needed?"

"Thanks for your help," Reese says. "You can get back to your lunch."

"See you after practice?"

"Yep."

He smiles and kisses her once more. Then hesitates and grabs another brownie. "Bye, Aubrey. Thanks for the brownies."

I wave. "Ugh. You guys are so cute I want to vomit."

"Thanks." She beams for another second, then taps the table. "Okay, do it."

I stuff a fry in my mouth. "And say what?"

"*Umm...*oh! How about, 'remember that time your tongue was in my mouth?'"

"Nice. Subtle." I grab my notebook and program the number into my phone as *Holland, probably.* I tap out a few different texts, delete each one, and finally shove the phone back in my bag without sending anything. "Maybe later."

Reese lets out an exasperated sigh and throws a fry at me. I catch it in my mouth. We both go wide-eyed with our hands up for a celebratory second, then her shoulders sink and she says, "You know what I think? I think your expectations are too high."

"You think *my* expectations are too high?"

"Yeah, you're looking at this all wrong, like a text is some kind of commitment. Just keep it casual."

I give her a pointed look.

She lifts her hands. "Okay, obviously that advice is kind of ironic coming from me. But just because I always end up in a relationship doesn't mean you have to."

"True..."

Reese perks up. She has me on the line now and isn't letting go. "Bayes' rule!"

"What?"

She claps her hands, apparently thrilled with herself, which makes me even more wary. "We learned about it in stats class. So basically, with Bayesian probability, you update your beliefs...or like, the probability that something you think you know is actually true, as new information comes in. *So*—you think dating is a waste of time. But you had fun with Holland on New Year's, right?"

"I mean…yeah. I did."

"So what makes you think you won't have fun again? The more you hang out with him, the more information you'll have to inform your decision." She picks up her fork and spears her last bite of salad triumphantly. "Don't think of it as *dating*, think of it as gathering evidence."

My mouth twists to the side. Reese really does know me too well. "We have a home game next Friday, right?"

Reese puts the lid back on her empty salad Tupperware and folds her arms across the table. "Why yes, we do. Against West Rochester, in fact. Might you be interested in attending?"

"It *has* been a while since I came to watch my favorite cheerleader." The bell rings to signal passing time. I shove my last few fries into my mouth and swing my backpack onto my shoulders. "Here." I wrap up the rest of the brownies and drop them into her tote. "In case you need a snack before practice."

"*Ooh*, thank you." She loops her arm through mine as we walk out of the caf. "Seriously though, I'm excited about Holland. There's just one issue we haven't talked about…"

A traffic jam forms as everyone files into the hallway. We stop behind a few slow-moving sophomores, and I glance over at her with a stomach-clenchy feeling. "What?"

"Just…do you think Holland will be jealous of your illegitimate child with Webster?"

I blink at her, then shake my head and start walking again. "I hate you."

She snorts a laugh and squeezes my arm tighter, tries to slow me down. "I'm kidding! Holland seems like a stand-up guy—I'm sure he'll love the baby like his own!"

★ ★ ★

I count myself lucky to have Anatomy at the end of the day. Especially now that we're starting our dissection lab. I take my seat in the back and my lab partner, Veronica, nods her head in a greeting.

"Hey."

She's not the chatty type, which is half the reason I like working with her. She takes this class as seriously as I do.

Back in ninth grade, Veronica was fully integrated in the popular crowd. Friends with people like Sam and Mike, though the two of them weren't together yet. I'm pretty sure Veronica's antisocial attitude stems from when Sam allegedly caught her hooking up with the guy Sam liked at some party. Which probably also explains why *Veronica King is a slut* was scratched into the wall of the girls' bathroom.

Regardless of the validity of those rumors, they don't affect her ability to finish lab work, so I really couldn't care less.

"How was your break?" I ask while everyone gets settled.

"Mediocre. Yours?"

I glance at my phone. My thumb hovers over *Holland, probably*'s number. Reese did make an interesting argument at lunch. I spent the last two passing times reading about Bayes' rule, and while I'd normally do a lot more research before making a decision…Reese's whole point was to keep things casual.

I can totally be casual. "Yeah, same."

She gives a half smile before slipping back into her usual poker face.

In the last few minutes before class gets started, I open a text message and type out, Hey. It's Aubrey Cash.

I debate typing a longer explanation about how Webster gave me his number, but duh, he would know that already. I hit Send and shove my phone into my bag. We're not supposed to have them out at school, and anyway, I refuse to sit here staring at the screen, waiting for him to reply.

"Okay," Mrs. Landis says to get everyone's attention. "Today is the big day. In a moment, you will be assigned a cat to dissect over the next two months. But before we get into that, let's cover some ground rules. Safety goggles must be worn at all times..."

Mrs. Landis spends the next twenty minutes going over the proper way to hold and pass scalpels, and a long list of unacceptable behaviors that include, but are not limited to: using your cat corpse as a puppet, taking any portion of the body out of the room, or recording choreographed videos of the cats "dancing." The truly horrifying thing is that everything on this list must have been done by previous students at some point. She reminds those who look squeamish at the mention of skinning the cats that we all knew this was a requirement of the course, and that with time we'll all get used to the smell of formaldehyde.

Granted, I have a pretty strong stomach. But as we pick out a cat wrapped in a thick plastic bag from the literal BARREL OF DEAD CATS in the back of the room, and pull it out and onto the metal tray on our table, the smell hits me and I start feeling really sorry for the kids who have to take this class right *before* lunch.

Veronica blows out a long breath. "Maybe we should name him?"

"Really?"

"Is that inappropriate? I was just thinking it would help humanize him. I don't want to become one of those doctors who forgets their patients are real people, you know? Or cats. Whatever."

I've heard about that. How surgeons sometimes become so desensitized in their jobs that they barely treat the patients like humans anymore. Of course, in my case, the patients *would* be animals. Veronica knows I want to be a vet, and she's planning on going pre-med.

"Did you hear back from MSU, by the way?" she asks without looking up from the still-unnamed cat.

"Yeah. I got in." My shiny acceptance letter to the Michigan State Honors College came right before Christmas.

She smiles, a little fuller than I've ever seen before. It erases her sharp edges and even draws out dimples. It's unnerving. "Good. I knew you would."

"Thanks. Any news on your end?"

"My top choice is in Boston. They don't send decisions for another month."

"Well, keep me posted."

She nods, then returns her focus to the cat. "Okay…so…I guess we just…"

She gestures to the cat with her scalpel. I glance enviously at Veronica's ponytail and take off my gloves to dig through my bag for a couple bobby pins. Once my hair is secured out of my face, I pull my latex gloves on again, then clear my throat. "We can do this."

We both make cuts on opposite side of the cat, and like Mrs. Landis demonstrated, we start swiping the scalpel along the thin line of fascia connecting the skin to muscle.

"This is weirdly satisfying."

Veronica cuts a look at me.

I wrinkle my nose. "Does that make me sound like a psychopath?"

Her face remains expressionless. "Little bit. But you're right, it kind of is."

We work in silence for a few minutes, until Veronica cuts free the first patch of fur. She stares at it in her hand for a moment, lips smashed together in what looks like a mixture of disgust and curiosity.

"Guess this is good practice," I say. "You'll need a strong stomach in med school."

"That's one way of looking at it."

We manage to make some progress over the next half hour...which is a weird way of thinking about skinning a cat. In the last few minutes of class, we put it back into storage and clean up our lab.

As we're walking out, I say, "How about Salem? He is a black cat, after all."

Veronica's face is a neutral mask, but she nods once. "I dig it."

We part ways and I stop by my locker to get the books I need for homework. Due to the unfortunate alphabet system, my locker is positioned right beside Webster's. Thankfully, he hasn't actually visited his locker all year. Huddled against the metal door, which holds pictures of me and Reese, and one of my old guinea pig, Rosie, held up by a cake-shaped magnet Reese got me for my last birthday, I pull out my phone and check for messages.

My stomach does a little flip. He wrote back.

Aubrey TBD Cash! Good to hear from you—I thought for sure you'd lose my number.

I type out a reply: Not yet.

Right away a bubble appears to indicate he's typing. He sends a new picture of Lucy the pit bull. Dude really does know the way to my heart. I reply with a series of exclamation points.

Plenty more where that came from. So, how was your day?

I shut my locker and head to the student parking lot, nearly bumping into someone every few feet as I try to type and walk at the same time. It takes everything I have not to touch my phone once I get in the car. And for the first time since I can remember, I'm smiling the whole drive home.

5

FAMILY DINNERS ARE an increasingly rare event at my house. Mom works late more often than not, which means there isn't much cooking going on in general, which usually gives my dad an excuse to meet up with his golf buddies after work. When the weather was nice they'd play a quick round, but now that it's winter, I'm pretty sure they just go to a bar.

Anyway, we're all here tonight. Twirling spaghetti around our forks in a frigid silence until finally my mom sips her red wine and asks what my plans are for the night.

"I'm going to the basketball game."

"Really?" My dad looks up from his plate. I can't remember the last time he was this interested in my social life. Though to be fair, my response is almost always "hanging out with Reese." So. I kind of get it. "That's great, honey. Who are they playing?"

"West Rochester?"

He nods seriously, as though he's been keeping up with the stats for the local high school basketball league. "That should be a great game. You going with Reese?"

"She's cheering. So I won't see her until after."

My mom seizes the opportunity to point out she knows something my dad doesn't. "Honestly, John. Reese has been cheering for years."

He ignores her. "Home game though, right?"

I nod.

"Good. It's supposed to snow again, so I don't want you driving too far. You still have plenty of windshield wiper fluid, right?"

This is what passes for affection at my house. Checking up on automotive fluid levels. "Yeah. I think I'm good."

"Doesn't the team usually go out after Friday games?" my mom asks.

"I don't know." And I *especially* don't know why my mom would have this information.

"Well, if people are doing something after, I think you should go."

..."Why?"

Mom laughs and looks at me like I'm being funny on purpose. "Because you're young! And it's nice seeing you get out a bit more."

"Don't push her, Irene," Dad interjects.

Mom's grip tightens on her fork. "I wasn't pushing her."

He rips off a chunk of garlic bread. "I don't want you drinking at this party."

"I'm not even going to a party."

"See?" my mom scoffs. "Now you've made her feel like she can't go out and have fun with her friends."

"Well, if she has to drink to have fun—"

"Don't put words in my mouth. Of course that's not what I meant." Mom looks at me, even though I'm pretty sure this has nothing to do with me anymore. Not that they ever actually talk about *why* they're fighting. "She knows that's not what I meant. Don't you?"

"Mm-hmm."

They snipe at each other for a few more minutes, then my mom lets out a big huff and we go back to a soundtrack of silverware on ceramic plates. It's so quiet that I can hear my dad's jaw click when he chews. Apparently my mother can, too, because she keeps shooting him salty looks like he's doing it on purpose.

Back when these dinners were an everyday thing, I used to put in a lot more effort. I'd try to carry the conversation— a difficult feat considering my life pretty much consists of school then homework then sleep, repeat. But especially after walking in on my mom and *David from work*, it seemed important to steer the conversation away from any touchy subjects, to fill the silences that sprang up like leaks in the family ship.

Sometimes I think I should have just told my dad what I saw. Because keeping it a secret doesn't seem to have made any difference. Their fighting still got worse, and now there's no such thing as a safe subject, and I wish we could just go back to eating in different rooms. That I could pick up my plate and go sit in front of the TV, or eat at my desk with my door closed. But my mother makes me sit there until we've all finished, and she intentionally takes forever to clear her plate.

The second she does, I'm out of there.

I get in my car, and it's not until I've backed out of the driveway that I notice Webster standing in his. He has the hood of his car propped open and is staring at the engine with both hands on his hips. I shift my car into Drive and ease my foot off the brake. Whatever he's dealing with, it's not my problem.

Ugh, *except*. As I slowly roll down the street, all I can think is: it's freezing out, and he's wearing his warm-up sweats because he's clearly headed to the game, and I'm driving there anyway, so it'd be an asshole move to just leave him there.

I sigh and pull into his driveway. I roll down my window and stick my head out. "You need a ride?"

Webster looks from me to his car and back again. "Um. Yes, actually."

I roll my window back up and wait for him to close the hood and grab his bag from the trunk. He slides into the passenger seat of my car, clutching his duffel to his chest and eyeing me suspiciously. Hard to say if it's because he's not sure why I offered him a ride (same, to be honest), or because some part of him suspects I'm responsible for his car not starting. I decide not to comment either way.

"Thanks for the lift," he says. "You have great timing."

"No big deal. I'm going to the game anyway."

"Right. Well…still." We pull out of the neighborhood, and Webster glances my way again. "Don't think I've seen you at any of my games before. Any particular reason you're going to this one?"

"No." I'm so not falling into the trap of talking about Holland with him again. "Reese just wanted me to come."

Webster nods, but I get the sense he doesn't remotely believe me. I turn up the radio, only to realize the song currently playing is one Webster sent me that summer. Back when we were constantly trading recommendations on movies and music and books, when we were hungry for details about each other, so supportive of each other's interests.

We don't talk the rest of the drive, and when I park it's made slightly more awkward by the fact that I don't move to get out of the car.

"I thought you were coming in," Webster says, hesitating with one foot out the door.

"Yeah, I am." But it's super early, so I was planning to sit in the parking lot and read for a bit. "Just...not yet."

"Okay... Guess I'll see you later, then."

Webster goes, and I pull up an article about Bayes' theorem that I bookmarked on my phone. The past few days, I've pored over real-world examples of Bayesian probability—like how it applies to poker. If all the players have an equal understanding of the game, then poker boils down to standard probability: the chance certain cards will appear. But if you know the person sitting across the table from you, know how likely they are to bluff or how to identify their tells, then you can use that information to reassess your own hand.

That's what I like about Bayes'—it takes into account how unpredictable people can be. The focus is on *why* things happen. And that's the question that's haunted me ever since Webster stood me up at homecoming.

But I'm still figuring out how to use it in the context of my love life. I close out the article and open my text thread with Holland. We've been messaging all week. Reese says we're in a full-on flirtationship, but for now I'm just focused on getting to know him better, one tidbit at a time.

More people have started to funnel into the gym. I drop my

phone into my bag but don't move yet. I haven't been here at night in a long time. Since last year's homecoming, to be exact.

My fingers tighten around the steering wheel and, for a moment, I consider turning around and going back home. But finally I blow out a deep breath and join the stream of people moving toward the gymnasium.

The reason I don't generally attend athletic events isn't that I'm wholly against sports. I do understand the appeal. It's the logistics that have always kept me away. None of my friends outside of Reese's core group are the type to come to games, and since she's down on the court cheering, I'm left in the bleachers…by myself.

I brought a notebook with me, because I figure multitasking will help me look like I actually chose to sit alone. But discreetly as possible, I scan the bleachers for someone I know. The first person I spot is Phil Marlow, whom I was sort of friends with when we had orchestra together, but haven't spoken to since I quit last year to fit in an extra science elective. Then, to my surprise, I spot Veronica a few rows behind him, surrounded by a bunch of girls of similar height. I'm pretty sure this group makes up the girls' varsity basketball team, and I'm not sure if I'm allowed to sit with them, but when she sees me she gives her usual nod, so I figure I'll give it a try.

"Surprised to see you here."

"Likewise." She scoots down the bleacher to make more room for me. "Coach makes us come to three of the boys' home games. Solidarity, or whatever. This is my last one."

"Oh. Cool."

I settle in, dropping my bag and propping my feet on the empty bench in front of us. I scan the sidelines and see the new vice principal, Mr. Davis, beckon a couple sophomore girls wearing crop tops over to him. They both end up putting their coats back on before finding a seat. Ever since he started fall semester, he's been strictly enforcing the dress code—even, apparently, at extracurricular events. I roll my eyes as he continues to stroll in front of the bleachers with his hands folded behind his back.

"So, what number do you like?" Veronica asks.

"Sorry?"

The game is just starting, and she keeps her eyes on the court until tip-off, then faces me. "I figured that's why you're here. To watch a guy you have a crush on?"

Oh. She means jersey number. I feel my face heat up. "That's not a very feminist assumption. But also…not incorrect."

She smirks and raises an eyebrow. "So?"

We're not this level of friends, Veronica and me. We don't gossip, especially about who we want to make out with. And I'm generally not the type to go blabbing about a crush. And yet…the answer slips off my tongue.

"He actually plays for West Rochester. Holland Sawyer?"

Veronica barely reacts. "Yeah, I could see that," is all she says.

"You know him?"

She shrugs. "Not well. He's a good point guard, though."

I turn back to the court and squint. Despite how many times I've heard Reese use that term, I still don't know what the hell a point guard is, so it takes me a moment to pick him out. The back of his jersey has the number 14 on it. When the whistle blows, he jogs to the visitor bench, and I finally get a good look at him.

My stomach does a little squeeze because, even flushed from running around the court, he's exactly as cute as I remembered. And so tall. And his arms are sculpted and I didn't even know that was a turn-on for me, but apparently it is. I can't stop staring as he reaches for a water bottle and takes a drink.

We just watch the game for a bit, in the casual silence I've grown used to with Veronica. Somehow I have no trouble spotting Webster. My gaze follows him down the court. He gets passed the ball and in one smooth motion makes an impossible-looking shot.

"Oh, sick," Veronica says, and a bunch of the other girls start shouting and whistling. I look below, and Reese and the others are shaking their pom-poms in the air. My molars clench.

"So number 23…" I lower my voice a little. Though only a few people witnessed it happen, practically everyone heard about the stunt Webster pulled on me at homecoming. And while I'm pretty sure most people have forgotten by now—if they ever cared in the first place—I still don't want the world to hear me ask about him. But after all the rumors that have gone around about Veronica, I trust her not to bring up any of mine. "He's pretty good, huh?"

"Web? Yeah, he's solid. Has a few scouts looking at him, I think."

I knew this already, so I'm not sure why I bothered asking. I guess I hoped since Veronica actually plays basketball, she'd see something I didn't. That she'd say, *Webster Casey? That guy is so overrated.*

Whatever. I came here to see Holland play, anyway. I keep my gaze trained on him all through the first half. As far as I can tell, he's every bit as talented as Webster. And way more fun to watch. In fact, I practically forget Webster's even on the court until he gets fouled a few minutes into the second half.

He lines up to take his free throw, dribbles the ball twice. I watch him bend his knees and lift the ball, and something about it takes me right back to that summer. His body behind mine, showing me how to position my feet. His hands at my elbows, mouth close to my ear as he reminds me to snap my wrist, to always follow through.

I don't watch him take the shot. Don't cheer with the rest of the crowd when he makes it.

We end up winning by nine points—thanks in large part to Webster, who scores a few more times in the final minutes of the game. After the clock winds down, the teams each form a line and walk past each other to slap hands and make other sportsmanlike gestures. When Holland and Webster meet, they do one of those handshake-turned-bro-hug maneuvers. And apparently Webster says something witty, because Holland's head tilts back in a laugh and he claps him on the shoulder.

The bleachers are clearing out quickly. I focus my attention on not face-planting as I step down the risers toward Reese, who's still talking to some of the cheerleaders. Veronica follows me to the bottom but then glances awkwardly toward the cheerleaders. I follow her gaze and catch Sam glaring at her.

"See you Monday," she says, and hitches her bag higher on her shoulder as she weaves her way out of the gym. I'm tempted to follow her—partly because my feet are getting cold, but mostly because I know how shitty it is to feel like you're not welcome somewhere you have every right to be.

But the next moment, Reese reaches me. She rustles her pom-poms against my waist, apparently still burning off energy from the game. "You actually came!"

"Yep. Great job boosting morale."

Sam is still looking out the door Veronica left through. Her face has softened somewhat, and now she looks a little like she wishes she could follow Veronica. She turns to me, her perfect smile back in place. "Thanks for coming, Aubrey." She taps Reese's arm and reaches down for a duffel bag stashed under the side of the bleachers. "I'm going to change."

"Okay, me too." Reese turns to me. "Walk with me to the locker room? I just have to clean up, and then we're all heading to Oscar's."

Oscar's is a vintage car–themed diner on Woodward Ave. They specialize in cheese fries and mozzarella sticks, and don't even serve alcohol. So, not exactly the rager my mother had in mind. But infinitely more appealing to me.

"Sure." I follow her off the court.

"God, I'm so sick of this," she says once we're away from all the other cheerleaders.

"So why don't you quit?" I know Reese is friends with the other girls, and that she wanted to join the squad ever since she saw Rachel cheer at her first football game, back when we were still in middle school. But given how obviously her feelings about it have changed, I don't understand why she won't give it up.

Like every other time I've made that suggestion, Reese simply shrugs. "The season's almost over. Besides, I'd still be coming to the games to support Kevin."

She folds her arms. "So. Your boy looked pretty good out there tonight."

The hallway is filled with sweaty guys, most of whom are wearing our school's colors. The away team walked off the court first and are already hidden away in the visitors' locker room. In a low voice I say, "He's not my boy."

"Did you tell him you were coming?"

We've reached the girls' locker room. I drop my bag by my feet and lean against the wall. "I told him I might make it."

"Look at you, playing hard to get." She hitches her bag higher and tugs a lock of my hair. "You got this, okay?"

She goes in to change, and I watch as the sea of proud parents sporting our school's heinous purple and gold colors flows out of the gym and heads through the double doors to the parking lot. A few families linger down the hall, presumably waiting for their kids to come out of the locker room.

My thumb picks at the nail on my middle finger, right along the side until it catches and tears and then I have no choice but to bite it. Which is not my best habit but a hard one to break, because the second my nails get long enough to look nice, they get weak and bendy enough for me to start fiddling with them.

Right as the nail finally tears, Holland walks out of the visitor locker room. When he spots me, he says something to the guy walking next to him before veering over. I'm trying to be discreet as I scrape off the bit of nail stuck to my tongue and flick it away. Needless to say, I'm feeling super attractive by the time he reaches me.

My insides do a little dance. I can do this. I'm going to do this. "Hey."

"Hey, glad you made it." His dark hair is glossy and damp, and I can't tell if it's from sweat or a shower. Do the guys actually shower after games? It doesn't seem like they would have had enough time and, besides, why would you shower here when you're headed home right after? I try not to be grossed out by the fact that it's probably sweat. "Guess your resolutions are off to a good start."

"Yeah, so far so good." The hall is more crowded now, so I reach for my tote bag. My fingers curl around the strap. "Great game, by the way."

He winces a little. "Thanks."

"I mean, I know you lost." *Yes. Good. Definitely remind him of that.* "But…you looked great out there."

"Thanks. Coach might not agree, but…" His cheeks are a little pink. And sure, it's probably because he's still overheated from all that running. But it's still completely adorable.

Down the hall, the boys' locker room door opens again, and Webster walks out with a few other guys. He sees me, too. And despite the good deed I did earlier, he doesn't even attempt to control the look on his face—eyebrows puckered and lip curled, like I'm a groupie standing outside a stadium, pathetic.

I stand up a little straighter and try to remember what I'd planned to say, the words carefully chosen to sound casual, confident. Except now all I can think is, what if Webster said something to Holland? Or what if he's waiting, biding his time until the two of us make plans, and then he'll tell Holland terrible things about me, ruin everything just because he can?

But Holland wanted me here. I have the text chain to prove it. So screw Webster and his pretentious little smirk. His stupid, floppy hair. He's probably just jealous because Holland got all the good genes.

"I actually have to run," Holland says before I can get anything out. "Coach makes us take the bus back together."

"Oh." This isn't going the way I pictured. I mean, it's not like I thought he'd come with me and a bunch of players from the opposing team to Oscar's. But I guess I figured we'd have a little more time to talk. That I wouldn't feel Webster watching me, waiting for me to stumble and fall flat on my face. "Yeah, of course."

Reese and Sam and a few other cheerleaders come back into the hall then. She stops right behind Holland, not even trying to hide the fact that she's totally eavesdropping.

Now or never. "Before you go… I was wondering if you're free next weekend?"

Holland smiles, the same parentheses-in-his-cheeks smile he gave me on New Year's. "Yeah, I'm free. What'd you have in mind?"

"I'm seeing a movie with Reese and her boyfriend Saturday. You want to come?"

"Definitely." His attention snags on the area down the hall, where his coach is waiting. "So, I'll call you."

"Great."

He flashes another smile and then heads to where the rest of his team is gathered. Once he's out of earshot, Reese nudges my ribs. "See, that wasn't too painful, was it?"

"Relatively pain-free." But since I apparently have to find *something* to fixate on, my thoughts immediately latch on to the next pressing problem: I have a date. And even if it's for the good of science, that's a scary prospect. I link my arm through Reese's, and together we start toward the parking lot. "Here's hoping the guy actually shows up this time."

6

MY MUSIC IS *shake the mirror on the wall* loud. It is *feel it in your teeth* loud. It is *probably going to have hearing damage* loud.

It is not loud enough.

My hand trembles as I put on my mascara, and I have to use a Q-tip to get the black mess off my eyelid. I take a deep breath and try to drown out the voices.

It's not like my parents ever had a perfect marriage. They fought when I was a kid, too, but back then it was in the way normal people who spend all their time together fight. The way I argue with Reese. Over petty things that end in a huff and a few minutes of silence while we cool off. Fights that are forgotten when the commercial break ends and our favorite show comes back on.

The way they fight is different now. With slammed dresser drawers and kitchen cupboards. With heavy stomps up the stairs that are too loud to be by accident—like toddlers throwing a tantrum. I'm not sure which of them deserves more of the blame for the way things are. Obviously there's *David from work* to consider. Plus, my mom's the type to find fault in everything. She's never satisfied, nothing is ever good enough for her. So eventually my dad stopped trying to make her happy, and then he just…stopped trying altogether. Stopped taking care of himself, stopped keeping his promises. Which is probably why the *David from work* incident happened in the first place…and around and around we go.

In the gap between songs, my parents' argument filters in through my closed door. The usual stuff: my dad doesn't listen and my mom treats him like a child and *maybe if you didn't act like such a goddamn child…*

I focus on finishing my makeup. Look myself over in the full-length mirror hanging from the back of my closet door. It feels like there's more I should be doing to get ready. In romantic comedies, getting ready for a big date always becomes a montage of makeup and wardrobe choices. But Reese helped me decide what to wear days ago. I've already washed my hair, and I even blow-dried it so that it's all straight and smooth, albeit *still* at an unfortunate, in-between length. I'm wearing sparkly eye shadow and this tinted lip balm I like because it tastes like cherries and makes me look like I've been sucking on a Popsicle. In a good way. I think.

Point is, I'm ready. Antsy.

A door slams across the hall, followed by a few grumbles from my father and vibrations as he flies down the stairs. Headlights flash across my window a few beats later as he backs out of our driveway.

I turn down my music and move to my bed. Even though

the house is quiet again, still and peaceful like the aftermath of a storm, I don't want to be here. I wish I could kill time at Reese's, but she's not there. She and Kevin are at his place "studying," and are going to meet us downtown.

I reach for my computer and pull up the Pinterest board I've dedicated to dorm-room decor. It's full of ideas like temporary wallpaper and ways to hang curtains with suspension rods. I'm 99 percent sure I won't actually try to do any of this. For one thing, I probably can't afford this temporary wallpaper because it comes in tiny rolls and is stupidly expensive, and for another, the school will assign my roommate, which means I have no idea if their taste will mesh with mine.

I've tried to make my bedroom feel like my own space, but with walls this thin, it's hard to feel truly isolated from the rest of the house. Never mind the fact that it's still home to numerous items I've outgrown, like the stacks of paperback romances I loved to read when I was a baby freshman and still haven't gotten around to donating. Anyway, at college I'll probably settle for a few movie posters and a paper lantern light, but it's still nice to think about having my own place—even if it is essentially a cinder-block cell shared with another girl. I just pray that whoever they are, my roommate and I get along okay. That once I move out of this house, I won't have to absorb any more yelling.

I type *Bayes' rule* into a new tab and copy and paste the equation that pops up in the search results into a new document. Not that the equation is actually all that useful for my purposes. But the principle itself is about how every theory is a work in progress, taking into consideration every scrap of information you receive. So, I start a list. *David from work* goes at the top, followed by every terrible fight I can remember, all the times my parents said or did something that made me question why anyone would want to get married. All the evidence I have that love does not, in fact, conquer all.

And at the bottom of the page I write Webster's name. *You make it easy.*

I stare at the list and realize I'm still skewing the evidence toward my own pessimistic opinions. Trying to prove my own existing belief, rather than treating my theory like something to be updated and refined. I do know *some* couples that seem happy, after all. Like Reese and Kevin. And I should be giving those examples equal weight, looking out for new evidence instead of lingering on the past, but I can't get over this feeling that happiness like theirs is always temporary.

Suddenly I wish Bayes' theorem worked like a reverse online dating algorithm. That it could help me predict more than just the probable outcome of a relationship. Not just *why* it will end, but *how.* Because there have to be certain ways of falling out of love that hurt less than others, and I want to know what those are.

"Aubrey, honey?" Mom's knuckles rap against my door.

I shouldn't have turned down my music. At least then I could have pretended I didn't hear her. Ignored her until she went away.

"Come in." I don't look up from my computer as Mom steps inside and perches on the foot of my bed, hand smoothing out wrinkles in the duvet.

"You look nice," she says. "Going out with Reese tonight?"

I nod and switch back to scrolling through Pinterest. It's not like my parents would have a problem with me going out with Holland. In fact, my mom would be thrilled—she'd want to see his picture and ask me a million questions about him and might even go so far as to call Webster's mom and gossip about it with her.

So. That's pretty much exactly why I didn't tell her. I don't want her making this into a bigger deal than it is. And I sure as hell don't want her dating advice.

Mom doesn't say anything else, so eventually I lift my gaze and say, "Did you need something?"

She draws in a deep breath, and for a moment I think she's going to apologize for fighting like that in front of me. Reassure me it didn't mean anything, that it will all blow over, the way she used to when I was little.

Instead she shakes her head and says, "I don't know what to do with your father. He's driving me crazy, he really is. If I have to ask him to take down the Christmas lights *one more time*—I mean, I work full-time, then I come home and I cook dinner, I do the laundry, I clean the house. I ask for this *one thing*, and do you think he can do it?"

I'm not sure if I'm actually expected to answer or not. I settle for a noncommittal grunt and continue scrolling on my computer, seeing nothing.

Eventually Mom heaves another sigh and pushes herself off the bed. "Anyway. I shouldn't be talking about this with you."

"No, you probably shouldn't," I say, a little sharper than I intended.

Mom shifts and clears her throat. "So, what are your plans?"

"Movies." I close my laptop and reach for my bag. "Actually, I should run. We're getting dinner first."

That part isn't even a lie. We are eating first, though technically not for another hour. But I can't be here another minute. She makes me so fucking stressed. God—it's no wonder my dad is never home anymore.

"Oh! Okay. Guess I'm on my own for dinner, then."

A twinge of guilt hits me, but it's tempered with the same exasperation that's been pulsing through me the past hour. "Guess so. See you later, okay?"

"Home by eleven," she tells me as I head down the stairs.

I walk through the garage, past Dad's empty parking spot, and vow I'll never end up like them. I don't even understand how it happens—how you can fall in love with someone and be so sure about them, so committed to building a life with them, and then one day wake up and realize the love you shared was only as stable as water cupped in your palm, slipping through the cracks little by little until there's nothing left.

I may not understand the *why* yet, but I've seen it happen. And once you do, it makes you realize it's safest not to fall in love in the first place.

1

HOLLAND AND I sit side by side in a small booth near the back of Oliver's, a seating arrangement that sounds more romantic than it actually is. Every time I want to ask him something, I have to turn my head at an awkward angle, and his limbs are so long that we keep bumping elbows as we eat. It doesn't seem to bother Reese and Kevin, probably because they've been together long enough now that his arm has become a permanent fixture across her shoulders.

Meanwhile I can't stop worrying about how I smell, or whether I have food in my teeth. Reese nudges my foot under the table. When I meet her eye, she takes a visible inhale, drops her shoulders on the exhale—telling me to relax.

In turn, I tell myself, *if Holland puts his arm around my shoulders, it means he likes being this close.* Because Reese was right. Tonight is all about gathering evidence.

Here are the observations I've made so far: Holland is extremely polite. He always thanks the server and holds doors open for people and has excellent table manners. He laughs easily and listens well, and I keep looking for flaws—surely he has flaws besides being clumsy—but I can't find any.

Our waitress, a girl only a few years older than us, comes by to ask if there's anything else we need. Holland asks for a refill on his Coke, and as soon as she walks away with his glass I say, "You sure that's a good idea, Spiller?"

He tilts his head and groans. "Never gonna live that down, am I?"

"Nope." I bite the straw of my own pop and grin at him.

He slides his arm around me. My cheeks warm, and I keep chewing on my straw as I meet Reese's gaze across the table again. Her eyebrow raises, which makes me thinks she's reading as much into his body language as I am.

His refill arrives, and Holland's deep blue eyes hold mine as he reaches for his glass with both hands. He moves as slowly as physically possible, making a show of how careful he's being not to spill. By the time the glass reaches his lips, I'm losing the battle of hiding my grin. Holland gets this pleased look on his face, like making me smile is some kind of prize.

When it's time to head to the theater, Holland pays our half of the bill before I even have a chance to react, then we file outside after Reese and Kevin. We trail a couple yards behind them, salt crunching under our boots and twinkling lights hanging off trees that line the road. Holland's stride is almost comically long compared to mine. It looks like he's walking in slow motion, but at his normal pace I'd probably have to run to keep up.

"Uh-oh," Holland says. He clenches his teeth and makes

a face at me, and for a second I think I've read the signs all wrong. He's going to make some excuse and bail before the movie.

"What?"

"Don't look now, but...there's a dog up ahead—"

I honestly don't even hear the rest of what he says. My senses all tune in to the dog, who is sitting like a very good boy, watching people pass by on the sidewalk while his owner scrolls through her phone. My fingers curl around the ends of my scarf and I veer over to them, slowing as I approach.

When the woman holding the leash notices me lurking, I blurt out, "Can I pet your dog?"

She smiles. "Sure."

I crouch down and offer the dog my hand to sniff. "What's its name?"

"Harvey."

"Of *course* it is," I say as I scratch Harvey behind the ears. "Hi, you're a good boy."

Suddenly Holland is crouching beside me, looking equally thrilled to make Harvey's acquaintance. "Is he a goldendoodle?"

She nods, and a beat later Holland stands up again. I give Harvey one last pet and reluctantly follow. "Thanks."

Reese and Kevin are waiting for us in front of the next shop. "Can't take you two anywhere," Reese says when we catch up.

Holland laughs and turns to me as we start walking again. "I'm guessing you make a lot of dog-related detours?"

The way he says it isn't judgmental. More like he totally gets it, has a hard time passing a dog without stopping as well.

"Well, I generally like meeting dogs more than people, so."

"This is why I've got to introduce you to Lucy. You'll definitely like her more than you like me."

"I mean…probably yes."

His smile draws parentheses on his cheeks again. He nods like he knew that would be my response. "Yeah, but see, we're kind of a package deal. So if you fall for her…"

"I'll be stuck with you?"

"Exactly."

My mouth scrunches to the side, and I tilt my head, gaze at him like I'm considering. "That might not be so bad."

"Warming up to me already." He bumps his shoulder against mine. "What about you—do you have any pets?"

"Sadly no. My parents never let me get a dog. I did have a guinea pig for a while, but it died last year. I thought about getting another, but I knew I wouldn't be able to bring it to college, and I don't trust my parents to take care of it while I'm away, so."

"Bummer."

"Yeah. But I volunteer at an animal shelter over the summer, so I get some quality animal time in that way."

"Nice. You'll make a great vet one day, Aubrey TBD Cash."

"Thanks. I'm sure you will, too." We've reached the theater now, and get in line for the ticket window. "Do you know where you want to go to school?"

"It's looking like North Carolina State."

"Oh, nice."

"What about you?"

"I just got accepted to Michigan State. That's my top choice right now."

"That's awesome, congrats. Well, who knows—maybe

we'll end up in the same program for grad school. Or work together one day."

My mind flashes to *David from work* and my smile gets stiffer. "Yeah. Maybe."

It's our turn at the window. Holland reaches into his pocket automatically.

"I can get this," I offer, but just like at the diner, he waves me off.

"You get the next one."

The next one. The way he says it isn't even a question. He wants to go out again. Which simultaneously sends a warm thrill down my spine and has me fighting the urge to pump the brakes. But this is going so well—and Reese was right, I *am* having fun. So as long as I stick to the casual dating deal, I'll be in control of how much I let Holland in. We can keep having fun and I won't be blindsided or hurt if Holland turns out to be, say, a liar or someone who thinks it's okay to ghost me.

Kevin pulls Reese a little closer, so that her neck rests in the crook of his elbow. He plants a kiss on top of her head, and she tilts her face up toward his, turning in his arms so she can slide her hands around his waist. They look like the kind of couple that's grown so secure in their relationship that they actually believe they're going to make it. That they're invincible. It sets off a destructive streak in me. I want to point out that they're going away to different colleges, slide up beside Reese and whisper *it's never going to last* in her ear.

Seriously, why am I like this?

I mean, I know why. Living with two people who seem to hate each other is bound to give you a complex eventually. I just wish my brain didn't work this way. I'm on a date with a perfectly decent guy, who also happens to be super hot, and all I can think about is how almost half of all marriages end in divorce.

Kevin moves to the concession stand, orders Reese a Diet Coke like it's all part of the routine at this point. And I don't know why it irks me. People are allowed to have a go-to drink. It's really sweet that he knows what she likes, gets it for her without even asking. But again, this voice in my head asks what the point is of getting to know someone that well. There's nothing stopping them from getting bored with you. From changing in ways you could never have seen coming.

"You want anything?" Holland asks.

"I'm good. Thanks, though."

He nods, and we wait near the front of the line for Reese and Kevin to get their drinks. People keep weaving around us, balancing their popcorn and frozen Cokes, until finally Holland grabs my hand and gently pulls me over to the wall, out of the way.

And then he doesn't let go.

If Holland holds my hand for another thirty seconds, it means he likes being seen in public with me.

It goes longer than thirty seconds. We stay that way as Reese and Kevin rejoin us, up until we reach the guy taking tickets.

"Oh, hey, man."

I look up and see Kevin hand his tickets to Webster, who is wearing the same black polo shirt as the rest of the employees. God—since when does Webster work here? And *why* does he have to be working right now?

Webster tears their tickets and Kevin walks through with Reese. Holland fist-bumps Webster when he steps forward—apparently he's not the least bit surprised to see him here—but I notice something tight in his expression. In *both* their expressions, actually. Webster's jaw knots, and his gaze flickers between us as Holland drops my hand to pull the tickets out of his pocket.

When Holland passes the tickets over, Webster reads each one carefully, as though it's not completely obvious we're seeing the same thing as Reese and Kevin. He tears them and hands back the stubs.

"Theater seven, cuz."

"Cool. We still watching the game next weekend?"

"For sure."

Holland nods and passes through. I follow him, but Webster taps my arm on my way by. When I turn around, he's wearing a bland smile that's possibly supposed to be professional but is more likely meant to antagonize me. The corner of his mouth twitches, like he's barely resisting the urge to crack a joke. He finds it so damn funny that I'm out with his cousin. I glare back, daring him to say shit about it.

He gestures conspiratorially for me to come closer. I hesitate. He cocks his head and beckons again, as though he has a secret to tell me.

This feels like a trap. Down the hall, Reese is throwing popcorn kernels that Kevin tries to catch in his mouth. Holland is joking around with them, laughing with Kevin like they're old friends, not two guys who tried to kill each other on the basketball court last week.

"What do you want?"

Before Webster can answer, another guy wearing the theater's uniform polo swoops in and says, "Hey, Web. Bossman says you can take your break in fifteen."

"Cool, thanks, Henry." As soon as the other guy's gone, Webster leans close enough for me to smell his shirt, which somehow doesn't carry the butter-popcorn scent I assumed it would—instead he smells citrusy and earthy, almost like tea. His eyes flash over my shoulder to Holland, and back again. He keeps his voice low, confidential. "The father did it."

"What…" I blink at him. "Wait. Did you just give away the ending to the movie I'm about to see?"

"Enjoy the show."

He sits there with a shit-eating grin and, oh my god, I want to smack it off his stupid face. "You're an asshole."

He shrugs loosely, completely unbothered by this. "Yeah, that seems to be the consensus."

I spin on my heel and hightail it to Holland. My hand slips into his again, fingers lacing together, and this time it feels like a perfect fit. Because I deserve to have someone like Holland interested in me. Someone who doesn't play mind games.

He squeezes my hand, a quick pulse accompanied by a soft smile, and I realize I have all the evidence I need to keep seeing Holland. I like him, and he likes me, and that's enough for now. So as we head toward our theater, I don't spare Webster another glance.

8

AFTER THE WAY he acted at the movie theater, I fully expect Webster to give me a hard time at school Monday morning. I'm bracing for his ridicule on my walk to Life Skills, but when I get there, he's outside the door, flattened against the wall with his tongue in some poor sophomore girl's mouth. It's not the first time I've seen him demonstrate PDA in the hallways. There always seems to be a queue of girls—and possibly guys, but if so they're less public about it—waiting for their chance to date the star of the basketball team. I remain completely baffled by the cultlike following he's developed. And while I get the urge to take the sophomore aside and gently question her life choices, I suppose I should really be thanking her. Because by the time he walks into class, he's in a great mood. So great that he barely acknowledges my existence.

This goes on for the rest of the week. And don't get me

wrong, I'm completely okay with not talking to Webster. It's not like baking requires a whole lot of discussion anyway. But our peaceful silence finally breaks on Friday when he won't stop eating the coconut we need for German chocolate frosting.

How many times do I have to explain to him the importance of having exact measurements? Finally, I smack his hand away from the bowl.

He finishes chewing and frowns at me. "You need to loosen up."

This is a common theme throughout our admittedly sparse conversations. I'm uptight and no fun and if I just relaxed a little, we'd get along fine. Because of course our dynamic is my fault and has nothing to do with the fact that Webster is an entitled ass, or that he's about as mature as a fourth grader.

"If you don't want me sampling the ingredients, you should give me something to do," he says.

"I'm not stopping you from helping."

He rolls his eyes. "Please. You have a hissy fit if I so much as measure out a cup of flour."

"Because you never level it off!"

His mouth twitches and I could swear he wants to smile.

"Fine, if you want to be helpful, why don't you line the baking tin with these." I pass over the package of white cupcake liners.

"You got it, boss."

He's only halfway through the task when Anna Simmons comes over and perches at the edge of our table. "Hey, Web."

The cupcake liners are quickly forgotten. "What's up, Anna?"

She shrugs and slouches closer with her elbows on the counter. "So bored. What flavor did you guys pick?"

He looks at the recipe, because apparently he's so invested in our efforts he can't even remember. "German chocolate. What about you guys?"

"Red velvet."

"Oh man, that sounds good. Save me one?"

She grins widely, her teeth perfectly straight and intensely white. "Sure. So listen, I'm having a party tonight…"

At this point I know Webster's a goner. He never made it sound like he was super popular at his last school but, considering how much attention he's been given since starting here, it's no wonder his ego has gotten so out of control.

I reach across him and grab the muffin tin. I finish the job and measure out batter into each of the liners. I'm closing the oven door when Anna finally walks away.

I start making the frosting, which is more complicated than the buttercream I usually put on cupcakes. Instead of just beating all the ingredients together with the mixer, this frosting has to be cooked in a saucepan. And it's totally going to be short on coconut, thanks to Webster.

Webster goes to reach for the cupcake liners, realizes the tin is gone, and leans back to peek in the oven. "Oh. Thanks for finishing up."

"No worries," I say in a saccharine voice. "I mean, why should you be expected to pay attention to something as trivial as our assignment when there's a party to plan?"

"Well, you know what they say. All work and no play…"

I'm pretty sure this is Webster's way of calling me dull. I scowl and dip under the counter to check on our cupcakes, and only after I'm lifting myself up do I realize how close my head just was to Webster's crotch. He clears his throat, and I reach for my notebook, flip to the syllabus taped inside the front cover. Only a few more weeks left in this segment of class before we move on to reproductive health. We'll be switching to more complicated doughs next week, starting with making a pizza from scratch.

"Think we get to pick our own toppings?" Webster asks, making it clear he's been reading over my shoulder.

"We're not putting black olives on," I say flatly. "I don't care how much you like them."

Webster's mouth quirks. He looks at me for a long moment, a tightness to his dark eyes like he's remembering his first summer here, too, all those pizza nights at his place, the two of us balancing plates on our laps while we watched movies on his living room floor. How we could never agree what kind to get and always ended up ordering different toppings on each half.

And now I'm remembering the last night pizza night of that summer. When we were finished eating, our backs against the couch and my hand resting on the carpet between us, he inched his own hand closer and closer until our pinkies touched, and when I looked up he was already watching me. The way he leaned in, I was so sure it was finally going to happen, that he wanted to kiss me. Only then his mom walked in, and I never got to find out if I was right.

"So…" He straightens, looks away. "You coming to Anna's party?"

The question actually sounds genuine. Not like he's setting me up for another joke, or making fun of the fact that I

clearly wasn't included in Anna's invitation. It's almost like…
he's trying to be nice. Weird.

"I have a date," I finally answer. Holland and I have been
texting all week, and a couple nights ago he asked me out
again. We're going to dinner, just the two of us this time.

"With Holland?"

I nod and check the timer again, because even though I just
looked, I didn't actually pay attention to what it said. Seven
minutes left. I swear, every time our assignment goes in the
oven I'm tempted to flee, just so we're not forced to make
this kind of small talk.

Webster drums his pen against the counter a moment, then
tucks it behind his ear. "So what is it about him?"

I pull the finished frosting off the stove to cool. "What do
you mean?"

He leans against the counter, facing me. His lips pout as
he shrugs. "Just wondering what you like about my cousin."

I squirm in my seat. This is so uncomfortable. Whatever I
say he'll probably relay right back to Holland, and it's not like
I'm going to sit here and gush about the guy. We've only been
on one date. Besides, Webster knows him better than I do,
and he should know what makes him likable. "We have a lot
in common—we both want to be vets. And he's nice to me."

"He's nice to everyone. But hey, I'm sure you haven't given
him a reason not to be, right?"

I can't tell if Webster's implying I don't deserve a nice guy
or that it's just who Holland is and I shouldn't read anything
into it. Possibly both. "He's smart, too," I add in a tight voice.

"Smart." Webster nods, his gaze fixed on me for a long
moment. "That's true, he's a smart guy."

Ignore him. I have to ignore him. This is what the past year of practice was for. I squeeze my fingers into fists and press my knuckles against the cold countertop. But something is swelling up inside me. Taking me back to junior year, the homecoming dance. Asking him for an explanation and getting only, *You make it easy*. And that laugh.

Because everything is a fucking joke to him. Especially me.

"So then what do you two talk about? Articles you read in medical journals? The latest NASA findings?"

"I get it," I snap. "You find it shocking someone would actually want to date me. But here's the thing—it's really none of your business. So would you shut the fuck up about it?"

I manage to keep my voice quiet, but not as steady as I would have liked. Webster freezes, and my cheeks are too hot and I want to cover them, want to harness the adrenaline causing my hands to tremble and use it to stamp away this pressure building in the back of my throat. I swallow hard and study the frosting recipe like it contains the answers to my math test next week.

"Aubrey... I wasn't—"

"Don't. Okay? Just..." I shift my jaw and shake my head.

The timer goes off before he can say anything else. Webster shoves an oven mitt on his hand and pulls the cupcakes out of the oven. They look atrocious.

I test them to make sure they're cooked through and scowl. "Shit, why are they so flat?"

"Maybe you should have let me help more."

I just look at him.

He swipes his finger in the bowl of frosting and licks it off.

Unbelievable. "What? Only trying to get a rise out of you."
He waits a beat, then nudges my arm with his elbow. "Get it?"

I know what he's trying to do. He's trying to backtrack,
trying to say: *just kidding, no hard feelings, don't tell Holland I
was such a dick to you.* But I don't have it in me to pretend any
of this is funny.

We move the cupcakes onto the cooling rack in silence.
Until finally I say, "Look, you obviously don't think I'm good
enough for Holland—"

"That's not what I said."

"It doesn't matter. Just…leave it alone. Leave *us* alone. Don't
screw this up for me, okay? Please."

Webster huffs out a humorless laugh. "You think I'd do
that?"

"I know you would." I start slapping on frosting even
though the cupcakes are definitely still too warm, because
everything's already ruined, so who cares if the frosting melts?

Webster starts packing up his stuff, even though there are
still ten minutes left in class. I'm frozen with a cupcake in
one hand and a spatula full of frosting in the other. I want to
fling it at him, get him right in the face.

"You don't know shit about me," he says without looking
up. Only a beat later, he does, and his gaze is so unfriendly
that I physically recoil, hip bumping against the counter.

An entire summer, seeing each other almost every day.
Lying side by side in the sun, talking for hours about our
families. The way his jaw knotted when he'd tell me about
his dad's new girlfriend. The way his eyes watered when I
got him to laugh hard enough. I know what his favorite pizza

toppings are and what book he rereads every year and what his voice sounds like late at night when he should be asleep.

But sure. Fine. I don't know shit.

I'm smooshing the cupcake. I loosen my grip and finish frosting it, and lick the excess off my thumb.

"I'll finish these. I would hate to see you overextend yourself."

Across the room, Anna is trying to get his attention by waving a perfectly frosted cupcake at him. He pushes away from the counter and casts one more look at me before going over.

This is what I get, I remind myself. This is what happens when I let myself believe Webster can be nice.

9

REESE COMES OVER after school to help me pick out something to wear on my date. We grab snacks from the kitchen and go upstairs, where I stand in front of my closet and try to will something new and cute into existence. But Reese isn't with me. When I poke my head out of my door, I find her stalled at the top of the stairs. Then I see why.

A flush works its way down my neck when I realize the reason she's lingering. The guest room door is open. She can see the unmade bed, the clothes my dad wore yesterday still crumpled on the floor. She finally comes into my room and perches on the edge of my desk. Hands me my can of pop. She already knows about *David from work* and what my parents have been like the last couple years, but judging from the embarrassed look on her face, I'm not sure she fully got it before now.

"He doesn't sleep in there every night," I say before she

can comment. "Just when he has to get up early for meetings and stuff."

It doesn't feel like a lie until it's already out of my mouth, when I realize he *has* slept in there every night this week.

Reese sips her Sprite and nods thoughtfully. "Right, makes sense."

"Yeah." My thumb indents the side of my can. I shove a few hangers aside with my free hand. "Anyway, I hate all my clothes."

She gets up and starts sorting through my closet. "I know the feeling. I'm pretty sure ninety-five percent of my closet is stuff Rachel picked out and wore first. Okay, how about this?"

I veto the first two options she picks because they're skirts and it's twenty fucking degrees outside, and settle for the jeans I wore to school and a cute V-neck sweater in a shade of purple that she says makes my brown eyes pop.

Reese keeps looking through my clothes while I get changed. "*Ooh*, mind if I borrow this?"

I glance at the sequined top she's holding—one my mother bought that I still haven't worn because it's much more her style than mine. "Go for it."

She puts it on and we move to the bathroom, where Reese pulls a makeup bag from her backpack. I run a brush through my hair, then tap the bristles against my thigh in an erratic rhythm.

"Nervous?" Reese pulls out an eyeliner and uncaps it.

"No." I toss my brush onto the counter and fiddle with some of her makeup, swatching metallic gold eye shadows on the back of my hand. "I mean. A little, maybe. But I think things are going pretty well so far."

"Definitely. Even Kevin thinks you guys make a cute couple."

"*A cute couple.* Kevin used those exact words?"

Reese leans close to the mirror, a half smile tugging at her lips. "*No*, but he said you seem good together." She finishes lining one eye and pulls back to look at it. "But if you want a buffer, you could always bring him to Anna's party."

I scrub the eye shadow off my hand. "I think it could actually be good to have some time alone with Holland." Besides, I can just picture how awkward this party would be. First of all, Webster will be there. So there's that. Plus if we hang out with the same people he met on New Year's Eve, Holland will eventually realize I'm not actually friends with any of them, and while I'm sure Webster has warned him that I'm a complete outcast, I don't feel the need to demonstrate the veracity of that claim.

"*Alone time*, huh?" She wiggles her shoulder at me and goes back to doing her eyeliner. "The four of us should hang out again soon, though."

"Yeah, for sure."

She recaps the eyeliner and reaches for her pop. "Speaking of which, the Snow Ball is coming up in a couple weeks…"

My head snaps up and I meet her gaze in the mirror.

"I was thinking we could all go in the same group," she adds.

I twist the bottles of face wash and toner and moisturizer sitting on my counter so the labels are turned out.

Reese fiddles with the tab on her pop can. "Do you not want to go because of what happened last year?"

"What? No." I send her a sidelong glance. "I never even think about that anymore."

She cocks an eyebrow, looking as though she didn't believe that any longer than it took me to say it. And she's right, because suddenly I'm back to wondering if this might be some sick joke on Webster's part. A long con to get me into the same situation all over again. How can I trust Holland when we've had only one date? After all, I trusted Webster. I'd spent way more time with him, *thought* I really knew him, and look what happened.

Of course, I don't say any of this out loud. It's not that Reese wouldn't be sympathetic, but even I recognize I'm thinking like a conspiracy theorist. I'm trying to get better about using Bayes' theorem properly—using it to update the probability of a hypothesis based on available evidence. And, well, I don't have any evidence to support the hypothesis Holland would do something like that. In fact, aside from their shared interest in basketball, so far Webster and Holland are nothing alike.

"Then what's the problem?" she asks a moment later.

"It's just not really my thing, you know?"

Reese's lips purse. "I'm just saying, we have a limited number of opportunities left to make memories—"

"Okay, are you dying or something?"

"Before graduation," she finishes with an eye roll. "So why not replace a bad memory with a good one?"

Before she can continue the hard sell, her phone buzzes. She sighs. "I have to go—I promised Becca I'd drop her at her friend's house before the party."

I help her pack up her makeup, and the two of us make

it downstairs right as the garage door rumbles open. My mom's home.

Reese hangs back to say hello to her, and her eyes widen as soon as my mom walks in. "Whoa, Mrs. Cash. Love your new hair."

"Thank you, honey."

She's completely changed the style. Dyed it auburn and cut at least six inches off. "Wow."

Mom redirects her attention back to me. "You like it? I thought it was time for something different. Actually, I had a very similar haircut to this when John and I first met."

Even though I know these superficial changes are the only ones Mom ever makes—new clothes, new makeup, new hair—I still get a flicker of hope that this means something more. That my mom is trying to rekindle things with my dad, that this is the start of something new. "It looks great," I tell her, and Reese nods her agreement.

Mom beams. She sets down her bag and sheds her coat. "So, what are you girls up to tonight?"

"I was just heading out," Reese says. "I have to drive my sister somewhere and then I'm heading to a party. I just stopped by to help Aubrey get ready for her date."

"Yes! With Holland," Mom says, like she earns points for remembering my date's name. "You've met him, right, Reese? What's he like?"

"He's great," Reese assures her. "Super nice, and smart. I'm sure Aubrey told you he wants to be a vet." Mom nods—that's pretty much the one piece of information I volunteered. "He's cute, too. You want to see a picture?"

"Yes!"

"Wait, what?" I turn to Reese. "Why do you have his picture?"

I lean over her shoulder while she pulls up his Instagram account. Mom moves around to Reese's other side.

"Wow, he is cute," my mom says when Reese tips the phone toward her.

"Uh-huh." I'm biting my nails again. I curl my fingers into my palm to stop myself from doing too much damage.

Once upon a time, talking about a crush with my mother wouldn't have warranted the throat-squeezing hesitation hitting me now. I used to open up to her quite regularly on the subject. Of course, that was before she encouraged me to act on a particularly ill-advised crush, completely setting me up to fail.

"Have you guys kissed yet?"

My face. It is on FIRE. "Mom. Can we not?"

"I'll take that as a yes," she says.

I stare at the ceiling and shake my head. We had the sex talk when I was ten, and again when I started high school. We are not going there now. And sure, her question may seem innocent, but I know a can of worms when I see one.

Reese is still laughing, which only encourages my mother.

"Well, you should bring him over sometime. Soon, okay? If you're going to keep seeing him, your father and I want to meet him. I'd insist you introduce us tonight, but your dad and I are meeting for dinner and I think we'll be gone before he picks you up. Maybe when he drops you off?"

Mom and Dad haven't gone out together in *ages*. I'm so distracted by this new information that all I can do is nod.

Reese's phone buzzes again and she grabs her backpack. "Okay, I really have to go now."

I walk her out to the garage, arms crossed against the chill. "Have fun tonight."

"You too." She walks backward down the driveway toward her car. "And promise me you'll think about the dance, okay?"

I hold up my pinkie in a silent swear. "It's officially under consideration."

I have no reason to be this nervous.

Holland and I are having a great time. He took me to a sushi restaurant for dinner, and we talked the whole time, not a single awkward silence, and now he's holding my hand as we walk back to his car. The worst thing that can happen is he'll say no.

Immediately a voice in my head steps up to remind me that's actually not the worst-case scenario, that there are several ways he could respond that would be infinitely more hurtful and embarrassing.

But I don't even care about this dance so *why am I still thinking so much?*

We're at his car now, and he's opening the passenger side door for me like a total gentleman, like someone out of a movie. I slide into the car and, while he walks around to his side, I check my reflection in the side mirror to make sure my nose isn't running too bad. I discreetly wipe it on my mitten as Holland gets in and starts the engine.

My palms start to sweat as we wind down the parking structure. I yank off my mittens with my teeth and sit on my hands while Holland feeds his ticket into the meter and pays.

"Everything okay?" Holland asks when the gate lifts. "You've gotten awfully quiet over there."

"Yeah, I'm great."

Holland nods, and we pull out of the structure, heading toward Woodward Ave. and hitting the first red light. Holland fiddles with the radio, and I stare at the center console. A small metal pin inside one of the cup holders snags my attention. I pick it up to get a closer look. It's made of brass and navy enamel, with the caduceus medical symbol.

"What's this?"

Holland spares a quick sideways glance before turning his focus back to the road. "I got that when I finished the junior EMT program."

"Wait, you're an EMT?" I look down at the pin, then back at Holland.

"Technically I still have to be certified."

"But you've gone through the training? Have you ridden in an ambulance?"

Holland laughs. "Yeah, I have. But just as an observer. Now that I'm eighteen I plan to get certified, though. I want to volunteer as a full EMT this summer."

"Wow. Guess I know who to call if I'm feeling faint."

I set his pin back where I found it, and spend the next mile or so mulling over this newly unveiled side of him. And possibly picturing Holland in an EMT uniform.

The distraction lasts until we get caught at the next red light, at which point Reese's voice starts to play in the back of my head again.

I'm not going to pretend to be as sentimental about high school ending as she is. But it does seem very un-Bayesian to form an opinion of school dances based on *one* bad experience with someone completely different. That night sucked because of Webster, not because of the dance itself. And not asking Holland *because* of Webster would be just as counter-productive as sitting back and waiting for him to interfere with our relationship. It'd be giving him too much control.

The light turns green.

"So there's this thing," I blurt out.

Holland glances sideways at me. "A thing," he repeats ominously.

"Yeah. Like, a school thing. A dance thing."

"I see."

"And I know school dances are kind of awful. Or—I don't know, maybe you're like Reese. Reese loves them. I'm not the biggest fan."

"Okay…" I risk a glance at him, and his brow is furrowed, teeth caught on his bottom lip. He must feel my gaze, because he sends me another quick sidelong glance. "When is this dance-type thing?"

"Um." I wipe my palms on my jeans. So sweaty. "Friday after next."

Holland nods. His fingers drum against the steering wheel. "So…to clarify, are you asking me to be your date?"

"Oh. Yes." I frown. "Did I not say that part?"

Holland laughs softly. "Not yet."

If my face wasn't red before, it sure is now. Like, to the point where I can't even blame the cold.

"You're pretty cute when you get flustered."

"I'm…" I shake my head. "Not flustered."

"Oh, okay." He's smiling harder now. It's as adorable as it is obnoxious.

"God." This is excruciating. He's actually going to make me say it. "Okay. Holland, will you go to a dance with me?"

He pulls up to another red light. "I'd love to."

"Yeah? Okay. Cool. Thanks."

"You're welcome." His amusement is evident in his voice.

I groan and sink back against the seat, half smiling and half cringing until we pull into my neighborhood. Holland knows his way around it well after visiting Webster so many times.

"It's funny," he says as he turns onto my street, "because I was actually planning on asking you to the dance at my school, but it's the same night."

"Oh. Would you rather go to that one?"

"Nah. Besides, you asked first."

He sounds sort of happy about that. Flattered, even. Heat kisses my cheeks for an entirely different reason.

"Plus, this way we'll be able to go in a group with Webster."

My smile freezes. Holland pulls into my driveway, and I glance over my shoulder at Webster's house. I want to tell Holland I already agreed to go in Reese's group, but I know that's a weak excuse, since there's no reason Webster couldn't be included. Besides, with others there as a buffer, I probably won't even notice Webster.

So I ignore the tightness building in my chest again and brightly as I can, I say, "Can't wait."

10

REESE IS (OBVIOUSLY) ecstatic when she finds out I've asked Holland to the Snow Ball. But the closer we get to the dance, the more I have to remind myself of Bayes' rule. Of the low probability this dance will turn out anything like the last one.

Too many variables have changed. The biggest being Holland, of course. With a different date, I have every reason to expect a different outcome.

So I buy my ticket the first day they go on sale. And I put up with Webster appointing himself the leader of our group and subsequently choosing an Italian restaurant for dinner, despite the fact heavy pasta is probably the worst food to eat before a night of dancing.

And then the day of the dance arrives.

It's been more than a month since Reese and I last stood outside Webster's door, waiting to be let in. I can't stop fidgeting, just like on New Year's, though there are a few notable differences between then and now. For starters, I was actually invited this time.

Webster's mom opens the door, and I try to ignore the wave of déjà vu that washes over me.

"Don't you girls look beautiful!"

"Thanks, Mrs. Casey," I say. Reese beams and looks down at her dress: a high-neck red gown with a cutout in the back and a high slit in the front. She looks completely fierce in it. I'm wearing one of her old dresses, too—well, one of Rachel's, technically. It's made of black lace, floor-length and strapless with a sweetheart neckline. I refused to make as big a deal out of this dance as I did homecoming, which meant turning down Mom's offer to buy me a new dress. Though there was no stopping her from coming over to take part in the picture-taking.

"Carol, so good to see you," Mom says as she walks in behind me. Even though Mom knows Webster and I had a falling-out at the homecoming dance, I never got into the details of what happened with her. Mostly because I didn't actually have answers to any of the questions she asked in the days following the incident. I have to believe she pumped Mrs. Casey for details, too, but whatever was said between them, my drama with Webster never affected their friendship.

I was hoping Holland would arrive before us, but so far the only other person here is Kevin. Reese heads straight into his arms, which leaves Webster and me. Standing close enough that we probably should be talking but aren't. He's wearing a black suit that makes him look serious and broad-shouldered. The pants are just a little bit too short on him, revealing a sliver of hot-pink socks. My eyes drag back up to his face in time to see he was checking me out the same way, a deep furrow in his brow.

Well. I don't know about Webster, but I for one am definitely not thinking about that time I asked him to homecoming and he acted like he wanted to go with me but then stood me up to go stag instead.

Definitely not thinking about that.

His mother reaches for my shoulder. "Aubrey, that's such a pretty dress! Webster, doesn't she look stunning?"

Just kill me.

Our mothers become absorbed in their own conversation again, and the question just hangs there. Webster tilts his head and gives his answer. "You look…"

"What?" My voice is entirely too eager. I pull out my phone, desperate for a reason to divert my attention.

"Never mind."

Without looking up, I say, "It's super annoying when you do that. Just FYI."

He rattles some loose change in his pocket. "You look different. From how you normally look, at school. That's all."

I pinch my lips together and try to find some way that could be construed as a compliment. But no. "Okay. Well, thanks for your input."

"Why does it matter what I think, anyway?"

"Oh, don't worry, it doesn't."

Caitlin Pratt—Webster's date—walks in then, followed by Sam and Mike. I scroll through my messages, even though I know Holland is probably driving and won't be able to text me.

After a few more minutes of catching up and complimenting each other's hair and dresses, the group gathers in front of the fireplace for pictures. I stand to one side, out of the shot. Check my phone again.

Holland would've told me if he had to cancel, right? He would have called, or at least texted me, and told me he wasn't going to make it. Because Holland isn't Webster.

Reese pulls me over for a few girls-only pictures. I try to smile like normal. Try to shake the growing sense that the whole room is watching me.

Next each couple takes a few pictures together, and once Reese and Kevin have finished with theirs, Reese goes over to Webster—who is standing alone while Caitlin texts on her phone across the room. I can't help but notice Webster has barely said two words to his own date. Though the question of whether they're actually into each other or not is quickly pushed out of my head when I overhear Reese ask if he's heard from Holland. Webster shakes his head. Reese stares at him with a fierce set to her jaw.

"I don't know where he is," Webster insists in a low voice. His eyes flicker toward me, and I drop my gaze to the floor.

I remember sitting in this same room that first summer, holding Webster's hand after his dad canceled a visit last-minute. Webster had been crushed. It was written all over his face—the disappointment, the insecurity—despite how hard he was trying not to let it show.

I don't know what my expression looked like to him in that moment, but if I had to guess…I'd say it was probably close to the way Webster just looked at me now. Like he wished he could do something, anything, to make it better.

The group is getting antsy. Even Mom and Mrs. Webster are trading whispers, Mom sending me nervous glances from across the room. We're supposed to be leaving for dinner now. I'm about to fake a migraine—because there's no way I'm going to sit through dinner knowing I've been stood up—when finally Holland arrives.

He hurries over to me, pausing to hug his aunt along the way. He dips to kiss my cheek when he reaches me. "I'm so sorry I'm late. Traffic."

"It's fine," I say automatically. Because it is. And now I feel silly for getting worked up over nothing, for letting myself spiral like that. "You didn't miss much."

"You look...wow." His blue eyes quickly map me, head to toe. "Here, this is for you." He holds out a corsage inside a clear plastic box. White, which is a smart choice because it goes with everything, and I never did tell him the color of my dress. I let him slip it over my wrist.

"Thank you." I lift my wrist to smell it and take the moment to admire Holland's whole look. His navy suit fits him perfectly, and the color turns his eyes a shocking shade of blue. "You look nice, too, by the way."

My mom makes her way over to us then, and I cringe through the whole introduction thing. Holland is, of course, a perfect gentleman—shaking her hand and making eye contact, the two things required to pass my parents' first test. My mom tells him how great it is to finally put a face to a name and how she'd love to have him over for dinner sometime but don't worry, she'll order a pizza, *ha-ha-ha*. She appears to be under the assumption I've talked Holland's ear off about her, like her bad cooking is some kind of inside joke between the three of us.

The meet and greet is mercifully cut short so that we can take a couple more group pictures before dinner. Once everyone's satisfied with the photographic evidence of this night, we all pile into Mike's mom's giant SUV to head over to Antonelli's. Mike and Sam are up front, with Kevin, Reese, and Caitlin claiming the middle. Which means I'm crammed in the back between Holland and Webster.

It's a short ride to the restaurant, thank god, and at dinner Webster and Caitlin sit all the way at the far end of the table, which I'm doubly grateful for. But then afterward, everyone climbs into their original spots in the car, like this is a classroom with assigned seats.

We make it to the school, and Mike parks way in the back of the student lot. At first I'm sort of irritated about how far Mike is making us walk in heels, but then he pulls a water bottle out of the center console and Sam opens a bottle of Coke, and I understand why he's parked so far from the entrance.

They each take a swig from the water bottle and chase it with the pop. Then the bottles get passed back. Kevin takes a pull, but Reese declines. It makes its way around until Webster is passing the bottle to me.

At this point, five other mouths have touched these bottles. Most recently Webster's. And since I'm me, all I can think about is catching mono.

I almost pass the bottles off without having any, but then I look at Holland beside me, fine as hell in his navy suit, and I want to take my mind off the pinprick of achy pressure on my chin, the telltale sign of a pimple forming, one that I keep wanting to touch but can't because that would just draw more attention to it. I want to go in there and have fun and not care whether I look stupid, or that last year my date didn't want me. I want to get rid of the tightness in my chest that still hasn't gone away even though Holland's been by my side since Webster's house.

I want to stop thinking. Isn't that why alcohol was invented?

I take a quick drink and pass that bottle to Holland while I take a big swig of Coke. He smiles and takes a pull from the bottle before passing it back up to the front. Suit jackets are pressed against both my arms. I'm starting to sweat. Since my dress is black, I shouldn't get any pit stains, but I keep my arms close to my sides just in case.

The water bottle makes another round.

Holland leans in close, hand warm where it rests on my thigh. His cologne stings my sinuses. He was a little heavy-handed with it tonight, but I'm sure it's mostly because we're trapped inside the car together, probably it will dissipate over the course of the night.

His breath is hot against my ear when he whispers, "You look really pretty."

I can smell the sharp alcohol on his breath and get paranoid that mine must smell, too. We have to show our IDs to get into the dance. I'll have to talk to a teacher. I'm so caught up in the possibility of getting in trouble before the night has even really started that for a moment I forget I'm supposed to respond.

"Thanks," I say. "You too. Handsome, I mean."

On my other side, Webster fidgets in his seat. He reaches forward and gently plays with one of Caitlin's curls, twisting it around his finger. She sends a secret smile back at him. A *just wait until we're alone* smile. I turn my attention back to Holland.

The water bottle gets passed back to us once more, though there's hardly any pop left to chase with. My next drink goes down a little smoother though, now that I'm ready for it. Already I can feel the heat washing down my body, spreading to my fingers and toes.

Sam passes back a tin of mints, and I happily pop one into my mouth. I get the impression they drink in the parking lot often—they certainly have the logistics down. Reese tips her head back and looks at me upside down. "Okay?"

I press a kiss into my finger and then boop her nose. "I'm good."

Still, she watches me wobble in my heels as I climb awkwardly out of the car and points to Holland. "Don't let her stumble in front of anyone."

"Don't worry, she's safe with me."

"Safety first," I say with a smile, poking my finger against Holland's ribs. "Right, Dr. Sawyer?"

The alcohol is hitting me fast, now that we're standing. But I keep my posture straight and focus on not tripping again in these heels. I show my ID at the door and sign Holland in as a guest without incident. Then he weaves his fingers through mine, and before I've had a chance to brace myself, he's pulling me through the doors to the gym.

I stare at the court lines painted on the floor. Focus on the feeling of Holland's hand in mine. Don't look at Webster.

"Oh…my god," Reese says ahead of me. She's staring at the side wall, her expression a mix of horror and amusement.

Since it's Valentine's Day weekend, the theme of the dance is "undying love," and the students responsible for the decor decided to take an ironic approach. A pair of skeletons holding hands are strung up on the wall, along with cutouts of vampires. It looks like they just used all the leftover decorations from the orchestra's Halloween concert. Reese curls her lips in and looks at Sam, who is senior class president and therefore kind of responsible by default.

"I'm going to kill her," Sam says through gritted teeth.

Kevin frowns. "Who?"

"Veronica. She insisted on joining student council this year, so I put her in charge of the decorating committee, because I knew she'd hate it, and then she does *this*."

I catch sight of a mummy with a black construction paper heart taped to its chest and burst out laughing. Because I've been so freaking nervous, and this…this is just…

Sam shoots a disapproving look my way, which only makes me laugh harder. Like, to the point where I'm crying a little.

Surprise etches across Holland's brow. "You're a bit of a lightweight, aren't you?"

"No." I rock closer, press a finger into one of his smile-parentheses. "Best smile."

Holland laughs at this and draws his arm across my shoulder. Dips his head so his mouth is close to my ear. "I like yours better."

Sam eventually gets over her dismay, and our group heads onto the floor. We end up near a cluster of juniors, including Phil Marlow, who's here with his boyfriend—a guy from a private school nearby. When they came to homecoming together, I remember there being a smattering of surprised reactions, as if everyone forgot Phil was gay until they actually saw him with another boy. Seeing them together now makes me wonder how people would react if Webster brought a guy to a school dance. I hope they would show him the same acceptance.

I'm thinking too much about Webster.

Phil catches my eye and lifts his hand off his boyfriend's waist to give me a wave, which I return before reaching up and sliding my arms around Holland's neck.

Suddenly it doesn't matter that we're in the middle of a crowded gym, doesn't matter what else has happened in this room. His hands are on my hips, keeping me close. I slide my hand into his hair—he has such soft hair—then wrap my palm tight around the back of his neck.

Holland dips his head and his lips graze the corner of my mouth. I can feel his smile against my skin, and it's contagious. I laugh and lift my gaze over his shoulder—and make eye contact with Webster. My lungs tighten and my smile freezes, my breath stuck somewhere in the base of my throat. One blink and he looks away, his attention back on Caitlin. And mine returns to Holland, where it belongs.

We dance for the length of a few songs, and when the music turns slow again, most of our group heads off the floor for a break. But Holland just pulls me closer.

"I'm glad you're here," I tell him.

"Me too. I know you said dances weren't really your thing, but I'm having fun."

"I'm coming around to them." I shrug. "I've actually only been to one other dance before, and it was kind of a disaster."

Holland nods slowly. He draws a deep inhale—I feel his shoulders rise under my wrists. "You mean homecoming?"

My head tips back so I can look at him properly. "What?"

"I didn't put it together when we first met, but...once I realized you lived across the street from Web." Holland's jaw shifts. "He told me about you, back when he first moved to town. You asked him to homecoming, right?"

Asking Webster out was like exposing myself to radiation. The humiliation is stored in my bones, apparently sticking with me for a lifetime. My pulse picks up, roars in my ears, and I'm left feeling like I've been caught in a lie. Only I haven't—I just didn't tell Holland about my history with Webster, that's all. It's not like he ever asked.

Until now.

"Right," I manage weakly. "So...sorry, what exactly did he tell you?"

His mouth opens, but he hesitates until I squeeze my arms a little tighter around him, urging him to say it. I laugh like it's nothing. As if to say, *We can talk about this. No big deal.*

Holland shrugs, clearly uncomfortable. "Just...you know, how he heard you were telling people it was a joke." I shake my head—I have no idea what Holland is talking about. "How you only asked him because you felt sorry for him or something? And that thing about him having a certain...*type.*"

Heat flares across my cheeks. I'm abruptly, painfully sober. And I remember: Reese waiting with me in the cafeteria line. Her then-boyfriend and a couple of the other basketball guys who'd become friends with Webster getting in line behind us and starting in on how I had a thing for him. Me telling them Webster and I were just neighbors, that my mom made me ask him. I said that—but only because they wouldn't let up, wouldn't stop joking that I was in love with him, and—ironically—I was worried that it would scare Webster off. But I felt bad as soon as the lie slipped out, for pretending even for a second that I wasn't thrilled to be going with Webster, so I added, *I doubt I'm even his type.*

And it got back to Webster. Oh my *god*. I can't believe I never realized that. I'm completely horrified by the way Holland said it—*a certain type*. Webster thought I was hinting at his sexuality. I never meant for him to hear any of that conversation in the first place, but now I feel extra terrible for not even realizing how my words might come off.

"That's not…" My mouth is dry. I swallow. My gaze snags on a medical poster of an anatomical heart on the wall behind Holland, with what appears to be a wooden stake taped next to it. I blink hard and refocus on Holland, my fingers twisting around back of his collar. "That's not exactly how it happened."

Holland is quiet for a beat. Then: "I figured there was probably more than one side to the story, now that I know you."

It's that last bit that has me on high alert. "What else did Webster say? Like, when you first asked him to give me your number?"

"He didn't bring up the dance again, if that's what you mean. He just sort of…said to be careful. Anyway…it's all in the past. Right?"

The way he asks—it isn't a rhetorical question. Holland

really wants to know. To make sure I'm over it, that my animosity toward Webster won't get in the way of us.

"Ancient history," I tell him.

But even as I make that promise, my head spins with memories of homecoming. *Find someone else to share a pity dance with.* Everything Webster said that night, the guarded way he spoke—it's finally starting to make sense.

The song changes, morphs into something faster, bass bouncing off the walls as Holland takes my hand and spins me around. My gaze meets Webster's as he leads Caitlin back onto the floor.

For a moment I watch him, his hands on Caitlin's hips, and I allow myself to wonder how that night might have gone if I'd known the whole story.

Then Holland spins me again, and my hand rests on his shoulder, the soft petals of my corsage grazing his crisp suit. But no matter how hard I try to conjure that feeling of just-us, it's gone now. I'm too aware of the music and the way my strapless bra is sliding down and the fact that the pimple on my chin is definitely getting bigger.

Too aware of Webster dancing nearby, and all the things we've left unsaid.

11

WHEN I COME downstairs the next morning, I find my parents sitting in the living room. Together. My mom jumps up and moves toward me.

"Aubrey. You're up."

"Morning," I say through a yawn. I check the clock on the TV—it's almost nine, and I'm not one to sleep in super late, so I don't know why she sounds surprised to see me.

Mom glances behind her, at my dad, sitting with elbows propped on his knees. He scrubs his face with his hands before finally looking my way. "Can you come in here a minute, honey?"

I do a full body clench. I'm going to get grounded. Although… I'm not sure what I've actually done to deserve it. Maybe they just want to interrogate me about the dance. Or more specifically, about Holland. Maybe they heard we're *sexually active*, as my mom would put it, except we're not, and besides, who would they have heard that from? The only person I can think of is Webster, if he mentioned something to his mom and it got back to mine. But that would be so gross and weird, and even though I wouldn't put it past him to try to get me in trouble, I can't imagine he'd go about it that way.

Still, as I walk into the room, I brace for my parents to start lecturing me about trust and acting like a responsible adult.

But when I stand in front of them, my mom just gestures for me to sit down. "Your father and I wanted to talk to you about something."

She looks at Dad cautiously, and he nods once. "We want you to know we love you very much."

Oh.

It's this conversation, then.

My hands slide under my thighs. I stare into the blank TV screen, at the way our shadow-selves are mirrored in the glass. Murky and blurred around the edges.

Mom runs a hand through her newly shortened hair. She tugs at the ends self-consciously, and I get the feeling she already regrets chopping it off. It doesn't look as good as it did when she came home from the salon. She couldn't re-create the stylist's perfect waves, couldn't get rid of the frizz. It was stupid of her—of both of us, really—to hope a haircut would make any difference. That one dinner together would be enough to fix things.

My parents look at each other for a loaded moment, and then my mom puts her hand on my knee and says, "Your father and I have decided to separate. A trial separation," she clarifies.

I'm still staring at the people in the television. Quiet versions of us.

"Aubrey?" My dad scoots closer.

"Why now?" I want a concrete reason, want them to explain to me what happened last night to make them change their minds—or make up their minds—after all this time.

But all my mom says is, "It's complicated."

A bitter laugh huffs out of me. *Complicated.* As if I didn't already know that much. "Does this mean you're getting divorced?"

"No," my father hurries to say. "We're just…taking some time."

"To figure out what we both want," Mom chimes in, and this is ironically the most in sync with each other I can remember them being.

I pull my palm out from under my leg and run my fingers through my hair. "What happens now? How does this work?"

My father's hands are clasped between his knees. He's frowning at the floor the way Mom might if she found a stain on one of the good rugs. "You and your mother will stay here in the house for the time being. I'll be signing a short-term lease on an apartment nearby."

For the time being. Which translates to: until I graduate. Then my mom will be living here alone, and the house is probably too big for that, and I don't even know if she makes enough money to cover the mortgage, or if they have the house paid off already, or if she'll want to move somewhere entirely different. Maybe once I leave for school, I won't even have a home to come back to anymore.

I look at Mom. She seems shocked. Stunned into silence for maybe the first time in my entire life. I turn back to my dad. "When are you leaving?"

He runs his fingers along the scruff on his jaw, the sound like sandpaper against drywall. "Well, I'll need to get a few things packed, and then…"

I shake my head. It was a dumb question. Obviously he's leaving today. Probably as soon as we're done with this conversation. I mean, why would he stick around? We're not going to sit here and play board games in front of the fire. We never do that shit, so why would we start now?

I stand up. Shove my hands in the pockets of my sweatpants. "Do you need my help with anything?"

"No, you don't need to…be involved in any of that."

"So is it okay if I go over to Reese's, then?"

He chews his bottom lip. "I think you should stay with your mother—"

"Let her go," my mom says quietly as she stares at her hands and picks at her nails.

I don't wait to hear them argue about it. I just leave. Get in my car and drive to Reese's house.

"What's wrong?" she asks when she opens the door to find me in my pajamas. I shake my head, hold it together until we get inside the house. And only when we're inside her room and away from the rest of her family, Reese's arms wrapped tight around my shoulders, do I finally break down.

THREE:

A Natural Disaster

REESE

12

ONCE I MANAGE to stop crying, Reese ventures downstairs for comfort food. She returns a few minutes later carrying a tray piled with Eggos, half a grocery-store coffee cake, potato chips, two Cokes, and a bag of marshmallows.

"Okay," she says as she sets the tray down on top of her duvet. "Talk to me."

"It's not like I'm surprised," I tell her. Because a part of me knows the separation shouldn't be so difficult to digest after the past couple years of their constant fighting. But something about making it official, turning their experience into another statistic—more proof that the odds are against every relationship—breaks my heart a little. "But at the same time, I kind of can't believe my parents' marriage might actually be over."

Reese smooshes a marshmallow between her fingers.

"*Might* be." She glances back up at me. "Nothing's decided yet, right?"

It's true, but I can't seem to stifle the questions that come up every time I think the word *divorce*—questions like when, exactly, my parents fell out of love. Or if their love was flawed from the beginning. A tiny imperfection, barely perceptible. Small enough to shove down and ignore until the crack grew so big that one day they couldn't anymore.

"I feel like a jerk for leaving my mom alone right now," I tell her. "But then I think about being there to watch my dad pack…or seeing his empty closet…"

"Your mom is an adult—she can manage on her own. Or call one of her friends to support her. That's not your job."

At the mention of Mom's friends, *David from work* pops into my mind again. The idea Mom might call him for comfort. But he hasn't come up once since the incident, and I'm sure Reese is right, that Mom would call one of her real friends if she needed to talk to someone—maybe even Mrs. Casey.

"Yeah." I draw in a shaky breath and pick up a fork. Take a bite of coffee cake straight out of the box. "You're right," I say, once I've swallowed. "Can we talk about something else for a while? Distract me."

She leans forward and props her chin in her hand. "Let's see. Kevin and I almost had sex last night."

"Um, *what?*" I shake my head, sufficiently distracted from my own issues. "Start at the beginning."

She leans forward to grab a scrunchie off her nightstand and throws her hair into a ponytail with a deep sigh. "Well, we were hooking up, and it's been getting harder and harder to stop before that point lately. And you know we've been talking about it."

I nod. This has been the subject of many conversations the past few weeks. Reese has been saying Kevin is "the one" pretty much since they started dating. Though I was never entirely sure whether she meant "the one I want to lose my virginity to" or "the one I want to marry." Knowing Reese, she probably means both.

"So I ask if he wants to…and somehow it turned into this massive fight. I've replayed the whole thing over in my head a dozen times and I still have no idea how we got there. But basically, Kevin kept asking if I was sure—like, to the point where it was no longer sweet or considerate and was just annoying, so I told him to stop, and he said, 'I just don't want you to do anything you'll regret.' So I reminded him I was capable of making my own choices and didn't appreciate him taking away my agency, and it sort of spiraled from there."

"Huh…" I chase another bite of coffee cake with a few potato chips and a sip of Coke. "Well. It's good you guys were talking it out beforehand. It sounds like nerves just got in the way of things. Which is understandable."

"Yeah. Like, I'm ready. I *want* to, but obviously I'm still nervous. I don't want it to change anything between us."

"Well…it's probably going to change things a little. But not necessarily in a bad way."

She tucks her ankles under her and hugs a pillow to her stomach. "Maybe you're right."

"Totally. As long as you're really honest with each other, it could be great. I mean, the way I see it, it's probably better to do it with someone you know you won't stay with forever anyway. There's already so much pressure on first times, why add to the expectations, you know?"

Maybe it all boils down to being female. A girl's virginity is always treated like something precious we're meant to protect, because once it's gone we can never get it back. But what are we supposed to be losing, aside from a thin membrane that would probably disappear anyway if I took up horseback riding? If it was called something other than Losing Your Virginity, would anyone even care?

Reese's hand lifts to her face, fingers twisting and pulling the short hairs of her eyebrow. "Okay… Do you not like Kevin or something?"

"What? No. I mean, yes, of course I like him. Why would you think that?"

"Because, I'm telling you how freaked out I am that sex will change our relationship and you're just like, *whatever, sex is no big deal, better to do it with someone you know you won't end up with*. Which…is not exactly the kind of advice I was looking for. And this isn't even the first time you've said something like that, about how Kevin won't be around forever."

"I didn't mean it like that," I say in a rush. Even though… well. A part of me did. But to be fair, Reese does this all the time. Her parents were high school sweethearts, and sometimes she seems determined to force the same fate on herself. Every single one of her exes has been "the one" at some point or another. Because Reese can't wrap her head around the idea that she might find a better match once she's out in the real world, instead of surrounded by people she's known her whole life.

Still. There's a difference between me being honest with her and being just plain insensitive.

"I'm really sorry," I tell her. "I'm probably just projecting on you. This morning kind of messed with me."

"And I get that," Reese says quietly. "I know you're having a hard time, and I'm trying to be supportive, but I need your support, too."

"You're right." I gnaw on the inside of my lip for a moment. Pick up a marshmallow, just to have something to do with my hands. "I do like Kevin," I tell her. "I think you guys are great together."

Reese manages a small smile. "Let's just forget about it, okay?"

We go back to picking at the food, though my appetite isn't nearly what it was a few minutes ago. Once we've had our fill of the sugary stuff, Reese announces she wants a smoothie next, so we carry the remaining food down to her kitchen. Her dad looks up from the paper he's reading at the island and smiles. "Good morning, girls."

"Morning," Reese mumbles as she opens the refrigerator door.

"Sorry to show up so early," I say.

Mrs. Daniels waves her hand dismissively. "You know you're welcome anytime."

I slide onto a seat at the kitchen table and soak in this moment of normalcy. I've always loved the Daniels' brand of morning chaos, the way their family feels *together*, in some intangible way, even when they're bustling around different rooms, even with Rachel away at school. Though right now it makes me homesick for the routine my family had when I was little, when Dad still made a big pancake breakfast every Sunday.

Mrs. Daniels drains the last of her coffee, then pushes to her feet. "Reese, make up your mind or close the refrigerator. You're letting all the cold air out."

Reese grabs a bag of spinach from the drawer and asks, "Where's the almond milk?"

"I think your sister used the last of it. But there's regular milk in there."

Reese huffs and grabs a carton of orange juice instead, then closes the door. Then she takes the blender out of the cupboard. "You want one?" she asks me.

I eye the bag of spinach warily. Reese's smoothies tend to be alarmingly healthy. "Um…sure."

"Okay, we're about to head out," her mom says as she puts her mug in the dishwasher. She turns to Reese. "Make sure you pack everything you need for Kalamazoo tonight, okay? We have to leave at seven tomorrow. And I need you to pick Becca up at the school this afternoon. She's covering the softball game for the newspaper."

"Volleyball tournament," Becca says as she shuffles into the room.

"Right," Mrs. Daniels says. "So, can you go get her at four thirty?"

Reese is visibly put out by this. "I'm supposed to meet up with Kevin around then."

"Well, then I guess you'll have to tell Kevin you're going to be late."

"Fine," Reese mumbles. She peels a banana and dumps it into the blender, then adds half an avocado, ice cubes, and a few handfuls of spinach. She flicks a glance at her sister and says, "You better be ready to leave when I get there."

"Fine," Becca echoes, sounding equally exasperated. She puts her camera strap over her neck and tucks her phone in her back pocket.

Mr. Daniels puts his plates in the dishwasher, too, and the three of them herd toward the door to the garage. Mrs. Daniels pauses at the edge of the kitchen. "Okay, so it looks like you have breakfast covered," she says as she scans the room, looking like she's worried she's forgetting something. "And I'll have my phone on me if you need anything."

Reese pours some juice into the blender and turns it on. "Love you, *byeee*," Reese calls over the high-pitched whine.

She keeps blending until they're gone. When she cuts the machine off, the sudden silence is unnerving. Reese frowns as she reaches for two glasses in the cabinet next to the sink.

"What's with the face?" I ask when she turns back around.

She shakes her head. "Guess I'm just stressed. Between the Kevin drama and that college visit tomorrow… Plus I have so much work to do, and Kalamazoo is like a two-hour drive each way, and I don't even know if I want to go there."

"Isn't that…kind of the point of going, though? To see if you like it?"

She narrows her eyes at me. "Yes, smarty-pants. But I'm still stressed."

I grin as she pours the smoothies and slides one over to me. "Fair enough."

"I keep thinking about being far from you and Kevin." She sticks out her bottom lip. "I've started reading up on long-distance relationships, though. Tips and tricks. We should set up a monthly movie date. We can FaceTime while we watch together."

"That sounds great. And I bet you'll have fun once you're on campus," I say to lighten the mood again. "You'll be able to picture yourself there. Check out the dorms and imagine rolling out of bed five minutes before class starts and moving one building over."

Both in terms of the campus and the student body, Reese's liberal arts college is a tiny fraction of the size of my state school. Sometimes I think it would have been smarter for me to apply to a place like that. Somewhere I might not get lost so easily.

"The cafeteria food will probably be better at State," she says, as though she's reading my mind. "You'll have way more options."

"Well, when I took a tour, I did notice they had about twelve different kinds of cereal, so I'm *pret-ty* excited about that."

Reese doesn't laugh. She turns the smoothie glass around in her hands and says, "Guess you won't have much reason to come home, will you?"

I've just crammed half a waffle in my mouth, but I stop chewing for a second. I hate when Reese gets all nostalgic and sentimental like this. Mostly because I hate thinking about how far apart we'll be next year, too. "It's not like I'll want to stay in an empty dorm for all the breaks—"

"But you'll stay for some, I bet. And you won't really be alone. You'll meet so many new people and at a school that big, a bunch of them will end up staying on campus over breaks."

It always strikes me as ridiculous when Reese acts like *I'm* the one who will make a whole new set of friends as soon as I set foot on campus. But in a way it's reassuring. Kind of like when Mom and I are home alone and there's a spider, and even though I hate spiders, I'm always the one to kill it, because seeing her scared makes me feel braver. If Reese is worried about us growing apart, then I know we'll both put in the work it takes to make sure that never happens.

"I might stay for a couple of the small ones..." Reese's frown deepens, and I hurry to make it better. "But we'll talk all the time, and have our movie dates, and we can visit some weekends."

"Promise?"

I hold out my pinkie. "Swear it."

She loops her pinkie around mine, and the corner of her mouth ticks up.

"Just think how much easier this would all be if you'd decided to come to State instead," I say.

"I *knowww*. Don't rub it in."

"We could've lived together—"

"And eaten all our meals together—"

"And then you'd get totally sick of me and by Thanksgiving you'd be begging me to stay in the dorms just so you wouldn't have to endure the two-hour car ride home with me..."

Jokes like this are easy to make, because I'll never have to find out if there's any truth to them. I don't have to worry about the chance she wouldn't have wanted to room together, don't have to brace for that awkward conversation about how she'd really rather room with someone random or with one of the other kids from school who are going there. How I'd be so much better off opting to live on the Honors floor instead. Because as far as either of us are concerned, living together would have made us even more inseparable. We definitely wouldn't have driven each other bonkers and started fighting over who left the cap off the toothpaste.

Reese's smile grows wider. "Lies. I'd make you do all the driving, especially in the winter." Something catches in her smile. "Actually, freshmen aren't allowed to have cars on campus at my school. So I guess you'll be doing the driving regardless."

"Good thing I like long drives." I lift the smoothie, then hesitate.

"It doesn't taste as green as it looks, I promise."

I smile and take a cautious sip. "Not bad."

"See! Told you."

We spend the next few hours snacking and watching Netflix, and by the time I go home, any lingering tension between us is long gone. Because Reese is the one person I can talk to about anything, and vice versa. And no matter how stressed out we are, at least I know that will never change.

13

"HOW WAS THE rest of your weekend?"

It's the first thing out of Webster's mouth Monday morning. I freeze, hands covered in flour. We're making a pie today, and I just got started on the crust. I cut butter into the dry ingredients, keep my focus on that, because it's easier than wondering if Webster's only being nice because he heard about my mom and dad. Or worse—because Holland talked to him after the dance, gave him the same sort of pep talk he gave me. Asked him to be more friendly.

After what went down with my parents, it was easy to push what Holland told me out of my mind for a couple days. But now, standing shoulder to shoulder with Webster, it's all I can think about. How he must have felt overhearing me, and how differently things might have turned out if I'd just kept my mouth shut.

Pointless to go down that rabbit hole.

Instead I blurt out, "My parents split up."

Webster blinks at me. "Wait, for real?"

I nod and dust the flour off my hands. He braces an arm against the countertop, leans closer. "Damn. I'm sorry to hear that."

"They're just separating for now. So. We'll see how that plays out." I glance sidelong at him and something deep inside my chest flutters at the way his eyes have gone soft, gentle. He feels sorry for me. God—why did I tell him? I haven't even told Holland yet. "It's probably for the best."

Webster scrunches his mouth to the side. "Doesn't mean it isn't hard, though."

The mixture is coming together in the bowl. I flour the work surface and dump it out. I knead the dough together for a few more seconds, then reach for the rolling pin and smack the dough a few times to flatten the top.

"Why don't I do that part?" He gently takes the rolling pin and nudges me out of the way.

I watch him methodically roll out the crust, rotating it and sprinkling the surface with flour when it starts to stick to the wooden pin. My gaze drifts up his arm, lands on his face. Brow furrowed in concentration, the same look he gets when he's setting up for a free throw, and the fact I recognize this proves he was wrong that day, when he said I didn't know him.

He knew me, too. Knew how to make me laugh and what my soft spots were and what I look like when I sleep, even, and I don't understand—still—how he could have believed I didn't care.

What I told Holland was true—this is all ancient history. Webster probably couldn't care less anymore.

Or maybe he's been carrying the same hurt I have for the past year and a half.

Maybe it's only fair that I apply Bayes' rule to him as well. Because everything has changed since that summer, but I'm still me and he's still him and he's not all bad. I mean, yeah, he was an asshole at homecoming. And…on numerous occasions since. But he's also the guy who shut down Ted Turner's misogynistic story the other week in class, and the guy who used to watch every movie I recommended, just so we could talk about them.

And frankly, now that I know *why* he was such a jerk to me, it's a bit harder to hold it against him. Given my immature retaliation the night of homecoming, I'm not sure I can claim I would have acted any differently if the roles had been reversed.

I promised Holland this wouldn't get in our way. So if that means clearing the air once and for all…

"Holland told me," I say on an exhale. "About last year—what you heard me say about asking you to homecoming."

Webster freezes with the rolling pin under his palms.

"Why didn't you just talk to me?"

His gaze eventually lifts from the counter, but the crease between his brows doesn't budge.

"When you heard I'd said those things, you could have backed out then," I press. "Or you could have asked me about it—"

"Can you really blame me?" He sets the rolling pin aside, presses his thumb into a scrap of dough. He keeps his voice low so no one else can hear, starts talking fast, the verbal equivalent of ripping off a Band-Aid. "I was having a really rough time back then… I barely knew anyone, and the classes were harder than my old school. And you…you were the only person I'd come out to here, and so when I heard what you'd said, about the dance and about my sexual preferences—"

"No," I say quickly. "I said I didn't think I was your type. I didn't mean— I was just talking about *me*. Specifically. Not your type in general."

Webster frowns. I can't tell if hearing that after all this time has made any difference. "Well…I thought that was what you meant," he mumbles. "And it just felt like…the one good thing that happened to me when I moved here wasn't even real."

And he couldn't even talk to anyone besides Holland about it, because that would inherently mean coming out to them. Thinking about how lonely that must have been makes me feel terrible. But at the same time…I just wish he'd had a little more faith in me. I know how it must have sounded to him in the moment, but he still should have talked to me instead of jumping at the first chance he got to hurt me back.

"I would never have hurt you on purpose," I whisper. My palms start to sweat, and I drag them down the denim on my thighs. Maybe this was a mistake. I should have listened to the voice in my head telling me to leave it alone. "I wasn't… It was just—"

His eyes tighten. "What, Aubrey?"

My chest feels like I've just run a few miles in the freezing cold. Sharp and tight and icy-hot. "A misunderstanding. That stuff I said about asking you because my mom made me...it was just a stupid thing I said to get those guys off my back. It wasn't true."

A loaded pause stretches out between us. Webster doesn't seem to know how to respond, so he just keeps staring at the recipe sheet sitting between us on the table, until finally he clears his throat. "So...you really did want to go with me." He glances my way and I nod. "And I stood you up." I nod again. Webster blows out a long breath. "Wow."

..."Yeah." I rub my opposite arm and scramble for some way to make this whole situation less horrifyingly awkward, but I come up empty.

Finally I shove down any lingering embarrassment and look him in the eye. He's watching me without any trace of the annoyance that's been a near-constant presence the past few weeks. Instead there's a rawness to his expression, and I get the feeling if I asked him something personal right now, he might actually give an honest answer.

So that's what I do.

"Why did you sit next to me the first day of class?"

Webster curls the corner of our recipe sheet around his pencil. "Holland asked me to talk to you. I guess...I was also trying to watch out for him." He looks at me for a long moment. "But clearly I didn't need to. So...sorry you got stuck with me."

"I suppose it could have been worse." I glance behind me at Ted Turner, then back at Webster.

He smiles, but it's a flimsy thing. Like he's still not quite over the shock of all these revelations. Which makes two of us. He takes a deep breath and refocuses on our assignment, transferring the rolled-out crust into the pie dish. "Not sure if that's thin enough. What do you think?"

"I'm sure it's fine." My head is spinning, cheeks blazing, and all I can think about is how I should have made more of an effort to get him to talk to me last year. Should have let him cool off after the dance and then walked across the street and insisted we talk. I try to distract myself by stirring the chocolate filling.

"Oh, come on. No one likes a soggy bottom."

My mouth twists in spite of myself. "Was that a Mary Berry reference?"

"Maybe."

I snort and drop my gaze to the pie dish, then let out a sigh. "That's still way too thick."

He grins and steps to the side so I can fix it. We don't talk for the rest of the hour, but the pie turns out to be the best thing we've made together.

As I'm leaving school after the final bell, Kevin falls into step beside me.

"So I was wondering if you could help me with something," he says.

"Um…sure. I mean, maybe. What's up?"

"Well, Reese and I have our three-month anniversary coming up."

I raise an eyebrow. Who celebrates a three-month anniversary? "Wow. Time flies."

This earns a lopsided grin. "I know, right?" He holds the door open for me and we head outside, following the flood of upperclassmen headed toward the student parking lot. "Anyway, I'm making her dinner this weekend, and I want to make chocolate lava cakes for dessert. Like the ones they have at Mariposa's? That's where we had our first official date."

"Okay…" I'm still not sure what my role in this is.

"And I want it to be perfect, so I thought I'd better do a trial run. They…did not turn out like the ones at Mariposa's."

I make a sympathetic face. "Yeah, lava cakes are notoriously tricky."

"So you've made them before? Because I know you like to bake—those brownies the other day were great—and I was hoping you could take a look at the recipe and maybe give me some pointers?"

"Oh. Yeah, I can do that." We've reached my car now, so I slow to a crawl. I offer Kevin a smile—this really is sweet of him. Reese is going to love the gesture, regardless of how the dessert turns out. "No problem."

"Awesome. I'll send you the recipe this afternoon."

When I get home, I scroll through the recipe Kevin texted me. The flour ratio looks a little high to me, so I do some research and end up sending him a different recipe from a more established food blog. I write up a few notes about oven temperature and timing, and how to properly measure your dry ingredients, since if Kevin is anything like Webster, he may not be leveling them off. That said, Kevin is whip smart, one of those people who's so good at math that he actually has trouble explaining it to people who aren't on his level (which, yes, I know from experience). So as long as he follows this new recipe, I'm sure he'll be fine.

Feel free to call if you have questions when you're making them, I add before hitting Send.

He texts back: thanks Aubrey! I owe you one.

Since my laptop's already open, I pull up the Bayes' list I started the night of my first date with Holland. I wrote it so quickly—fueled by chaotic energy from my parents' fight—and it's riddled with typos as a result. But I scroll down to the bottom and add a new line to cover my parents' separation. Almost this entire page is about them, and their relationship. And maybe it's sort of telling that I keep fixating on this one example of a ruined relationship.

Earlier today at lunch, Reese and I looked through pictures from the Snow Ball, and I filled her in on what Holland told me and Webster's reaction when I brought it up in Life Skills.

"So what does this mean?" she asked when I'd finished catching her up to speed.

I didn't know how to answer that. I *still* don't.

Bayes' theorem shows us how to change our minds when we have new experiences. To acknowledge new evidence might be explained better by some other theory, instead of your own. And if everything I believed about Webster's motives was wrong, then I guess I can't be 100 percent confident in my other beliefs related to love.

Whatever happens with my parents' marriage, I can't keep using them as an excuse to negate every other relationship I see. Especially my own.

Before closing the document, I highlight what I'd originally written about Webster. And then I hit Delete.

14

MY ACCEPTANCE LETTER to North Carolina State comes a few weeks after the Snow Ball. Michigan State has been my top choice for so long that once I got in there, I stopped worrying about the other schools I was still waiting to hear from. I wasn't even that interested in NC State when I first applied. But circumstances have changed since then.

Holland and I have been dating for a couple months now—though the actual number of dates is still relatively low, given our schedules. It's strange dating someone who goes to a different school. I see the way Reese and Kevin interact every day—the way they're so comfortable around each other, the way they touch—and it's easy to understand why sex has been on her mind so much lately. To be honest, ever since she and I talked about it the other day, it's been on my mind, too.

I see Holland only about once a week, so things haven't

gone too far between us yet. But we talk every day. And last night, even our phone call somehow turned physical.

"What are you doing right now?" I asked when Holland answered his phone.

"Studying. But I can barely keep my eyes open."

"So you're saying I'm a welcome distraction?"

"Always," he said, and I could hear the smile in his voice.

"Where was this studying taking place? In your *bed*?"

Holland laughed at that. "Yes. Would you also like to know what I'm wearing?"

"Oh, no need. I'm already picturing you in basketball shorts. No shirt."

"Lucky guess." He lowered his voice like he was afraid his parents would overhear. Or like talking this way made him shy. "What about you?"

"Don't you want to guess?"

"My imagination isn't quite as colorful as yours. I think you'd better describe it to me."

So I did, embellishing the details only slightly, and by the time I'd finished, Holland's breath had grown heavy in my ear. I slid under my covers, feeling the sudden urge to hide, even as I whispered, "Your turn."

"God, this is…" He huffed an awkward laugh. "I'm so turned on right now."

"Me too."

"Yeah?"

I nodded, then remembered he couldn't see me. But there was a heaviness between my legs, and I slid my hand down, fingers trailing over my waistband. "Are you…doing anything about it?"

He was quiet for a moment. I pictured him swallowing, the way his Adam's apple would slide in his throat. "Yes. Is that okay?"

I turned my head, pressed my smile into the pillow. "Yeah, it's okay."

"Does that mean you are, too…?"

Heat bloomed all over my body. I pulled the covers over my head, needing the darkness they provided. "Maybe. I mean, not yet, but…"

Holland made a soft, tortured sound in my ear. "Please. I want you to feel good," he said when he found his voice again.

My lips curled in, trapped between my teeth. Then my hand slipped into my underwear.

The whole scenario has been playing in my head all morning. I expected to wake up feeling awkward about the things I said, embarrassed in the light of day. But instead I feel electric, my skin buzzing in anticipation as I park in front of his house.

My excitement doubles when I hear a bark from inside as I make my way to the door. Today I finally get to meet Lucy the pit bull. Needless to say, it's shaping up to be a pretty epic week.

Holland opens the door before I even have a chance to knock, Lucy having alerted him to my presence. We grin at each other, and then Lucy pushes her way past him to lie belly-up at my feet.

"Oh, *hello.*" I crouch down and immediately commence giving her belly rubs.

"Well, clearly she hates you," Holland deadpans above me.

"I'm not even sure which one of us you're talking to, but it doesn't matter, does it, Lucy?"

Holland laughs and bends down a beat later to hook up Lucy's leash, which gets her back onto four paws fast. "You ready?" he asks.

Lucy wags her tail and I nod once. "Ready."

We take Lucy to the dog park first, and once she's worn out, we stop by a pet store so Holland can pick up dog food.

I get to hold her leash while he lifts the heavy bag of food into the cart. And then I refuse to give her up as we wander through the aisles of the pet store, watching Lucy's reaction to the birds and other animals. She's a shy girl, curious but mildly wary of everyone she meets.

When we reach the hamster cages, I snap a picture and send it to Veronica, who I recently learned has a pet hamster named Garbanzo, which she revealed with a completely straight face despite my squeals of delight.

"Did I tell you about these pictures I saw online?" I ask over my shoulder.

"I don't think so…"

"Okay, so, this girl took a picture while she was in the shower—not of herself or anything, but because her dog comes to check on her every time she goes in there. She assumes the dog thinks she's upset, because he hates baths so much. So anyway, he sticks his head behind the curtain, and just like…watches her with this sullen expression. And then in the second picture, he comes back with his toy, to cheer her up. And she said he doesn't want to play with the toy— he just brings it to make her feel better. Isn't that the purest thing you've ever heard?"

Holland laughs in that gentle way of his and nods. "Pretty

sweet. Hey, how come your parents always said no to a dog? Is one of them allergic?"

"No." I scratch Lucy's neck and say, "But every time I begged for one, it would turn into a massive argument between them, about how my dad wouldn't be enough help taking care of it, and how my mom always made him out to be the bad guy. Eventually I just…stopped asking."

"Oh." Holland frowns and holds his hand out to help me up. Once I'm standing again, he pulls me close. He's so tall, my forehead falls against his shoulder, each inhale smelling of clean laundry. He dips his head to nuzzle his smile against my neck.

All at once, the sparks are back in my stomach. I feel the same playfulness, the same boldness I felt with Holland on the phone last night. No one else is in this part of the store, so I lean into his touch, lift onto my toes and catch his mouth with mine.

My fingers curl around the fabric of his shirt while my other hand tightens its grip on Lucy's leash, and if we were not in public, I am not entirely certain how much longer my bra would stay clasped.

His phone buzzes in his pocket and he pulls away to read it. "Sorry, Adam's been texting me about tonight."

"What's tonight?"

Holland rests his forearms on the cart handle. "His party. You're still cool with that plan, right?"

Oh right. I kind of forgot I'd agreed to meet Holland's friends. Or maybe I was trying to will it out of my mind, since the prospect inexplicably makes me feel a bit nauseous. But since we've spent a disproportionate amount of time with my friends so far, I couldn't think of any reasonable excuse for us not to go.

"Right, of course." I flash him a smile and then turn back to Lucy. Press my face into her neck.

Holland pulls me up to standing again and hooks his arm around my waist. "I promise we'll have a good time tonight."

"Definitely. I'm excited—"

He gives my favorite cheek-parentheses smile and dips his head to kiss me. "Sure you are."

"I am!" I'm not. But I appreciate that he already knows me well enough to understand I'm not big on parties. That he wants to do everything he can to ensure I have fun. Besides, I don't want him to think I have a problem with his friends. Or that we always have to do the things I want.

"Well, just to be safe, I told the guys we might have to take off early so I could get you home by curfew."

See? He just gets me.

"Though I feel the need to point out that parties do occasionally have upsides." Holland lifts an eyebrow. "We met at a party."

The memory is like biting into an unripened strawberry; it should be sweet but tastes like nothing. It's unfortunate that the story of how we met will always make me think of Webster instead.

I swallow and try to sound as playful as Holland. "Oh, so you think I'll meet a cute guy tonight?"

We make our way to the toy aisle, and Lucy starts to wag her tail. Total kid in a candy shop.

"Maybe we *should* stay home…" He narrows his eyes at me, then smiles.

Lucy nose-nudges a plush duck, and I pull it off the shelf. Squeak it at her. Her tail goes into overtime. Holland drops the toy into the cart and moves with us down the aisle. Lucy takes interest in a pull toy next. She looks at the toy, then looks at me and licks her lips. Clearly she knows which one of us is the pushover. I grab the toy and head toward the checkout lanes. "I'll get this one."

"Softie. You're gonna spoil her."

I gasp and look at Lucy, who tilts her face up toward me. She starts panting, and her tongue flops out of the side of her mouth. "But just look how happy she is! Tell me that smile isn't priceless."

He grins and shakes his head, like I'm a lost cause, but a cute one.

After I pay for Lucy's present, I scope out the impulse buys—individually wrapped dog treats and catnip—while the cashier rings up everything in Holland's cart.

"Looks like someone's getting enough toys to last her awhile," the cashier says as she lifts the bag for Holland to take.

He laughs and glances over his shoulder at me. "I think my girlfriend would disagree."

It's the first time he's referred to me as his girlfriend. The first time anyone has, actually. The labels of the treats in front of me go fuzzy—I can't focus, can't see anything under the buzz of fluorescent lights. I take Lucy outside before Holland has finished paying and try to breathe around the sudden tightness inside my chest.

Lucy sits by my feet and looks up at me, panting heavily. She really is a great dog. Of course Holland doesn't want to give her up. But it's not like he can keep fostering her forever. Eventually his family has to commit, make it official.

It's the same with dating. You can't just casually date someone for months and months without it getting more serious at some point. Either it gets more serious, or it ends. Those are the only options.

Lucy keeps panting, her tongue coated in white saliva. She looks around like she's trying to find water.

"I'm sorry," I tell her. Because I don't have what she needs.

Holland comes out a moment later, and we walk to his car. I help Lucy into the back seat while he stuffs the bags in the trunk. Then I climb into the passenger's seat, and the second he shuts the driver's side door I blurt out, "Girlfriend?"

He smiles, but the longer he looks at my face, the deeper the crease in his brow becomes. "Yeah, I thought... Is that okay? We haven't really talked labels, so..."

"Yeah, it's..." I lick my lips and glance out the window at the yellow Lab pulling its owner toward the store, the woman holding the leash struggling to dig her heels in, to stay in control. I blink and shift to face Holland. "What about after we graduate?"

He starts fiddling with the center console, opening and closing the top. "What do you mean?"

"Well, we might end up going to schools in different cities, so..."

He glances at me, and there's a tightness to his eyes. The way you brace when you didn't know how sunny it was outside and left the house without sunglasses. Like he didn't see this coming. "So...what? You want to break up when we leave for college?"

He seriously sounds like this hadn't even occurred to him. Like he was just working under the assumption we'd be together forever. The same way Reese is always talking about Kevin—all those articles she's been reading about maintaining healthy long-distance relationships—and I can't decide if they're both in denial, or if I'm the anomaly here. The one making this more difficult than it has to be.

"No, I'm not—I'm not saying that." I twist the seat belt around my hand. Let it go again.

"Then what are you saying?"

"I don't know!" I take a slow breath, fiddle with the air vent and then realize the car's not even on. I slouch low in my seat and cover my eyes. Deep breath. I'm messing this up and I don't even know why. Holland is great. But if I'm Holland's girlfriend, then I'm one step closer to becoming an ex-girlfriend—to all the pain and anger and loneliness Reese has gone through countless times, and my parents are going through right now.

I may not believe in the longevity of most high school relationships, or that following your heart leads to happily-ever-afters, but I do believe in making informed decisions. That choosing to surround yourself with people who share your interests *can* lead to happiness. I'm just not sure how to weigh all the different factors that go into that decision yet.

"I got into NC State," I mumble from behind my palms.

"What?" Holland tugs my hands away from my face. I let them fall into my lap and look over to see him wearing an incredulous smile. "Aubrey, that's awesome. Congratulations!"

"But I don't know if I want to go there," I clarify.

"That's okay, you have time to figure it out."

I nod. Slide my hands under my thighs and sit up a bit straighter again. "It's not that I haven't thought about how nice it would be to end up at the same college—"

"Hey." Holland's blue eyes soften. He reaches over and tucks my hair behind my ear. "I would love that, obviously. But you have to do what's right for you, and…if that means we go to different schools, we'll work it out. Right?"

Maybe it isn't denial. Maybe this is just part of what makes him Holland—the fact that he's *always prepared* means he never sees a problem as too big for him to handle.

"Yeah," I say, even though I'm not sure I believe him. That things will just *work out*. But I do feel better having told him about this, hearing how supportive he is.

"You're right, nothing needs to be decided right now." I blow out a big, shaky breath. "Wow, I just freaked out a little bit, didn't I? Sorry, I'm just…not good at this. I've never been someone's girlfriend before."

Holland laughs softly. "It's okay. I've never been anyone's boyfriend before, either."

"So we're okay?" I ask.

"Yeah." He leans back and turns the key in the ignition. Behind us, Lucy's tail thumps against the seat back. "We're good."

I watch Holland's profile as he backs out of the parking spot and heads toward the road. Nothing about our relationship has been what I expected. We're not casual anymore. And the longer we're together, the less temporary it feels. But as I turn the word *boyfriend* around in my head, I decide I like where we've ended up.

15

THE FOLLOWING WEEK starts with a snow day. Ten inches of fresh powder, which for most of my classmates is probably a happy surprise. They get to sleep in and feel vindicated about their decision not to do their homework after seeing the weather forecast last night. But I've never not done my homework, and I have a hard time sleeping in, and since I haven't owned a pair of snow pants since the fifth grade, I'm basically just a caged animal.

Thankfully by midday the roads are clear enough for Mom to go to work and for me to venture outside. Holland takes the opportunity to go skiing with some friends, and I call Reese to see what she's doing. Since she was already on her way back from dropping Becca off at a friend's house, she swings by to pick me up.

Reese is a cautious driver at the best of times, but with snow on the ground…let's just say I'm surprised she even got behind the wheel today. We head out of my neighborhood at a crawl.

"Have you eaten lunch?" she asks as I buckle up.

I glance at the clock. I knew vaguely what time it was, but it doesn't hit me until now that I haven't anything but a Pop-Tart today, and that was hours ago. "No."

"What are you in the mood for?"

We pull onto the main road and I stare out the window at the pristine white banks of snow on the side. Not enough cars on the road to dirty them up yet. "Whatever. You pick."

"Okay…" Reese's voice is quiet. Careful. When we stop at a red light, she looks at me for a long moment. And I recognize the apprehension in her eyes, the forced lift of her eyebrows, same as when she's trying to psych herself up before a game, trying to convince herself she still cares about cheerleading. Except now her attention is focused on me. Like it's taking a lot of effort to be upbeat around me.

"We should get fries," I say to make things easy. "And a chocolate milkshake."

The light turns green. Reese gingerly steps on the gas. "You got it."

We hit the drive-through and sit in the parking lot, me with my feet up on the dash and Reese twisted in her seat so she can face me. She dunks a fry in my chocolate shake and shivers as she bites down. I reach forward and turn the heat up another notch.

"Why didn't I apply to schools somewhere warmer?" she asks ruefully.

"Doesn't the western part of the state get even more snow than here?" I ask, just to be obnoxious.

"Stupid lake effect." She slouches lower in the driver's seat and sighs. "On the plus side though, as you've pointed out, campus is the size of a postage stamp, so I won't have to be outside too much."

"So you've decided, then?"

Reese hugs her forearms to her chest and lifts her shoulders toward her ears, lips twisted into a smile that seems equal parts nervous and excited. "Sent in my deposit yesterday. Now I just have to decide on a major. And, you know, what I want to do with the rest of my life."

"Little things," I joke. Reese's answering smile is barely more than a twitch. "Well, you're one step ahead of me. I'm still not sure where I want to go."

Reese tosses another fry into her mouth and uses the steering wheel to pull herself up straighter. "It's hard to imagine you anywhere but MSU," she says. "You've been talking about it for so long."

"I know. And that's probably where I'll end up. But talking to Holland and hearing how excited he is about NC State… I mean, it is ranked higher than MSU for pre-vet programs. Plus, better weather. I feel like I have to give it a fair shot, consider all my options."

"Definitely." She's fiddling with another fry, squeezing it between her thumb and forefinger. I offer her my milkshake for dipping. She grins and dunks it, and after she swallows, she says, "If you do end up at MSU, I can send you some articles on long-distance relationships. Kevin said they've been really helpful. Just, you know, for setting expectations. Of course, it basically all boils down to trust." She dunks another fry. "Speaking of which, have you told Holland about your parents yet?"

"Yeah. I mean, I mentioned it. But we don't really talk about that kind of stuff."

"What do you mean?"

"You know." I take a sip of my milkshake and shrug. "Heavy stuff."

Reese gets her *barely restraining myself from saying something you won't like* face, and I roll my eyes.

"What?"

She dunks another fry. "Just…you guys are getting more serious, which is great. But don't you think you should be able to talk to him about personal stuff?"

"I *can* talk to him." I lean over the console and rest my head on her shoulder. "But that's what I have you for."

She tilts her head so it hugs mine. "That's true."

"Besides," I say as I straighten in my seat again, "just because he's my boyfriend now doesn't mean I'm going to abandon Bayes' rule."

"Okay, first of all—*boyfriend!*" She reaches over and presses her finger to my cheek, right where a dimple would go if I had one. I lean away and roll my eyes. She pulls back and reaches for another fry, brandishing it as she says, "Second, don't you think you're taking this Bayes' stuff a little too seriously? I mean…the point was to give Holland a chance. Get to know him and decide if he was boyfriend material. And now you have, right?"

"Yeah, I guess." I frown at my milkshake. "It just…helps me make sense of things. Compartmentalize, you know?"

It helps me keep everything happening with my parents

separate from my relationship with Holland. Keeps me from giving up on the idea of dating altogether.

Reese chews her fry and leans back against the headrest. "I know. But sometimes, I think you just have to let yourself feel what you feel."

Easier said than done.

After we've finished the last of our food and I've given myself a cold headache from sucking down my milkshake too fast, Reese takes me home. I wave as she reverses down my snow-covered driveway, and then trudge the rest of the way up to the house. The garage door is closed, and it isn't until I nearly face-plant into the now-locked front door that I realize I don't have my keys.

I call my mom, who tells me she can't leave work for at least a couple hours. "But the Caseys still have a spare key," she adds helpfully.

Fantastic. I hang up and squint across the street. For a moment I debate calling Reese and asking her to come back to get me. Or maybe pulling up a YouTube video on my phone and attempting to pick the lock. But reason eventually wins out, and I head across the street. In the glass of their front door, I quickly check my reflection. I pull off my knit hat and try to flatten all the little hairs around my ears that are now so staticky they stick straight out. I put my hat back on.

Mrs. Casey opens the door shortly after my knock. "Aubrey!"

"Hi, Mrs. Casey. Sorry to bother you, but I got locked out."

She ushers me inside. "Oh, no problem. Let me find the key your mom gave me."

As I step into the foyer, the smell of warm cookies hits me, and I immediately start to salivate.

"Should be right in here," she says, gesturing for me to follow her into the kitchen. "And help yourself to some cookies if you're hungry! They're fresh out of the oven."

I turn the corner and my eyes fall on Webster, who is transferring cookies from a baking sheet onto a wire cooling rack and wearing an apron. A floral-patterned apron.

His grip on the spatula visibly tightens when he looks at me. "Hi."

"Hey." I reach up to pull my hair into a ponytail, which is, of course, futile. My hands drop to my sides and I step forward to survey the cookies. "Oatmeal chocolate chip?"

He moves the last one and sets the spatula down. "Yep."

"So. Sorry, are you practicing for our midterm right now?"

"I just…" He shakes his head. "Had a craving. Thought I'd try out a new recipe."

"Uh-huh." I sneak a piece of one and pop it in my mouth. It's fucking fantastic. "Not too shabby."

"I aim to please." He glances up, but his forehead wrinkles, and his gaze zeroes in on my mouth. I freeze under his scrutiny, transfixed by the way his own lips part. We're trapped in this charged silence, and I don't understand what's happening until finally, hard eyes flicker back up to mine. "You have chocolate on your face."

My hand flies up and I wipe my mouth against the back of my palm. Heat prickles along my hairline. The way he said it—it's like he's back to finding everything about me annoying.

Fortunately his mother locates the key and saves me from having to respond.

"So, Aubrey, your mom told me you're heading to Michigan State in the fall." Mrs. Casey drops the key on the counter in front of me on her way around the island to Web. "That's wonderful."

"Yeah." My smile feels flimsy. But I'm so tired of thinking about college, it's easier not to elaborate or correct her. "Thanks."

"We're still waiting to hear from a few schools," she says, and puts her hand on Webster's shoulder. He's staring at his mom with wide eyes, as if willing her to drop it. "Just have to keep our grades up this semester."

As ridiculous as it is to see Webster wearing that apron with a smudge of flour on his right jaw, there's something distinctly unfunny about it, too. He's trying. Suddenly I feel bad for giving him a hard time earlier this semester, for saying he can't take anything seriously.

I knew better than that. I was there when he worried over every detail of starting at a new school, from where he'd sit in the cafeteria to whether he'd be good enough to make the basketball team. When Webster cares about something, he *really* cares.

And I'm starting to understand he feigns indifference to protect himself—because if you don't seem to care about something, no one can use it against you.

He shoots his mom another look, and she seems to take the hint this time, because she refills her water glass and makes her way back to the living room.

"So…do you bake on your own a lot?" I ask when she's gone.

He shrugs. "It's really not a big deal. We had some spices that were going to go bad."

"Right. Well. Thanks for the cookie." I lift the key and turn to leave. But after a moment's hesitation, I spin back around. "Hey, you've probably got your own system down, but if you ever want to study together…I'm great at making flash cards."

"I'll bet you are," he says with a slight smirk. "But I'm all set."

His voice has an edge to it, and I get the sense his college prospects are a bit of a sore spot. I don't want to say the wrong thing, so I start to go again, and this time I make it all the way into the hall before he calls me back. I glance over my shoulder.

"Thanks for the offer, though."

I nod once. "Anytime."

16

MY DAD INSISTS on taking me out to breakfast before school on Tuesday. Which means I have to get up about an hour and a half earlier than usual. I can barely keep my eyes open as I sip black tea at the kitchen table and wait for him. Mom waits with me, but instead of stumbling around in her bathrobe, half-awake and shushing anyone who tries to talk to her before she's finished her first cup of coffee like she normally would at this hour, she's already showered and wearing a full face of makeup.

She moves around the kitchen, frying bacon and scrambling eggs. She brings me a plate with both, plus a side of dry toast.

"You know we're going out to eat, right?"

"Yes, of course. I just want to make sure you have something in your stomach, in case your father is late or the service is slow and you don't have time for a proper breakfast."

Up until this moment, a "proper breakfast" has always consisted of cereal or Pop-Tarts or anything else my mom could shove in my hands on my way out the door. And I was fine with that. It was actually preferable, because she's clearly only doing all this to look good in front of and/or piss off my dad. But I eat a couple bites just to make her happy, then set my fork down again. Mom taps her nails against her place mat and under the table I type out a text to Reese that says, I'm starting to wish my parents would just divorce and get it over with.

When we hear Dad's car pull into the driveway, I sling my backpack onto one shoulder and head to the door. Mom follows me like a shadow. She scoffs when she sees Dad isn't getting out of his car.

"I'll see you after school." I hop down the porch steps and look back. Mom is hovering in the doorway, hand on hip in a practiced pose designed to make her look slimmer. She waves, and I duck into Dad's car.

"Morning, sweetheart." He kisses my cheek, and I try not to lean away from his coffee breath.

"Morning."

"So, where do you want to eat? Anything in particular sound good?"

"Anywhere close to school is fine."

We end up at a diner on one of the mile roads. I order the short stack of pancakes, because even if my mom does start cooking breakfast on the regular (which I doubt will happen), this is one thing she always burns.

"How are things going with school?" Dad asks when he swallows the first forkful of his omelet.

"Fine, I guess. Second semester senior so…not much to report."

"Right." He smiles awkwardly and tucks into his food again. He glances out the window and I notice a fresh nick on his throat where he caught himself shaving.

"How's the apartment?"

"Oh, it's fine. Nothing special. When I get a bit more furniture, you'll have to come over. We could have dinner."

So much of that sentence depresses me. I picture my dad alone in a dingy apartment. An empty living room with battered carpet and bare white walls. Eating frozen dinners and fast food every night because he sure as shit doesn't know how to make anything besides grilled cheese, and even that would probably be too much effort. The fridge is probably filled with old take-out boxes and beer, nothing else. The trash crammed with empty pizza boxes.

"Sounds great. Just let me know when." With my fork, I pick at my pancakes. Slide the pat of butter around the top until it melts.

"And uh…" Dad chews and swallows. Tugs at the collar of his shirt. "Holland? How's he doing?"

"He's good. We're good."

Dad frowns at his plate. He sets his fork down and reaches for his mug of coffee. "You sure you're holding up okay?"

I take a big bite of pancakes so all I have to do is nod. It's nice of him to ask and all, but honestly. What's he going to do about it if I say something different? How does he expect to help me when he's barely keeping his own shit together? Not that it matters anyway, because I'm fine. I had my crying jag, did the whole eating-cake-and-too-many-marshmallows thing with Reese. I'm over it.

Dad clears his throat and turns back to safe topics like senior year. He tells me all about the pranks his friends pulled when he was a senior—bringing garbage bags to school and two-liter bottles filled with water, so they could create a waterslide down the senior hallway. A food fight that broke out right before graduation, and how the administration actually suspended people, even though there was only a week left before finals.

"So I wouldn't recommend going that route," Dad says with a chuckle.

"Yeah." I smile and shovel in more pancakes. It's like cardboard in my mouth, so dry I can barely swallow. I pour a little more syrup on top.

My dad keeps one eye on his watch, and when it's time to take me to school, he waves the waitress over to pay the bill. He frowns at my half-eaten breakfast. "You sure you got enough to eat?"

"Yeah, I'm all set. Thank you."

We drive over to the school in silence, and just as I'm about to get out of the car, Dad opens the center console. "Almost forgot. I've got a check for this month's heating bill." He pulls out an envelope and hands it to me. "Would you mind giving that to your mother?"

I turn it over in my hand. "Okay."

Except, it's not okay. I shove it into my backpack and wrench the zipper shut. Pop open the door. But Dad catches me by the strap of my backpack.

"Hey, hold on a second."

"What?"

"You tell me. What's going on?"

I sink back into the seat and slam the door closed again. "I just don't see why you couldn't have given that to Mom yourself this morning. It was bad enough when you fought around me. Now you're going to fight through me? I'm not a carrier pigeon, you know?"

As it is, my mom will make me recount every moment of my morning with Dad as soon as she gets home from work. I can only imagine the things she'll have to say when I hand the envelope over.

Dad runs a hand along his jaw. "You're right." He looks me in the eye. "Aubrey, I apologize. I didn't think about it from your perspective, and I'm sorry."

I hug my backpack to my chest. "It's fine."

"It's not. I'll do better, okay? I'm trying."

"You both keep saying that. You say you're trying to work it out, but I don't see either of you really trying."

We both stare out the windshield for a long moment. "This isn't the sort of thing that can be fixed overnight. But I promise we are trying." Dad runs his hands over the steering wheel and frowns. "Kiddo...I know this isn't easy on you. I'm sorry."

"Yeah, it's fine." I reach for the door again, make it all the way out of the car this time. "I'll talk to you later. Thanks for breakfast."

I shut the door before he has a chance to respond, and head into school. I stop by my locker and check my phone. Reese responded with: You don't mean that.

She's right. Or at least she's *mostly* right. I don't like how things are now, but a divorce would probably just make them even more hostile toward each other.

I also have a text from Holland, who sent a picture of Lucy with the question, When can we see you?

Between his basketball schedule and various family obligations—which Holland admittedly has more of than I do these days—lately it's been hard for Holland and I to get together, even on the weekends. I pause at my locker and type out a response: This weekend?? but only if you bring Lucy...

You drive a hard bargain, Aubrey TBD Cash. Saturday, then. Lucy can't wait.

"Hey." Veronica leans against the locker next to mine. Webster's locker that he never uses. "Can I borrow your lab notes from yesterday? I feel like I missed some stuff."

"Yeah, sure." I rifle through my backpack for my Anatomy notebook and hand it over.

"Thanks. See you in class."

"See ya." I shuffle my books around, dumping the ones I brought home last week and replacing them with the ones I'll need for my first couple classes. That stupid envelope keeps jumping out at me, and all I can think about is having to give it to my mother later and what she'll say about my father when I do.

The shot of excitement I got from texting with Holland is already wearing off. It takes all my energy just to get myself to class. By the time third period rolls around, I'm exhausted.

I have bags under my eyes from lack of sleep, my entire chin is broken out from stress, and all I want to do is go home to my empty house and sleep for a million years and not have to talk to anyone.

And it isn't until I walk into Life Skills that I realize my day is about to get worse. Because today we start our reproductive health segment.

★ ★ ★

"Congratulations, everyone, you just became parents!"

Miss Holloway picks up the nearest doll and holds it like a real baby. "Some things you should know—these dolls are high-tech. Which means *I'll* know if you neglect your baby when it's crying, or if you forget to feed it, or if you let its neck snap back. Every day you will bring your doll to class and I will upload the data to find out how you did the night before.

"Your responsibilities should be shared equally between both partners. Traditional gender roles do not apply. If you have two men in your group, you still have to feed the baby. If you are the only woman in a group, you should not be doing all the diaper changing. Are we clear?"

A collective grumble fills the room in response.

"Super. Then one person from each table can come up and adopt your child for the next two weeks."

I go up and take the doll Miss Holloway hands me, along with the magnetic-tipped bottle and cloth diapers. Inside its carrier, the thing weighs a ton. I am not looking forward to lugging it around for the next two weeks. Which I guess is the point. Well played, public school system.

When I set the carrier on the table in front of Webster, he leans forward to get a better look. "Aw. She has your eyes."

A sigh is all I can muster.

"First order of business," he says. "She needs a name."

"So pick one."

"Okay," he says with enough enthusiasm to make me immediately regret giving him permission. "You know what name I've always loved? Imogen."

My jaw locks. I know for a fact I never told Webster that was my middle name.

"Doesn't she just *look* like an Imogen?" His eyes are too bright, a smile trembling across his lips.

He's trying to get under my skin again. It's like he feels compelled to make up for the fact that I witnessed him actually trying for once. And no matter how I react, I'll play right into his hand.

I decide to let it go. Not say anything. Always the safest bet with Webster.

Miss Holloway walks us through how all of the sensors work in more detail, then activates our dolls and immediately has to deal with one doll that seems to be defective. It won't stop making a monstrous screeching noise. Meanwhile, Webster has taken *Imogen* out of her carrier and is bouncing her in his arms.

"It's okay, Immy. Don't worry about the loud noise. Mom and Dad love you very much—"

Okay, I can't. "How'd you find out?"

"Hmm?" He raises his eyebrows, tilts his head like he doesn't understand the question.

"My middle name. Who told you?"

He grins. "I overheard your mom yelling outside once when you were in trouble."

I sigh, then face the front of the class.

"So anyway, I was thinking I could have her on Mondays, Tuesdays, and Wednesdays, and then you—"

"Wait, what?" I swivel back toward him. "You think I'm going to take her all weekend? I have a life."

He bites his bottom lip and squints at me as if to say, *Do you, though?*

"Shut up. I'll take this week, you take her next." I pull out my planner and write down a schedule.

"Sounds good, partner."

"Great."

"Maybe we should exchange numbers," he says. "In case anything comes up while I have Immy."

My hand stills over my planner. I'm reading too much into this. I know I am. Because all I can think now is that he could message me online if he needed to get in touch. So him asking to exchange numbers seems like it could mean something, like maybe we're becoming friends, except, literally every time I let my guard down with Webster, he makes me regret it. Either way, I'm glad I decided to delete his number from my phone last year, since he clearly deleted mine.

"Okay." I'm gripping the edge of the table so hard. My fingers will be frozen into this claw for the rest of the day.

He pulls out his phone and types in the number I tell him. Then he hits Call and holds the phone to his ear until he hears it ring.

"What, do you think I gave you a fake number?"

He makes a funny face, like that thought never occurred to him, because in the history of him getting people's numbers, it has probably never happened.

He lowers the phone and hangs up. "No, I was just calling so you'd have my number, too."

"Oh. Right." My vocabulary is just stunning today. It's no wonder I did so well on my SATs.

"So yeah, if you ever need a break…" he starts.

"Excuse me?"

He scratches the back of his neck, not looking at me. "Like, when you have Immy, if it gets to be too much. Or if you just want to get out for a bit…we could always take her to Chuck E. Cheese or something."

"That's maybe the creepiest idea anyone's ever had."

He tries not to grin. "I was just trying to think of somewhere kid-friendly."

It's entirely possible Webster is being nice to me for the obvious reasons. Because I'm with Holland, or because he still feels sorry for me. That first summer, Webster didn't talk much about his parents' divorce, but it was obvious how much it affected him. He had to move, start at a new school in a completely different state than his dad. He understands what the last few weeks have been like.

But as I watch the tips of his ears turn pink, I start to think it might be more. That maybe Webster feels as ridiculous as I do about how we've treated each other since last year. That he's ready to start over.

I glance down at the doll so I don't have to look at him. "Well, thank you. And if *you* end up needing anything when it's your turn…"

"I've got your number."

17

MY CURFEW ALWAYS comes too early when I'm with Holland. Especially tonight, considering I was forced to bring my Life Skills doll on our date, which means we spend the majority of the time wandering around a park with Lucy and trying to get the thing to stop wailing.

Poor Lucy is quite concerned by the whole situation and keeps licking the doll's face in an attempt to comfort it.

"Well, that's adorable," I say when we're back in the car—the doll *finally* quiet—and Lucy rests her head on top of the carrier, keeping watch.

Of course, now it's time for Holland to take me home, and I sigh as he pulls up to the curb in front of my house.

"She's quite a caretaker," he says. He's been much more patient than me about the whole thing, and grins over his shoulder at Lucy.

"Next week is Webster's turn, so you won't have to suffer through it again, promise."

"Except…next weekend I'm going up north. My dad wants a guys' weekend at the cabin. Ice fishing, that sort of thing."

"Boooo." I'm bummed to say the least. It sucks how little we get to see each other. "I've never understood the appeal of ice fishing. You just like…sit in the cold and stare at a hole in the ice, right?"

"There's a little more to it than that," Holland says with a grin. "But yeah, basically. It definitely wouldn't be your thing. It's sort of a tradition for me and my dad, though."

"Right," I say, suddenly remembering Webster once mentioned his cousin had a cabin on a lake. He was supposed to go up with his dad and uncle that first summer, and that was the trip his dad canceled last-minute. "Does Webster go with you sometimes?"

"He used to, when we were kids," Holland says. "He and Uncle Matt used to make the trip up from Chicago every summer, and we'd hang out there for a week or so. But that kind of stopped after his parents' divorce."

"That's too bad," I say idly, trying not to think too hard about how sad Webster had been to miss out.

"Yeah. Though to be honest, it was always kind of a disaster. I loved spending that time with Webster, but Uncle Matt never seemed that into it. Not a close-quarters, rustic-living kind of guy."

Not a nice guy on the whole, as far as I can tell. But I shrug and say, "Well, we can't all be as well-rounded as you."

I lean across the console to kiss him good-night before he can get in his rebuttal. After a moment, the kiss deepens. I wrap cold fingers around the base of his neck. Holland sucks in a surprised breath against my mouth, then pulls back.

"Hang on." He hurries to put the car in Park and unbuckle his seat belt, which reminds me I still have mine on, too. When we're both unrestrained, he strokes his thumb across my cheek. The gesture sends a shiver down my spine. He threads his fingers through my hair as our lips meet again. His tongue presses gently into my mouth, and he tastes like the mint he ate in the park, fresh and slightly sweet.

The radio is on, but too quiet to drown out our heavy breathing, and I don't want to ask Holland to turn it up because I sort of hate this song. That's one thing I've discovered— aside from Janelle Monáe, who Holland only listens to because I made him, we don't like the same type of music. But that's a minor thing, easy to overlook when he's got my bottom lip between his teeth, when he shifts his kiss to a spot under my jaw that always gets my pulse up.

Somewhere in the back of my mind I'm vaguely aware that we're on display here, the streetlamp above us like a spotlight. Anyone could see us. My parents. Neighbors taking their dog for a walk. Webster, if he were to look out the right window.

I dip my chin and catch Holland's mouth with mine again. He truly is the best kisser. I want more of it, more of *him*—I want to drag him to the back seat, crawl onto his lap. Slide my hands under his shirt and feel the heat of his skin against mine. But he's slowing down now, pausing for breath between our kisses. His forehead tips against mine.

"Your curfew…"

"Ten more minutes." I kiss the corner of his mouth and feel him smile.

Holland pulls back far enough to look me in the eye. His expression is teasing. He enjoys being the one to hold back. "I don't want your parents to hate me. Or for you to get in trouble. 'Cause...I kind of want to see more of you."

My hands are tight around the fabric of his sweater. "Yeah?"

"Uh-huh." He kisses my cheek once more, then retreats all the way to his side of the car. I release his sweater with a pout, which makes Holland laugh.

"I really am sorry about the whole screaming-baby thing," I say as I gather my stuff. "Kind of put a damper on our date."

"Nah. Imogen's not so bad."

"*Stop* with the name!" I swat his arm and give him a look. Ever since Holland found out how Webster co-opted my middle name, he's gotten a kick out of teasing me.

"Point is," he continues, "you know I don't care what we're doing, as long as we're together."

I shake my head in mock disappointment. "How do you even come up with these lines?"

He grins broadly. "It's not a line!"

"Sure, Spiller."

"I'm serious." He reaches over and catches a piece of my hair between his fingers. His head tilts, and he looks at me like I'm perfect, like I should be hanging on a museum wall. "I might love you, Aubrey TBD Cash."

It's ice water in my veins. Suddenly my whole body's on high alert. Mouth hanging open and whatever's written on my face, it turns Holland's smile self-conscious. He exhales a small laugh and wrinkles his nose like maybe he just realized it was only a couple weeks ago we were sitting in this very car, and I was fully freaking out over being called his girlfriend.

"Too soon?"

"*Way* too soon," I tell him. But the smile is still playing at his lips, and I can't help the way my lips curve to match.

He shrugs in a *sorrynotsorry* kind of way. "You should get inside."

He's giving me an out. Knows I can't say it back yet and understands why. I take a deep breath, then lean across the console to give him one last kiss.

"I'll call you," he promises when I pull away.

"And text me pictures of Lucy."

"So demanding."

"Hey, you knew what you were getting into." I grab the doll from the back seat and give Lucy one last scratch before shutting the door.

He waves as I walk around the car, and waits to go until he sees I'm safe inside. I head straight up to my room and leave the doll's carrier on the floor as I collapse on my bed. I touch my lips and remember the way Holland's felt against them.

We've been together long enough now it should be easy to prove why we'd never work together long term. The flaws in our relationship should be obvious. Only...they aren't. I'm not saying Holland is perfect, or even that we're perfect for each other. I'm still not sure such a thing exists—*soul mates* or whatever you want to call it.

I think back to when Holland and I first started dating, when Webster asked what I saw in him, why we were together. And I wish it was easier to pinpoint the answer. I wish it was possible to engineer a relationship like a recipe, that love made as much sense as science. But no—whatever biology may be behind physical attraction or attachment, relationships don't have a set of guiding principles you can follow to ensure success. There are infinite ways to fall out of love.

But that doesn't mean I didn't like the way it felt, to hear Holland say he loves me. Or *might*.

I grab my laptop and open up the spreadsheet I started the day my NC State acceptance letter came. A pro/con list with a column for each school. I've done so much research on the facilities available at each university, the specializations. As far as my academic criteria go, they're neck and neck. But now I add Holland's name to the pro list under NC State.

For just a moment, I let myself picture it: the two of us meeting on the quad for coffee every morning. Walking to class together. Meeting up again for dinner in the cafeteria. Driving home together on school breaks.

My heart is beating faster, and I can't tell if it's from excitement or something else. I mean—what am I even doing? I'm considering changing my mind about what college I attend because of a boy. That's not me.

I close the spreadsheet and pull up my Bayes' list. And in spite of the fact I'm vaguely aware that I'm backsliding, I start writing down the names of every one of Reese's ex-boyfriends, switching to all-caps for the ones she claimed to have loved, or who claimed to love her.

Proof, I think, that even when you learn from your mistakes and do your best to make contingency plans, when it comes to loving someone, nothing is in your control. Even if it was possible to predict which way you were going to fall out of love, and even if you could do something to prevent it, the universe would just find some other way to fuck things up.

Kevin, I type at the bottom of the list, fast as my fingers will let me. *Dating four months. R once again believes she's found the one. Will probably last a week once college starts.*

My fingers still on the keyboard, I close my eyes. My chest is wound tight and I focus on taking deep breaths. Finally I close my laptop and sink onto my back, staring at the ceiling as I talk myself down. Listing all of Reese's exes like that…it accomplishes nothing. I was trying to force a result, trying to twist Bayes' theorem into something it's not. I can't let myself do that—look to the past as if all the answers are written there.

I take another deep breath and tell myself, *you have time to figure this out.* Tell myself, *you're still in control—it's not like you love him back.*

Only I'm not sure if that part's true anymore.

18

THE NEXT DAY Reese recruits my help making a batch of cupcakes for the school bake sale, which raises funds for prom and is apparently mandatory for all the cheerleaders. We end up at my house again, mainly because I feel bad subjecting her family to the doll's shrill crying.

"So, how's it going with your bundle of joy?" she asks as she looks down at its spot on top of the kitchen table.

I groan and duck down to grab the mixer from the bottom cupboards. "At least it's finally quiet," I say as I straighten again. "I swear that thing is programmed to be most annoying right after school gets out."

"Man, I'm so glad I didn't take this class." She rocks its plastic carrier. "She is kind of cute, though. Wait—is it a she?"

"It's a doll."

"What's her name, though?"

I scowl. "She doesn't have a name."

"I always named my dolls growing up. My favorite was Alexandra, because she had this wire in her hair so you could curl it or braid it and it would stay. Anyway. You should give her a name!"

I open a drawer and pull out the measuring cups. "Can we just focus on the cupcakes, please?"

She holds a hand up in surrender. "Fine."

"Sorry. But the thing was wailing for like, half an hour before you got here, and I can't listen to it again."

Reese stifles a grin and glances down at the doll once more. "Some powerful birth control right here."

I snort a laugh. "No kidding. I had to bring it on my date last night, so I can attest that's true."

"And how is Holland?" she asks as she sidles up next to me.

"He's good…" I bite my lip and line up the measuring cups in order of size. "He sort of said the *L* word last night."

Reese's eyes go wide and she smacks her hand on the counter. "*What?* Why didn't you tell me this at lunch? Oh my *god*—what did you say?"

I make a face that's somewhere between a smile and a grimace. "That it was too soon."

"That's probably the most on-brand thing I've ever heard."

"Well, it was! But he was good about it." I turn and lean against the counter. "He didn't seem to expect me to say it back yet."

"*Yet,*" Reese repeats, like she's reading way too much into that single syllable. She smiles at me for another moment. "I'm happy for you."

"Thank you." I spin back around to face the counter, more

than ready for a change in subject. "But we should seriously get going on this."

"Okay, okay. So what're we making?"

I open my laptop to show her the recipes I've earmarked. "Up to you. I think we have the ingredients for any of these."

While she looks through the options, I go to grab ingredients out of the pantry. Flour, sugar, baking soda, vanilla extract. All the basics. I unload everything onto the counter next to Reese. "So what'd you decide?"

She doesn't answer. Instead she tilts the screen toward me. "What is this?"

My stomach drops when I catch a glimpse of Bayes' theorem—I left the list from last night open. Reese lifts a brow, waiting. My heart slams against my rib cage.

"Nothing," I croak out. My hand reaches, shuts the laptop, and tugs it closer to me. "That was just—"

"Will probably last a week once college starts?" Reese's voice trembles, and I am the *worst*. I should have deleted that stupid document. Should never have written it in the first place.

"God. Reese—listen. I was so worked up last night, so I was just... I was trying to use Bayes' theorem, like you said. To figure out how I felt."

"Yeah, it's pretty clear how you feel." She rocks back on her heels like she wishes my kitchen was bigger, that she could put more space between us. "You think I'm naive. That I'm kidding myself about Kevin."

I open my mouth, but nothing comes out right away. "No—I just think..."

"What?" she snaps. "Just say it, Aubrey."

"I told you, I was confused last night. And—look, I'm not

saying your feelings aren't real. But…you don't even know what your major will be in college. You have no idea who you'll be in four years." Reese flinches at this, but I'm not telling her anything she hasn't already said herself. "Or who he'll be. You're both in this little bubble, going to all the same parties and hanging out with all the same people, but things are going to change next year. Whether you like it or not."

"And you think I don't know that? You think I don't get how hard it's going to be? Or I guess you just think you know more about my relationship than I do."

I think of all those relationship advice articles she's been reading and cringe. I'm such an asshole. "No—I know. Reese, please—"

But already Reese is packing up her things. "Look, I get that you're dealing with some intense stuff right now. And I've tried to be supportive. I mean, god." Reese huffs a laugh. "I was standing here telling you how *happy* I was that your relationship with Holland is getting more serious. And meanwhile you were using all the personal stuff I've told you to fuel your cynical *bullshit*."

Her voice shakes, and it tightens my own airways, makes me have to swallow hard against the shame rising up the back of my throat.

"I'm really sorry," I finally spit out. "I didn't mean…" I shake my head, unsure how to finish that sentence. I didn't mean to sound like a condescending jackass. I didn't mean to hurt her. But I did mean what I said, at least some of it.

Why am I the bad guy for pointing out the super obvious fact that most high school relationships don't last?

"You did mean it, though. You've always thought this.

That I'm naive and you're *so* wise, except you can't even see the way you're hiding out in your own safe little bubble."

"Please." I'm stinging from her comments, and this comes out sounding less like a plea and more like a weapon.

She slings her bag onto her shoulder. "You know… You probably don't need to stress so much about all this stuff with Holland. Because at this rate, it's not going to matter whether you believe in love. You'll end up alone regardless."

My molars clench. "At least I *can* be alone. Unlike you, who jumps from boyfriend to boyfriend because you don't like yourself enough to be alone."

Reese's cheeks go ruddy. She looks as though I slapped her. "Fuck you, Aubrey."

With that she flies out the kitchen door, leaving an unsettling silence in her wake.

After a few breaths I turn back to the counter. Put the mixer away, then the measuring cups. Store the ingredients back in the pantry and dust off the counter, washing away the evidence that she was even here.

But I can't shake the feeling that this fight was different. The kind that leaves a scar. The kind you point to months later, when you never see or speak to the other person anymore, and you say, *that, right there.* That was the moment we fell apart.

FOUR:

Three's a Crowd

HOLLAND

19

THIS FREAKING DOLL will be the death of me. Every part of my day is ten thousand times harder when I have to lug it around. Fortunately I get to hand it back over to Webster next period. *Un*fortunately, I have about two minutes left in passing time and I still can't find its stupid magnetic bottle, which is the only thing that makes it stop crying—which it has been doing since my last class let out. I'm on my hands and knees digging through my locker when I spot Reese walking down the hall, gaze locked on me.

Which…to be fair, a lot of people are watching me, because it's probably pretty clear I'm about to join the doll and have a full-scale meltdown of my own. But I've been psyching myself up to see her today, thinking through what I might say. I even wore the shirt she got me for my last birthday as a sort of olive branch. It still had the tags on it—it's not really my usual style, but every time Reese sees it in my closet, she tells me how cute it would look on me.

I abandon my search and straighten as Reese slows to a stop in front of me. My stomach is heavy as cement. My hands smooth down my blouse—a black, off-the-shoulder shirt with a floral print that would definitely look better on Reese than me, but the point is I'm trying. When she reaches me, she doesn't even seem to notice. All her focus goes to the doll instead of my shirt.

"That's a cute sound."

"Yeah, I lost the bottle thing…" I turn back to my locker, shift aside a few books to search a spot I've definitely already looked in. "And I'm starting to think I left it at home, which is just…perfect."

Reese hitches her tote higher and takes a big breath. Now her gaze is anywhere but on me. The silence between us is thick, tangible in a way it's never been before. Although I half expected her to actively avoid me today, so I guess I should be glad she came over here at all. Still, it'd be nice if she actually said something. I know I owe her an apology—a better one—but I don't even know where to begin. So I mumble, "How's your day going?"

Her jaw shifts and she glances at me again. "Look, I'm going to be late for class. I'll see you later."

The bell rings a beat after she's gone, and then I'm standing in an empty hall with a doll that has finally stopped crying but is now staring at me accusingly.

I gather my books and slam my locker door. I'm still beating myself up as I race down the main staircase and head for my Life Skills class. I'm just outside the door and can already hear Miss Holloway speaking when I hear hurried footsteps behind me.

"Miss Cash." The vice principal stops a few feet away and offers a bland smile. "Could I have a word?"

I'm initially surprised he knows my name. But then I get a burst of adrenaline, because I hate getting in trouble, and I'm not even sure if I am in trouble, but I start apologizing anyway. "Sorry for running in the hall."

"I appreciate that, but that's actually not why I stopped you."

"Oh…so what is this about?"

"You're in violation of the dress code." He pivots back a step. "Perhaps we should discuss this in my office."

"The dress code? How?"

"It explicitly states that blouses may not expose shoulders."

I glance down. My shirt does sit low on my shoulders, but the actual neckline is high and the sleeves go down to my elbows. You can't even see my bra straps.

His gaze flickers behind me for a moment. I turn around to see we've captured the attention of my entire class. Miss Holloway makes her way over to us. "Is there a problem?"

"Miss Cash is in violation of the dress code," he tells her. He sounds like a robot, like he only has three set phrases programmed into him. His gaze turns back to me. "I'm afraid I need you to change."

"Change? I don't…I don't have other clothes here." I adjust the doll's carrier higher, which is digging into the crook of my elbow. "Can't I just go to class? I won't wear this to school again."

"Perhaps a coat?"

I shake my head. This is the first warm-ish day we've had in ages; I didn't wear a jacket to school.

"Gym clothes?"

I'm getting frustrated now. I couldn't care less what other people wear as long as it isn't like…a sexist or racist slogan on a T-shirt. And it only ever seems to be girls who get in trouble for breaking the dress code.

He takes my silence as an answer. "Well, then I'm afraid you'll have to go home. I'll put a call in to your parents, let them know why you'll be marked absent in your remaining classes. Do you need to wait here for someone to pick you up?"

"No, I— You're seriously sending me home? I have a test today."

"Is this really necessary?" Miss Holloway asks in an even lower voice than before.

"I understand this is inconvenient for you, but the dress code is in place for a reason. Clothes that violate it can be distracting and make it hard for others to learn. However, if you change into something in accordance with the dress code, you are welcome to come back to finish out the day. You'll just need to have a parent call ahead, and stop by the office to check in—"

"This is ridiculous. My mom is at work right now." My hands grip the handle of the doll carrier until my knuckles turn white. "I'm a good student—you can look at my record."

He sighs like he's feeling really sympathetic. "I know you're a good student. But—"

"But your concern is protecting my classmates from the

possible threat of my body to their education, even at the expense of *my* education?"

Mr. Davis shifts his jaw and stares at me in silence for a long moment, eyebrows raised as if to say, *Are you finished?* "If I make an exception for you…"

"Got it." I turn to Miss Holloway and hand her the doll carrier. Most of the room is laughing behind her—I'm certain Webster is one of them. But as I turn to go, I spot Webster in his usual seat, elbow propped on the countertop and his mouth pressed against his fist.

Miss Holloway tries to wrangle everyone's attention back to her while I follow Mr. Davis toward the exit. Why do there always have to be so many witnesses when something embarrassing happens to me?

Why did I even bother wearing this fucking shirt?

Mr. Davis walks with me to the doors that lead out to the student lot. He holds one of them open for me and says, "Please pay closer attention to the codes of conduct upon your return."

I hate myself for nodding, like this whole thing isn't completely asinine. But I'm shaking, on the verge of tears, and I don't know if it's because I got in more trouble than I thought, or because so many people saw, or because I'm actually really angry right now and don't know what to do about it.

When I get home, I drop my car keys on the kitchen table and head straight to my bedroom. In the middle of the day, my empty house is both too big and too small. It's uncomfortably quiet without my parents—*parent*—home. Like my voice might echo. But at the same time, the walls suddenly seem so close together; I need more room to walk off this itchy-crawly sensation on my skin.

I call my mom's cell phone and leave her a message telling her my side of the story, since I'm sure the school will be contacting her any minute, if they haven't already. The only silver lining is that she loves this top as much as Reese does, so she'll probably be angry, too. But even if she tears into Mr. Davis, it doesn't change the fact that it happened. And I want to talk to someone who will calm me down, who will understand how unfair it is.

So while I wait for my mom to give me the all clear to head back to school, I scroll through the recent contacts on my phone. The school will probably contact my dad, too, but he's not the best person to vent to about things like this, and I honestly don't even want to involve him—if only because my mom would be hypercritical of the way he handles it. Reese is in class, but even if she weren't, I'm not sure I'd call her, or that she'd *want* me to.

But at least I have Holland. I check the time—his lunch period is around the same time as mine and should still be happening—then hit Call.

"Hey, shouldn't you be in class now?" he says when he answers.

His voice is tinged with concern, and it wraps around me like a warm blanket. I'm suddenly so grateful to have him in my life. "I should be. But I got sent home."

"What? Why?"

"Some stupid dress code violation. I'm so pissed. And now I can't decide if I should even go back, or just…try to make up the work I missed tomorrow. I feel like I'm too rage-y to even think straight, you know?"

"Wow. So what were you wearing?"

I frown at my carpet. "Just…this shirt. It shows my shoulders—which is apparently *too distracting for my classmates*. Can you believe that?"

"Well. I know I'd be distracted if you were in my class."

I hear the smile in his voice; I get that he's kidding. Flirting. He means it as a compliment. But I'm not laughing. I don't find it funny that I am supposed to worry about the impact my clothing has on the boys in my class. That I got punished because the administration is worried they can't keep their eyes on their own papers.

I grip the phone tighter in my hand. If his voice was a comforting quilt before, now it's a whole pile of them, smothering me. Before I can even string a sentence together, Holland says, "Hey, the bell just rang. I gotta get to class. But I'll call you after school, okay? Hang in there."

"Okay," I say. "Bye."

I hang up feeling worse than before I called. I miss Reese. So much right now—because she would say the right thing, she'd make me laugh without belittling me. I keep thinking about the other day in her car, my head on her shoulder as I said, *that's why I have you*. Except I was wrong. She's not the friend I can always count on to be there for me, to make me feel better. Not anymore.

20

WEBSTER WALKS INTO class with Immy's carrier in the crook of his elbow just before the bell rings. He sets her down on the counter and barely glances at me before flipping through his notebook. I get a flash of him yesterday, hiding his smile behind his fist, and flush with a fresh wave of embarrassment.

Class starts and Webster brings Immy up to Miss Holloway's desk to get the data uploaded. When he gets back he sets her down between us and scratches under the collar of his T-shirt—a plain black tee that has what appears to be a grass stain on the shoulder. Not his best look.

He pulls a pen out of the spiral of the notebook and taps the clicky-end against the desk, then tucks the pen behind his ear. He's fidgety, eyeing everyone who walks past our desk like he's expecting them to stop and chat him up. Like he's just that irresistible. I roll my eyes and start reading ahead for fourth period English while I wait for Miss Holloway to finish the uploads.

It isn't until the end of class, when everyone is packing up their stuff and restlessly staring at the clock like horses at a starting gate that he finally speaks to me.

"You've got Mr. MacDougal for history, right?"

"Yeah," I say absently as I zip my bag up. "Why?"

"You ready for his test Friday?"

"Not yet. My Anatomy teacher is letting me make up the exam I missed, so I've been focused on that. You?"

"Yeah, not really. Actually…I was wondering if your offer to study together still stands?"

"Oh." I pull my backpack onto my lap, hug it to my stomach. "Sure."

"Cool. After school?"

"Okay." I'm not sure what to make of this squirmy-snaky feeling that winds through my gut at the thought of him being in my house. "You want to come over around three thirty?"

The bell rings, and he gets up from his seat and nods. "It's a date."

I head to lunch in a haze, Webster's last words rattling around in my head like loose change. My first instinct is to tell Reese about this—maybe she can talk some sense into me, keep me from obsessing over phrasing that's obviously meaningless—but when I get to our table, she's standing beside it.

"So, I was wondering if it'd be okay if I ate with Kevin today?"

"Oh." My thumbnail flicks against the edge of my tray. My

gaze slides to the back of the cafeteria, to the table where Kevin and Mike Chen and the rest of the jock guys who have lunch this period sit. Where she presumably sat yesterday. And that's the thing—we have *so much* to talk about. I hate not knowing where we stand, but it's like she doesn't care if we're on the outs. She hasn't even asked why I wasn't here yesterday—which must mean she's already heard. Which almost makes it worse, because it was the shirt *she bought me*, and she doesn't have a thing to say about me getting sent home for wearing it? "Yeah, that's cool."

"You can come. If you want."

A lukewarm invitation if I've ever heard one. It's pretty clear at this point that she's choosing to put more space between us. "No, that's okay. I have this Anatomy test to study for, anyway."

"Okay." Reese smiles weakly. "Well…see you later, then."

"Yeah. Enjoy your lunch."

I sit down, hard. Stare at my tray as she walks away. I pull my backpack up onto the seat next to me and root around for my Anatomy notebook, but the buzz of all the conversations going on around me seems so much louder than usual. I scan the caf and spot Veronica at one of the longer tables a few rows down. She's sitting at the end of a group of basketball girls but doesn't seem to be interacting with them much. It makes me wonder if she's been sitting with the girls from her team by default, if she's had any truly close friends in the years since her falling-out with Sam.

She's got her head down, like she's reading. And there's an empty seat across from her.

I turn back to my empty table. I don't have to stay here.

It's not like Reese is my only friend—she's not the only one who can find other places to sit. Before I can think about it too much, I gather my stuff and walk over to Veronica, stopping across the table from her. "Hey."

"What's up?"

"Could I...?" I point down at the empty seat.

She nods and pulls her lunch bag closer to make room. "Go for it."

"Thanks." I lower my tray and bag before squeezing into the seat. I glance at the girls next to us—most of whom I've never said two words to. One smiles at me, but otherwise my presence pretty much goes unnoticed. I'm about to ask Veronica how the Anatomy exam went when Webster's name floats up from the conversation her teammates are having. I listen harder as I pull my notebook out of my bag.

"So is he, like, a cross-dresser, too, now?" one of them asks.

An exceptionally tall girl everyone calls Wheels says, "He told Mike it was to prove a point. About how the school dress code is sexist."

"Wait, what happened?" I glance between Veronica and the rest of the group.

"Apparently Webster Casey is quite a feminist," a girl named Serena answers.

Veronica steps up to explain. "He came to school wearing a women's blouse. They yanked him out of first period and made him change under the pretense that the shirt violated the dress code. Though...I feel like it's more likely the teacher just didn't want to deal with an uproar in class. Anyway. Even though we know why he wore it, *some* people—"

her gaze cuts to that first girl who spoke "—are spreading rumors that it's because Webster's…"

"Because he's…what?" I ask.

Veronica raises an eyebrow at the first girl, prompting her to finish the sentence. Under our scrutiny, the girl shifts uncomfortably. "You know…bi."

"What does that have to do with it?" I ask, an edge in my voice now.

The rest of the table falls quiet. I get a sudden rush of sympathy for Webster—and something close to protectiveness. As far as I know, no one at school has been overtly shitty to him about his sexuality since he came out. But moments like this make it easy to understand why he waited to tell people, why he still doesn't speak openly about it very often.

Veronica turns back to her lunch. "Exactly."

The group goes back to talking amongst themselves, though the conversation immediately veers into unrelated territory. But I'm still fixated on the idea that Webster wore a girl's shirt to school…and said nothing about it to me.

"So what happened to you yesterday?" Veronica asks before taking a bite of her sandwich.

"Um…" I send a sidelong glance at the rest of the girls. I don't really want to draw their attention to something I'm probably reading way too much into anyway. Fortunately they seem pretty absorbed in their own conversation. "Yeah, so…I got sent home." I lower my voice. "For violating the dress code. And…Webster *may* have witnessed it go down…"

Veronica cocks an eyebrow and stops chewing for a moment. She appears to be fighting off a smile.

I rush to set the story straight. "No, but—I don't think this is about me. Like, I think he was just making a general protest. He probably would have done it no matter who got sent home."

She stares at me for a beat, then swallows and picks off a piece of crust. "Yeah, I'm sure you're right."

"You think?"

She snorts. "No."

It's just a figure of speech.

That's what I tell myself the rest of the day. Webster didn't mean it's a *date*-date. It's just a thing that you say when you make plans with someone. Means nothing.

And yet, after school I take the time to change my clothes and clean my room, even though I have no intention of letting Webster see it. I tidy the living room and then brush my teeth, and then I get some toothpaste on my shirt, so I have to change again.

It might seem like I'm nervous, but that's only because things have been going so well with Holland. And if they keep going well, I'll be spending more and more time with Webster and his family. So it's kind of important that he likes me. That things stay friendly between us, I mean.

I'm pouring a bag of microwave popcorn into a bowl when the doorbell rings. I take a deep breath and tell myself to CHILL THE FUCK OUT and then answer the door. And die a little bit inside. Because he's wearing the New Year's Eve shirt. Holland's shirt that's really Webster's. The Janelle Monáe shirt. For some reason it bothers me, seeing him in the shirt Holland was wearing when we met. I can't tell if he's trolling me right now. But as soon as I think that, I feel ridiculous because *it's his shirt* and he probably doesn't even remember loaning it to Holland that night.

I swallow hard and open the door wider. "Is that all you brought?"

He looks down. He has a notebook in one hand and Immy's carrier in the other. "Was I supposed to bring something else?"

"A textbook might have proved useful."

He grins and hands me Immy before he steps past me. "I might have misplaced that. Figured you had yours."

"I'm starting to understand why you need help prepping for the test." I shut the door and deposit Immy in the living room before leading him into the kitchen. He plops down at one end of the table and I head for the fridge.

"You want anything to drink?"

"Water, please."

I pour us each a glass and slide into the seat around the corner from his. He's flipping through my flash cards.

"Yeah, so, I thought we could start with the flash cards, to figure out what areas we need to spend more time on?"

"Sounds good."

He leans back in his chair, one hand still tapping his pencil against the table.

"Okay…" I pick up the first flash card. "Give me the main strategies of the New Deal."

Webster offers up the right answer but becomes distracted after a few more questions. He *tap tap tap*s the eraser against the table, starts using it like a mini hockey stick, flicking a kernel of popcorn back and forth across the place mat. I take his pencil away.

He slouches low in his chair. "Can we take a break?"

"You literally just got here."

He grabs a handful of popcorn. "Here, open your mouth."

…"No. Also, maybe don't ever say that to me again."

He grins and tosses a kernel in the air. He ducks to the side to try to catch it and misses.

"Oh my god, okay, can you focus for like fifteen more minutes? Then we can take a break."

Webster (reluctantly) agrees and we get through a few more questions. He actually seems to be paying attention now, because he asks to clarify one of the bullet points I have written on my card.

I lean forward to scan the textbook between us. I flip back a few pages to the passage I'm thinking about. My finger traces the lines as I read them. "Okay, so this is the quote I pulled, so I think if you read this paragraph…"

I don't realize how close we're huddled together until I glance at Webster to make sure he's paying attention and find he's already looking at me. He blinks rapidly, like he's coming out of a daze. Then pulls forward in his chair, eyes fixed on the open page.

"Okay, got it." He turns to his notebook and jots down the information. The tops of his ears have turned bright pink. He resumes tapping his pencil eraser. "Hey, um… Did you tell Holland I was coming over here?"

I straighten my flash cards. "No, I haven't talked to him yet today."

Webster nods. "Just curious."

"I'm sure he'll be glad, though. That we're friends now."

Webster piles popcorn onto his napkin with an expression of distaste, like he just found a hair on one.

Don't look so happy about it, Webster.

This is really bugging me, a sting inside my veins, and I hate myself for craving this validation, but…yeah. I'm gonna need him to back me up on this.

I fiddle with my pen, pushing the cap on and off with my thumb. "I mean. We *are* friends, right?"

"As long as your parents keep writing those checks."

Right. Because of course Webster would only be seen with me if someone paid him. Of course.

"So funny," I say in the driest voice possible. "Maybe I should let you study on your own from now on."

He glances back up at me and his face relaxes, eases back into a smile. "Kidding. It's just kind of sad you had to ask."

At first it seems like there's more he wants to say, but then he just tosses a kernel of popcorn in his mouth and gestures toward the flash cards. I ask the next question. The answer he gives doesn't match what I have written down, so I read it out loud to him.

"No, that's wrong. That happened in 1942. It was a completely different thing."

…"I'm pretty sure it wasn't," I say.

"How much you wanna bet?"

"I'm not going to bet anything—"

"Because you know you're wrong?"

"Oh my god. Fine. If I'm right, you have to write the final report on Immy."

"And if *I'm* right, you have to take her the rest of the week."

There's a loaded pause, then we both reach for the textbook at the same time. Webster manages to wrestle it from my hands, spinning in his chair with the book in his lap so that it's out of reach.

"Hey!"

He flips to the index and then fans through the pages. I tug on his shoulder. "Yes!"

I launch forward, practically climbing on top of the table to get a glimpse. "What? No. You're such a cheater!"

"Unless you're accusing the good people at—" he flips the book around so he can see the spine "—Heathrow Publishing House of lying, then you've got some babysitting to do."

I finally manage to yank the book out of his grip and scan the answer. I smack the book down on the table. "I can't believe you were right." Or that I wrote down the wrong information on my flash card. What if more of them are wrong? I start flipping through the cards we haven't covered yet.

"It does happen occasionally." He seems so pleased—and I get the feeling it has more to do with him showing me he knew the right answer than the fact he won the bet.

I shove his shoulder, and he rests his elbows on the table, looking down at the textbook with pride.

"I feel like you've been hustling me," I say.

He cocks an eyebrow. "That's a pretty serious accusation."

"Yeah, well, you like to keep people on their toes, don't you? Hence your stunt at school this morning."

He turns his head sharply. "You heard about that?"

"I think pretty much everyone heard about it," I say. "And look, I know you didn't do it for me, but...I still appreciate it. So thank you."

"Sure." A long moment passes before he adds, "For the record, it might have been a little bit for you."

His voice is soft, the way he used to speak to me that first summer. I can't help comparing his response to Holland's, the way he laughed it off. *This* is the reaction I expected from someone who's supposed to care about me.

Not that Webster cares about me. But still. I'm stupidly pleased by it—emphasis on the *stupid*, because I should know by now that Webster is quick to revoke his seal of approval.

I send him a small smile and say, "It meant a lot. Especially considering not many people seemed to get it. Even Reese."

He frowns. "You two fighting or something?"

"Sort of. Yeah."

"Sorry to hear that. I know how important she is to you."

"Thanks." I stifle another pang of missing Reese by focusing on my notes. But the harder I try *not* to think about our fight, the more I end up dissecting every second of it, until I feel sick to my stomach.

"Do you want to talk about it?" Webster asks after a moment.

"It's a long story…" I shrug and meet his gaze, expecting him to move on. But instead he leans back in his chair, eyebrows raised like he's ready to listen. "Okay, you swear you won't give me a hard time about being a nerd?"

Webster considers this for a moment. Then, with a smile tugging at the corner of his mouth, he shakes his head. "No, I can't make that promise."

I roll my eyes. "Fine. Well, have you ever heard of Bayes' rule?"

He tells me he hasn't, so I break down the theorem for him,

giving him the gambling example to help paint a picture. And then I tell him how I've tried to apply it to my own life, how it allowed me to take my emotions out of decisions.

When I'm done, Webster shoots me a skeptical look. "And how's that working out for you?"

"I'd say the results have been mixed." I wrinkle my nose. "I know it probably doesn't make a lot of sense, but...it has helped a little." I hesitate before continuing. "After everything that went down between us last year, plus everything leading up to my parents separating, I was kind of...closed off. Thinking about new experiences in the context of Bayes' rule made me more open to trying things. It didn't matter how things turned out anymore, because the point was just to find out."

Webster nods slowly. "That does make sense, actually."

I fiddle with a popcorn kernel. "I guess I kind of started using it as a crutch, though. I kept this list. Of like...evidence, I guess you could call it. Fights my mom and dad had, that kind of thing. And even though it totally went against Bayesian thinking, I'd use these examples to avoid doing the real work. To just...reinforce the beliefs I had about relationships instead of actually acknowledging my own feelings."

Webster is quiet for a long moment, and I become very aware of how much emotional baggage I just dumped on him. Just as I start to worry I've rendered him speechless, he leans forward and braces his forearms against the table. "I did something sort of similar back in middle school, when I first started to realize I was bi. Like...any time I was attracted to a guy or masc nonbinary person, I started wondering if maybe I was kidding myself. Maybe I'm just gay. But then if I was into some girl, I'd think, maybe *this* is who I really am.

Maybe I was just confused before, and I'm actually straight."
His teeth catch on his bottom lip and he looks up at me. "I
went back and forth a bunch of times before finally accept-
ing the fact that you can't help who you fall for."

His voice has gone sort of soft, and it makes something in
my chest squeeze tighter. It's been so long since we talked
like this—totally openly, like we could trust each other. And
god, I missed it.

"But yeah, combine that with my parents splitting up, and
I definitely get why you'd try to find answers in a textbook."
He shoots me a quick, crooked smile. "So—coming full cir-
cle, what does this have to do with your fight with Reese?"

"Oh." I clear my throat and wrinkle my nose. "So, the
other night I was just kind of worked up about—" *your cousin*
"—something. And I added the names of all of Reese's ex-
boyfriends to that list, to try to…I don't even know what.
Anyway, she saw it, along with some stuff I'd written about
her and Kevin…" I glance up at Webster again, who makes
a *yikes* face. "Yeah. So. Can't really blame her for being mad
at me."

"Well…everyone makes mistakes." Webster's elbows slide
across the table, closer to me. "Even healthy relationships take
work, right?"

"Yeah. I guess you're right."

Here's a thing I try really hard to ignore but never can:
Webster smells *sofuckinggood*. Citrusy and fresh. I want to go
get my pillow and rub it all over him so I can breathe it in as
I fall asleep tonight.

My eyes flicker down to his throat. He swallows.

If he reaches for the flash cards again, this is all in your head.

I thought I knew how Webster saw me. I thought I was still just…his neighbor, his cousin's girlfriend, someone he used to be friends with and might be friends with again some-day. But my level of confidence is shifting wildly because…I don't know how to explain the way he's looking at me. Why his gaze is now set on my mouth. And I'm grasping for some other theory, anything besides the most obvious one, because Webster can't have feelings for me.

I'm not thinking straight. I'm just… My heart is pounding, and it's creating these little flutters, this energy that shoots straight down to my fingers. Makes them itch. Makes them do things they're not supposed to. Things like picking at the corner of Web's notebook. And then he's tracing the veins on my wrist, and it's happening so fast, his eyes flickering to meet mine, head tilting like a question—

A not-quite-human wail sounds from the living room. Both of us jump, Webster pushing all the way to his feet. The skin on my wrist tingles. I flex my fingers.

"That's Immy," he says. "I should… I'm going to deal with that. Her."

"Right, yeah. Good." I straighten the index cards, pen-cil poised above my notebook even though the words are all scrambled together right now.

I can hear Webster in the living room, rifling through Immy's carrier. Apparently he's forgotten all about his bet, how I'm sup-posed to take care of her now. The screaming stops. I glance over my shoulder to find Webster holding her bottle to her mouth.

He meets my gaze and then glances back down at Immy, his brows pinched together. "I should probably head home. In case she starts crying again."

"Oh." Relief crashes through me, but it's tinged with something bitter. Disappointment. I focus on Immy, the way Webster's bouncing her like he has too much adrenaline to stand still. "Okay…"

"Thanks for the help."

"Totally. No problem."

He grabs his notebook and backs up toward the door. "See you tomorrow."

Once the door shuts behind him, I close my eyes and let out a long breath. The silence he's left behind throbs in my ears. I don't know what happened—or almost happened—between Webster and me. But I'm left with the heaviness of guilt, and a feeling like I owe that creepy little doll for interrupting when she did.

21

THINGS GET INCREASINGLY awkward with Webster over the next week. On Wednesday I try to make an effort, so I ask him how the history test went. He says "fine" and asks how it went for me, to which I reply "fine." And then we don't talk again for two days.

I also try not to look at him too much, because I've decided there is another explanation for what happened: this whole mess is because he shares some kind of family resemblance to Holland and my brain is just confused. And it's really not that difficult to avoid eye contact with him, because we're officially done with Immy, which means it's time to learn all about hormonal birth control and the right way to put on a condom, plus an overview of STDs, all while sitting so close our elbows almost touch. Good times.

By Friday, I've just about given up hope that things will ever resemble normal again. I'm texting back and forth with

Holland—grateful for the distraction while simultaneously undermining that distraction by worrying he'll remember this is the hour I have class with Webster and ask me to pass a message along to him—when Webster shifts to face me.

"So, I got some news today."

I leap at this offering like a dog after table scraps. "Oh yeah? What news?"

"It's not a big deal or anything, but…" He rubs his neck and shrugs. "I got accepted to MSU. So it looks like you'll be stuck with me another four years."

"Oh my god! Webster!" I tap his arm with the back of my hand. "That's great. Congratulations."

"Thanks."

Miss Holloway clears her throat and asks everyone to settle down. She's having an awful lot of trouble wrangling us this week. Meanwhile I'm still turning Webster's words over in my head. *You'll be stuck with me.* Because of course Webster will be at one of my top choices while Holland will be at the other.

I consider telling him I'm still on the fence, but decide this moment is about him, not me.

"We should celebrate," I whisper.

He shakes his head. "We don't have to…"

"It can just be something low-key," I backtrack. He sucks in his cheeks, like maybe he's figuring out the best way to reject me. But I'm only trying to take the practical approach, to maintain this friendly dynamic we've got going for Holland's sake, or in case I do end up at MSU and we end up having to share a ride home at some point. "Let me buy you a celebratory Slurpee or something. Just a quick trip."

Webster glances to Miss Holloway at the front of the class. Back to me. "Okay."

I smile. "Meet at our lockers after school?"

"Sounds good."

See? We can be friends. We *are* friends.

And I know Holland would be happy to hear it—he was happy when I told him Webster and I had studied together, though I did leave out any mention of perceived weirdness, since at this point I'm pretty sure it was all in my head. But if I tell him about today's plans, he'd probably want to join us, which would turn it into a whole big thing. It would make Holland think the three of us could hang out together all the time, which…just because we're getting along better now doesn't mean I want Webster around every time I see my boyfriend. It's better not to tell him, at least until I see him tonight and there's actually something to tell.

So as Holland and I text throughout the day, I stick to the subjects that come up organically. He asks if I've talked to Reese yet, and I tell him she's still opting to sit at Kevin's table. To which he responds: You'll make up soon. And look on the bright side—at least you're getting to know Veronica better! I make a face at my phone after reading that. It's a valid point, but…I'm not really interested in hearing the bright side of losing my best friend.

I scroll through my texts with Reese, though neither of us has sent anything since before the fight. With a sigh, I switch back to Holland. I don't want to be too hard on him—I don't want to be like my mother, nitpicking every offhand comment, never able to let anything go.

So I change the subject to Lucy, and he tells me his parents agreed to officially adopt her. I can tell how happy he is not to have to give her up, so we stick to that topic until it's time for my next class. He ends the conversation with a heart emoji, and I stare at it while I wait for the bell to ring. Holland hasn't said I love you again, but I don't know if this counts. If I'm supposed to send a heart back, or if that's like saying *I love you, too.* I can't make up my mind, so I lock my screen and put my phone away without sending anything.

In the next month, I'm supposed to decide where I'm going to school. NC State, with its highly ranked program and amazing research facilities, its warm weather and brand-new scenery. With Holland. Or Michigan State, with its not-quite-as-highly-ranked but still *very* reputable program, its big open campus and familiarity. And with Webster.

Seeing as I can't even figure out what emoji to send my boyfriend, I'm not particularly confident in my current ability to make huge, life-altering decisions.

Apparently I'm not the only one whose mind is somewhere else today. As Veronica and I are cleaning up our Anatomy lab, she lets out a sharp hiss. I look over and she's clutching her left hand over her right, squeezing her middle finger.

"What's up?"

Her nose is wrinkled, teeth gritted. She loosens her grip and looks down. Her glove is sliced open—she cut herself.

"Oh, ouch." I get the attention of Mrs. Landis, who takes one look at Veronica's hand and instructs her to go see the school nurse.

"You can escort her, Aubrey. Take your things, I'll finish putting everything away."

"Okay, thanks."

We both ditch our gloves and lab coats and Veronica grabs some paper towel from the sinks at the back of the room. With that wrapped around her finger, she picks up her bag and we duck out of the room.

"It's not that bad," Veronica says once we're in the hall. But she isn't looking at the cut. Her hand is in a tight fist around the paper towel and raised over her head. "We can just ditch."

"Okay, but think about what you cut yourself with. You need to get it disinfected, at least."

She sighs and hitches her backpack higher with her free hand. We round the corner and head down the main staircase. When we get to the landing on the first floor, Veronica's stride falters. Sam is right in front of us, having just left the girls' bathroom. She stops, too, arms folded over her chest. She eyes Veronica, her gaze seeming fixed on Veronica's hand, which she's only now lowering to chest level. Sam frowns and for a second I think she's going to ask what happened, if we need help, but instead she abruptly shifts her gaze to me and drops her arms by her sides.

"Hey, Aubrey."

"Hey…" I glance at Veronica, who is now staring at a spot on the floor.

"Did Reese tell you about the party at Megan's place next weekend?"

"Um…no, I hadn't heard."

"Well, you and Holland should totally come!"

I always thought Sam seemed nice, but the smug smile she's wearing now has me reevaluating. I'm not sure if she says it just to make Veronica feel excluded, or because she *knew*

Reese hadn't asked me and wanted to rub salt in the wound. Suddenly I wouldn't put either past her.

Veronica walks between us, a new determination in her stride as she heads for the school nurse's office.

"Yeah, maybe," I say, and sidestep toward Veronica in a way I hope conveys I have her back. "I'll see you later."

"Hey, word of advice?" Sam takes a step closer to me and nods her chin down the hall, the direction Veronica just went. "You might want to watch your back with her."

I stare at Sam for a long moment, a bit shocked. This is the most she's ever spoken to me, and now she's warning me about Veronica? Who I'm pretty sure she hasn't spoken to in years? "Thanks, but…Veronica and I are good. And I like to make my own mind up about people."

Veronica doesn't say anything when I catch up to her. The nurse isn't here, so we sit in plastic chairs and wait.

"You can take off," Veronica finally says. "I don't need a babysitter."

I pull my backpack onto my lap and hug it to my chest. "No worries. Only a few minutes left before class is out, anyway."

She drops her bag between her feet and tips her head back against the wall. "Didn't realize you and Sam Palmer were friends."

"We're not," I say automatically. "But we're both friends with Reese, so…" My lips scrunch to the side. "Though I think Sam sees more of Reese than I do these days."

A long silence stretches out between us. I haven't actually caught up with Reese in over a week now, despite the fact we're still technically not not talking. I take a deep breath through my nose to quell the queasy feeling that rises up every time I think about our argument.

Veronica stares straight ahead, her gaze unfocused, like she's seeing something other than the anti-smoking poster taped to the wall opposite us.

"You two used to be friends, right?" I hedge.

"Long time ago." She drops her gaze to her hand again.

Their history isn't any of my business. But I remember the way Sam looked as she watched Veronica leave the gym after that basketball game, the regret etched on her face, and I can't resist asking, "Do you think you'll ever be friends again?"

Veronica side-eyes me for a second, as though wondering how much I really know about what went down between them (which, admittedly, is almost nothing). Or maybe she sees through me, knows I'm also trying to figure out what to do about Reese. And about Webster. Finally she shrugs. "I think…sometimes you're better off going it alone. You know?"

The nurse walks in before I can answer, startling a bit when she sees us waiting. "Sorry to keep you waiting. What can I do for you?"

Veronica shows her the cut, which has pretty much stopped bleeding by this point. It takes her a few minutes to disinfect the cut and bandage it, and by the time she's done, the final bell is ringing.

We walk into the flooded halls and head straight for the student lot. We reach my car first, and Veronica pauses in front of the hood. "Thanks. For staying with me."

"No problem."

Her bandaged hand adjusts the strap of her bag. "See you later."

I nod and pull open the driver's side door. It takes forever to file out of the student lot, and my phone is blowing up with texts from Holland now that he's out of class, too. I wait to answer until I get back home. With the car in Park and the windows down, I scroll through the links he sent me—a dozen or so dogs available for adoption.

I type back: Are you trying to kill me???

Just another part of life after college to look forward to!

At his mention of college, my stomach drops. I completely forgot about my plans with Webster. *Shit.*

I close my conversation with Holland and send a message to Webster, asking if he's still at the school. A minute goes by. Two. No answer. School let out almost twenty minutes ago—there's no way he's still waiting for me. No point in driving back.

I get out of the car and cross the street to his house, taking a seat on his front porch step. I don't have to wait long—his car pulls into the driveway about five minutes later. I leap off the porch as he parks and meet him in the driveway.

"I'm so sorry," I burst out.

He shakes his head and locks the car behind him. "It's cool."

"No, it's not. I totally flaked, I know, but—"

"Really, it's no big deal." He moves past me, toward the front door. "Just…if you didn't want to go you could have said so. Or not said anything in the first place, since it was your idea."

"I did want to hang out. I *do* want to. But my lab partner cut herself in Anatomy, so I went with her to the nurse's office and the bell rang while we were in there and I kind of… forgot."

He looks at me for a moment with a tiny divot between his brows. Then he straightens and his arms fall to his sides. He stuffs his hands into the pockets of his jeans. "Is she okay?"

"Yeah, it was minor." I look at down at my feet. Back up at Webster. "Anyway, if you're up for it, we could go now?"

Webster's jaw shifts. "It's cool. Holland mentioned you guys have plans tonight anyway, right?"

"Yeah, later on."

"Seems like things are getting pretty serious between you two."

Not a question, but Webster's clearly waiting for a response all the same. "Yeah. I guess they are."

For some reason, admitting it makes me feel guilty. And maybe I *should* feel guilty, given the vibe between Webster and I the past few days.

He nods. "Well, I've got to get ready for a date, too, so…"

"Oh yeah?" The sun goes behind a cloud and I shift my weight, cross one leg over the other to stay warm. "Who with?"

"This guy Henry from work. He's been asking me out for a while, and he's cute, so I figured, why not?"

"Oh!" Part of me wants to play the role of supportive friend—especially since I didn't get to be that person for Webster when he first came out at school. But I also kind of don't want to hear about Henry. Mostly because I feel like an idiot for thinking there was anything at all between us the other day. Not only is he not interested in me, he's been interested in a boy this whole time and I didn't even know. "That's really great. I thought…well, I wasn't sure if you'd dated any boys since you moved here."

"A couple." Webster spins his keys around his finger, then grips them in his palm. "Is that a problem for you, Aubrey?"

"No! No, I'm glad. I'm really proud of you for…"

"Going on a date? Thanks. I'm proud of you, too. We're very brave."

My cheeks flare. "I just meant…have a good time."

…"Yeah. You too."

I can't tell if he's pissed or not. He sort of seems like he is, but also like he couldn't care less about me or the plans we make. I offer a smile and he just stares at me, his eyebrows lifted like he isn't sure why I'm still standing here. "Okay, so, how about a rain check? Tomorrow maybe?"

"I'll probably be busy." He takes another step toward the door. "And I should really get going."

"Sure…yeah, we'll talk later, then."

He nods and goes inside without another word. And I'm left wondering why I ever thought this was a good idea.

Why I thought *we* were a good idea.

22

SEEING MY DAD sitting on the sofa in our living room shouldn't be strange, but it is. Everything from his suit and tie to the way he announces he's going to get a glass of water— as if waiting for someone to grant him permission—makes him seem out of place.

He comes back and sets the glass on the coffee table. Then, a beat later, leans forward and slides a coaster underneath.

His gaze flickers from the TV, which is playing an episode of *Great British Bake Off*, naturally, over to me. "Have you been giving any thought to what college you want to attend?"

What kind of question is that? I want to respond. Like, *No, Dad, I haven't given any thought to the biggest decision of my life, but thanks for the reminder.*

Since Webster and I didn't end up going anywhere after school, I spent that time studying my pros and cons list. I even plugged the graduate stats for all my options—including a third school in Ohio I have no interest in attending—into Bayes' theorem to see which school was most likely to get me into a vet program. And then the stupid Ohio school came out with the highest probability, even though it finishes last in literally every other category. So that was decidedly unhelpful.

"Yeah," I finally say to Dad. "I keep going back and forth about it."

Dad nods, sends me a sympathetic smile like he can tell how stressed the topic makes me. "You've got time."

Everyone keeps saying that—I keep saying it to myself, too, but pretty soon it won't be true anymore. And I'm terrified of choosing wrong. Of that one decision causing a domino effect of life choices I can't undo.

I keep trying to visualize myself at both schools. Going to pre-med classes with Holland. Maybe even partnering up in labs.

But then it's just as easy to picture going to MSU—and I don't mean for my daydream to automatically include Webster, but there he is. Living in the same dorm as me, coordinating rides home for the holidays.

"So what are you and Holland up to tonight?" Dad asks next, snapping me back to the present.

"Not sure," I tell him. I hug a velvet throw pillow to my stomach and pick lint off the front. "We might go to that arcade that opened up near the mall."

"Sounds like fun," he says, but his voice grows distracted as Mom comes down the stairs.

It's been only the past week or so that I've noticed a difference in the way Mom talks about Dad. Saying things like, *He's made such an effort lately.* Which I guess is evident in the tie. The fact he made a reservation at her favorite Italian restaurant.

Mom beams when he tells her this, and I know I should be happy they're getting along. Part of me is. But something I can't quite define twists deep in my gut. Guilt, maybe. Because his name has been caught in my throat since this afternoon, since Mom told me she had a date tonight and I immediately pictured a BMW parked in our driveway, wondered if she was seeing *David from work*.

Because I'm pretty sure my dad still has no idea about that night, and I'm partly to blame.

"Have fun tonight, kiddo," Dad says as he pulls me into a side hug and pecks the top of my head.

"You too." I smile and shove my hands in my pockets, still hovering near the couch.

"We won't be late." Mom pulls on her coat and wraps a scarf around her neck. "Oh, and your father and I were talking about having a family dinner this weekend."

"I can grill," Dad says enthusiastically. "And maybe you could take care of the dessert? Your mom says you've gotten really good at baking."

"Sounds good," I tell them, already mentally cataloging the pie recipes I could try.

"And why don't you invite Holland?" Mom says.

My smile grows tight on my lips. Forced. But it's a bit of a stretch, isn't it? Asking Holland to attend a family dinner when this is the first time my parents have gone out together since the separation. "Holland's pretty busy with basketball," I tell them, even though the season is technically over. "But I'll see if he's free."

I move around the couch, herding them toward the door.

Desperate for them to leave before Holland gets here—I don't want them to put him on the spot.

Finally they go, and I try to get back into the show, but I'm too wound up to care about *creme pat*. I let it play in the background, my mind all over the place.

I keep thinking about that night I walked in on my mom and *David from work*. Maybe she wasn't lying—maybe it was nothing. But if that's true, why would she have asked me not to tell my dad? And if I tell him now, will that ruin any chance they have of working things out?

The doorbell rings, and I leap off the couch and race to let Holland inside. As soon as I open the door, he starts apologizing for being early. "I was over at Webster's, but he had to leave for a date, so I figured I'd just come over."

I plant a kiss on his mouth—his perfect lips that are never dry and always a split second late to react to mine, like he's still surprised I like him.

His hand slides into my hair. He twists a lock around his finger, then breaks the kiss to smile at me. "Missed you, too."

I did miss this. Ever since my fight with Reese, I've been so lonely. And I missed the way his smile takes over his whole face and how kissing Holland makes me forget about everything and everyone else, if only for a few moments.

"I'm glad you're here now," I say as I close the door behind him. "I was just watching TV and thinking about baking something. Would you be up for that?"

"Baking?" I nod, and Holland makes a face. "I don't know if that's really my thing."

"Well, have you ever tried?" I say with a laugh. "We can start with something simple. It'll be fun."

"I'm just…not that into desserts, I guess."

"Okay. It was just an idea." I shrug. "What do you want to do tonight, then?"

Holland gestures toward the door, his car in the driveway. "Maybe we could go see a movie?"

"Or…" I raise an eyebrow. Grab his hand and tug him toward the stairs. "Since my parents are out…we could stay here for a while."

Because I need more of Holland's dizzying kisses. Need his touch to blot out everything else on my mind.

He answers with a crooked grin and lets me pull him upstairs, where he releases my hand in favor of taking a self-guided tour around my room. I follow his gaze as it tracks the photos of me and Reese taped to the door of my closet, cringe as he notices the puppy-themed calendar hanging above my desk. But of course he just comments on how cute April's golden retriever is. When he walks past my bookshelf, he turns his head to read the spines of my old paperback romances—plus a sci-fi book I borrowed from Webster that summer and never gave back. I really should donate all of those.

Next he picks up the corsage he gave me at the Snow Ball. It's been sitting on my desk ever since, petals now brittle and brown along the edges, its ribbon creased and bent out of shape. I feel bad I didn't put it somewhere safer, hang it upside down so it could dry in a pretty way instead of one side getting smooshed. Then again, I'm not sure why I even held on to it this long. I haven't kept anything else. Not the ticket stub from our first trip to the movies. Not a pair of chopsticks from the sushi restaurant we ate at on our second date. Nothing cutesy that I can stash in a shoebox, forget about until one day when we're broken up and I feel the urge to remember the details of our first dates.

His fingers trail over the MSU sweatshirt draped over my desk chair, and for a moment I think he's going to bring up NC State. And then I'll have to explain to him how torn I am, how I don't know how to quantify things like being at the same college as my boyfriend versus knowing more people at MSU or being closer to Reese's college—all these intangibles that make the decision more complicated.

I close the distance between us, press my face against his chest, and inhale the scent of his shirt. Floral laundry detergent. It's not a bad smell. Just sort of…generic. A bottled scent that could belong to anyone.

I'm a freak. Honestly, who cares what he smells like? My palm presses against his stomach and I can feel the ridges of muscle. The sense of smell is overrated.

Together we move to sit on the edge of my bed. He kisses me again, soft and sweet. The way he's always kissed me. But tonight I'm not in the mood for sweet, careful kisses.

I nip at his lip. Kiss him harder. Try to show him he's the only person I'm thinking about right now, that I've been thinking about him all day.

One of his hands moves to my thigh. But he just leaves it there, an inch above my knee.

Don't get me wrong, I like that he always starts slow. Love that he never assumes we're going to do something, even if we've done it before. But my mind is moving faster than we are, stuck on inappropriate subjects like what Webster might be doing on his date, or whether Reese and Kevin have had sex yet. Which is why I need Holland to touch me in a way that makes it harder to think.

We lie back on the bed together. This is the first time it's been like this—in my room, on a bed instead of the back seat of his car. I move my hand from under his shirt and slip my fingers under the waist of his jeans, thumb rubbing over the button on his fly. He sucks in a sharp breath and I tip my forehead against his. "Do you want me to…?"

He kisses me with a renewed enthusiasm, but it's another moment before his hand leaves my leg to help with his fly. And even though we've done this before, it's still new enough my heart kicks up as my hand slides all the way under his boxers. I worry sometimes I won't do it right, or it won't feel as good as last time, but I relax a bit when Holland gasps against my mouth. I press my chest closer to his, and while my hand works slowly against him, his palm runs from my hip back down to my thigh. I nudge my knees apart and he gets the hint, starts rubbing at the seam between my legs.

My pants are a bit tight, so it takes more work for him to get them out of his way. I stifle a moan when his fingers first slip into my underwear.

It gets increasingly difficult to keep up a steady rhythm, which apparently is an issue for Holland, too, since at one point he stops moving his hand altogether. I lift my hips to encourage him, but when he starts up again, his touch doesn't really do anything for me.

I try to concentrate, to shift my hips in a way that will help him hit the right spot. I don't know how else to communicate what feels good. But he doesn't even seem to care anymore. His eyes are squeezed shut and his head is tilted back and a moment later he grunts and pulls his hand away from me. He places it over mine instead, holding me in place as he finishes.

I wait, semi-frozen with embarrassment because even though this was the intended result of my efforts, I'm not totally sure what to do now that it's over. Holland swallows hard and takes a few shallow breaths, then uses his free hand to reach for a box of tissues on my nightstand.

We don't look at each other while we clean up. Then he takes the tissue away from me and gets up to toss them in the trash bin under my desk. When he gets back he kisses my cheek. "Thanks. That was really great."

"Oh. Good."

"Your turn." He leans closer to me, but I've already zipped my pants again.

"No. That's okay."

He checks the clock, like he wants to make sure he actually has enough time to get me off before asking, "Are you sure?"

To be fair, maybe now that Holland's finished, he'd be able to focus. Maybe it would be better than before. But even if that's true, I can't get over the fact that his hands are no longer clean, and I know entirely too much about biology to let them anywhere near my crotch.

"Yep. I'm good." Not great, though. Because now I'm even *more* tense than before Holland got here, and I'm irritated by the fact that this wasn't mutual, and I get that he's trying to rectify that, but I also just kind of want this night to be over now.

Holland tucks my hair behind my ear and kisses my jaw and it takes everything I have not to lean away from him. He pulls back, drops his hand onto the comforter between us.

"You okay?"

"Yeah. Sorry." I huff and tilt my head back. Close my eyes for a moment. "I'm just kind of distracted."

Holland's voice is gentle and quiet. "Did I do something wrong?"

I blink my eyes open and turn my head to face him. He looks so worried. "No, of course not."

"Then what's the matter?"

"It's just…my parents," I offer up, because that's easier, safer than telling him I'm not enjoying myself right now. And it's not really a lie—I haven't been able to push *David from work* out of my mind entirely. I keep wondering what kinds of compromises or doubts are normal in relationships. How you're supposed to know if something is a red flag or worth working past.

"It's good they're talking again though, right? Maybe things will work out."

It's the same way Holland reacted when I first told him about their separation. Always optimistic, as though this might be the best thing for them in the end.

And in this case I don't even disagree, but something about that statement still bothers me. Because it's so like him to think the pieces will just fall into place, things will just *work out*. That's why he was so quick to brush off my fight with Reese, because he thinks we'll just magically make up. And it's why he has no problem picturing us together next year—he doesn't factor in any of the issues that come with being long-distance.

"Last time I got my hopes up about them having dinner together, they got separated like…days later. They even tried to rope you into a dinner this weekend. Don't worry, I told them you were probably too busy."

Holland frowns at this. "I'm not too busy."

I glance up from under his arm. "I just figured…it's a lot."

"Kind of sounds like you don't want me there."

"No! Honestly, that's not it." Not *entirely* it, anyway. "This whole situation is fucked up, you know? I just think we should wait and see how it goes before subjecting you to a dinner, that's all."

Holland nods, offers me an understanding smile. "I get it," he says. "Some other time."

But I can still see traces of the hurt in his eyes—and I can't blame him. His *I love you* is still hanging over us, unanswered. And even on nights like this, when all I want is to feel close to him—even as we spend the rest of the night cuddled under the same blanket, watching TV until he has to go—I somehow feel like I've only managed to create more distance.

After Holland goes home, I walk back upstairs and cast out a heavy sigh as I collapse on my bed. My room is still filled with the same crackling energy as before. My chest is still wound tight. It reminds me of the feeling I got when I had a palate expander in my mouth to fix my underbite. Every week my mom would have to wind it tighter with this needle, and that pressure bordering on pain would be all I could think about for hours afterward. My whole body is filled with that kind of tension right now, and I need some kind of release.

I shut my light off and slip my hand into my underwear.

I think about Holland's breath in my ear, about his hands on me. My brow pinches, trying to focus on that sensation. But my mind slides around: our midnight kiss, his body heat against mine at the Snow Ball, his mouth on my neck. My hand moves and my mind drifts with it, this time back to Webster's house. New Year's Eve. Focus on New Year's Eve. But without my consent I'm in Webster's kitchen. Chocolate on my lip and the way Webster stared at my mouth. Glared at it. Then the image of us at my kitchen table floods back, the way his eyes drifted down again, that same intensity in his gaze.

Because he wanted something he couldn't have.

My breath hitches. I've lost control of my mind now. It's taking me places that don't exist, memories that never happened. The two of us in the Life Skills lab. Webster and me. Alone. And when he sees the chocolate on my lip he rubs his thumb across it. And what's in his eyes isn't resentment. It's something else. Something that makes my tongue sweep down to lick the place he touched. Then he rocks closer, catches my mouth with his. It isn't a sweet kiss. Not soft or gentle. It's hands gripping my waist, hips rocking together, Webster hoisting me onto the counter so my face is level with his. It's my shirt tugged off my shoulder and his mouth following everywhere his hands go. Buttons undone and hands scrambling for hair, skin, balling up clothing and tossing it aside until there's barely anything between us, and—

My eyes shoot open. I'm panting, shaking. Moonlight stripes my ceiling, cutting through the blinds at a sharp angle.

I can't believe I just…while thinking about *Webster*.

Pretty much the worst person I could have fantasized about, to be honest. But it's not an actual fantasy. I don't even know where that came from—it's not like I have feelings for him. I mean, Webster…he drives me crazy, always pushing my buttons and getting under my skin.

I blink up at the ceiling. *Fuck*.

I might have a problem.

23

I SIT ON the edge of my mom's bed, watching her fluff her hair and try on different shades of lipstick in her bathroom mirror. She's going out with my dad again tonight. Says he might even stay here at the house for the rest of the weekend.

"What do you think of this one?" Mom asks as she turns around to show me a brick red that looks exactly the same as the last one she tried on.

"That's perfect."

She glances back at her reflection once more, then nods and drops the tube into her purse. She stands up and smooths out the wrinkles in her dress. Checks the time and then casts a desperate glance toward her closet. "Maybe I should change into something else."

I sigh. This is her third outfit. "Why are you so nervous? It's just Dad."

"I know," she says with a wave. "I'm being silly. But your

father has been putting in a lot more effort lately, so…I want to as well."

While Mom puts on earrings, I scroll through Insta on my phone. Reese posted a new picture with Kevin. Mom shuffles closer, and when she sees Reese's face on the screen, she says, "I've noticed you haven't seen much of Reese lately."

"Yeah. We're kind of fighting right now."

To my surprise, Mom doesn't pry. All she says is, "Why don't you just call her, sweetie? I'm sure whatever is going on with you will pass."

Right. Because she's such a relationship expert, all of a sudden.

"What makes you sure?" I challenge after locking my screen.

"You two are so close," Mom says easily. "You'll be able to talk it out."

"And what about you and Dad?" I say before I can stop myself.

"Well…your dad and I still have a lot to talk about, too. But we're getting there."

My fingers curl into a fist and I try to keep my mouth shut. But I can't stand my mom acting like she and my dad are so in love—ignoring all the evidence to the contrary. "Does that mean you've told Dad about David?"

Mom stills. Drops her hand away from her earring and turns to look at me. "Pardon?"

"David. That guy from work I saw you with."

Mom looks at me for a long moment, brow furrowed. I can't tell what she's more concerned about—the anger and hurt evident in my voice, or the fact her secret isn't safe anymore.

The doorbell rings. Holland's here to take me to a party. I slide off the bed and tuck my phone away.

"Honey…I want you to understand—"

I hold my hand up. "I don't want to hear what happened between you. But Dad deserves to know." I pause in the doorway of her room. "Especially if you're getting back together."

Holland heard about the party at Megan's from Webster. He was low-key shocked when I agreed to go, and I can't really blame him. But my desperation to avoid a repeat of our last date outweighs my reservations about seeing Webster (and most likely Reese) at this thing. Plus, Holland volunteers to be my designated driver, which is great since I have no interest in staying sober tonight.

The fact that this is a widely shared sentiment becomes clear the second we arrive. The party is downstairs, so we've been given instructions to go around to the backyard and come in through Megan's basement-level sliding doors. It's cold enough outside that the body heat from people dancing has already fogged up the glass.

Everyone here is already wasted. Well, not *everyone*, but enough people that all of the conversations within hearing range are semi-incoherent. I tangle my fingers in the back of Holland's shirt, and together we weave our way through throngs of sloppy classmates to the laundry room, where there's an actual keg. I kind of thought those were a thing only at college parties, but Holland automatically starts pumping the handle as though he's done this a million times before. He fills a cup for me and steals just one sip before handing it over.

We make our way across the basement until Holland spots

Webster, who is sitting on the edge of the pool table…with Caitlin Pratt standing between his legs.

Holland sidles up to them, does his bro-y handshake with Webster. "Hey, guys."

"Hey, Aubrey." Caitlin offers me a friendly smile.

"Hey." My gaze lifts to Webster, who is watching me over her head. "You guys having fun?"

Caitlin shrugs and looks around with a razor-sharp focus that tells me she's still sober. "Yeah. Though I'm driving, so less fun than some people," she says with a teasing look toward Webster.

Webster grins and loops his arms around Caitlin's waist.

I take a long drink. This beer is as cheap as it gets, but at least it's cold enough I can barely taste it. I focus on the retro green lights hanging above the pool table. On the smooth felt under my palm. The beer isn't settling quite right—my stomach is heavy with it.

"You guys want to play?" Caitlin asks, already picking up a stick from the tabletop. "Guys against girls?"

Holland starts emptying the pockets. "Sure. I'll rack."

He moves to the far end of the table and gets the balls inside the triangle thingy, while Caitlin goes to the other end to break. She sinks a solid and does a lap around the table, taking forever to make her mind up about her next shot.

Holland comes back to where Webster and I are standing and swats Webster's arm. "I thought you'd started seeing that guy from the theater?" he says in a low voice.

"Oh, yeah, we went out a couple times but…" Webster shrugs and leaves it at that.

"Well, Caitlin's cool. And cute," Holland says.

I drain the rest of my drink in two gulps.

"Yeah." Webster rubs the back of his neck. His eyes flicker to mine, back to Holland a split second later. "She is."

I mean, they're not wrong. Caitlin is a beautiful girl. Her straight blond hair is always shampoo-model shiny, and she's mastered the whole no-makeup makeup look. Thick lashes, flushed cheeks, full lips. I want to ask her for makeup tips, like what kind of foundation she uses, but I'm sort of worried she'll tell me she doesn't use any, that her skin is flawless and lightly bronzed all on its own, all year long.

"Must have good genes," I contribute. Holland and Webster turn to me and I realize that was a totally weird thing to say. My thumb indents the side of my empty plastic cup. I'm saved from making any other unfortunate observations when Caitlin misses her next shot and tells Webster he's up.

Webster puts a stripe in a side pocket, then misses, and then it's my turn. Webster hands me his stick and his fingers brush mine, and in that moment I'm back at my kitchen table with Webster tracing my wrist and tilting his head and a smoldering heat low in my belly. My gaze flickers to meet his and I shift away. Turn my focus back to the table.

I'm not surprised when I don't even come close to sinking a ball.

I pass the stick to Holland and announce I'm going to get a refill. He catches my sleeve and sweeps his palm down to my wrist. "Maybe you should slow down a little."

"I'm fine." Heat prickles at my hairline. I know he's just looking out for me, but it feels an awful lot like being told what to do. "And it's your turn," I mumble as I skirt around him.

At the keg I fill my cup and start to walk away before hesitating. Right in the middle of the laundry room, I chug my beer and fill my cup again.

On my way back to the pool table my limbs are looser, and I keep bumping into people. Cold air hits me when I move past the open sliding glass door. Outside, a group of girls are shivering in their tank tops, rubbing their bare arms as they pass a cigarette around, exhaling smoke up toward the blackened sky. When I turn away from the door, I spot Reese standing nearby with Kevin. Kevin spots me first, lifts his hand to wave. I don't miss the way Reese tugs at his shirt like she wishes he'd stop.

But I walk over anyway, because it feels supremely weird not to.

"Surprised to see you here," she says when I reach them.

"Yeah. Holland wanted to come," I say, like I need an excuse to be here. "I probably won't be staying for long." I turn to Kevin and nod a hello.

"I'm gonna get another drink," he says, even though his cup is full. I get the distinct impression he's just giving us space, and I feel a rush of gratitude toward him. Followed by a wave of guilt when I think about the stupid things I said about Webster junior year getting back to him, and the possibility Reese might have repeated what I said about her and Kevin after our fight.

When he walks away, Reese turns to me with wide eyes, like I'm some acquaintance from summer camp she hasn't seen in years.

"So…having fun?" I ask.

A beat of silence passes and I start to wish I'd stuck with

a wave. Nothing is worse than making small talk with the person who's supposed to be my best friend.

"Yeah. You?"

The only response I can muster is a shrug. "I'm so sorry, about everything. Can we talk?"

Reese's shoulders droop just slightly. "I'm not sure this is the best time, Aubrey."

She's probably right. It's loud. We've been drinking. But I've been trying to figure out how to bring up our fight for weeks, and she won't even meet me halfway. She's ignored me at school, and now her gaze keeps darting around the room like she's searching for someone to rescue her. "Yeah. Okay. I should probably be getting back to Holland, anyway."

"Right," Reese says, and she shifts to the side, already on her way to find Kevin. "We'll talk later."

"Sure." But I can't help thinking that if she missed me at all, she'd tell me to stay. She'd make the same effort I am. "Later."

Maybe it was inevitable, that our friendship would turn into this. That Reese would become the person you make plans with over breaks until it starts to feel like an obligation, so you stop making plans and settle for a vague *would love to catch up sometime!* But then never do. At least now I know where we stand.

It's my turn again by the time I get back to the table. Caitlin passes me the stick and I take stock of what's left on the table. Caitlin is pretty good—she's already sunk most of the solids. An easy shot is set up in a corner pocket, and I'm able to make that before missing again.

She offers me a high five as I pass my stick off to Holland.

"You're still kind of carrying this team," I say as I reach for my drink.

Caitlin shrugs easily. "I'm over here a lot, so I've had a good amount of practice." She turns to Webster. "I wonder if I could take billiards or something as a PE credit next year."

"I know MSU offers bowling…" I say.

"Already have the course book memorized?" Webster asks in a teasing voice. And maybe because it's the first thing Webster's said directly to me tonight, or maybe because it's the kind of thing he would have said a few months ago, my cheeks flush.

Holland scratches the cue ball and Caitlin jumps forward to fish it out of the side pocket.

"What'd I miss?" Holland leans his weight onto his pool stick and glances between us.

"Aubrey was just about to tell me about all the classes she wants to take at MSU."

"*If* she ends up at MSU," Holland says wryly before I can offer a comeback.

Webster's smirk falters. "I thought that was a done deal."

"She's still deciding," Holland says, answering for me again.

I lick my lips and try to ignore the crackle of tension that runs down my spine, the pressure like a storm brewing inside my chest. "I'm…yeah."

Caitlin sinks the eight ball. We win. Holland immediately demands a rematch, and while he reracks, I make another trip to the keg. I've had only two—or maybe it was three, but in any case, it's not enough.

When I return, Holland's arm slips across my shoulders. Webster has his hand on Caitlin's waist, and together the four of us look like a sketch of a double date, so cute I could scream.

It's Webster's turn to break, and then he's back on the sidelines with me. Only, he won't even look at me now. Instead he stares into his beer, swirling it around his cup. I watch as he tilts his head back and drains the rest of his drink in one go. He wipes his mouth on his sleeve and something about the way his lips twist makes him look a little ill.

I drain half my beer and move to take my turn. I get another ball in—though technically not the one I was aiming for, and when I hand off the stick to Holland, he trades it for a cup of water he got during my turn.

"Don't want you to dehydrate."

I take a sip and smile at the floor because I'm having trouble focusing on anything else. Having trouble standing without swaying, come to think of it. "Sure, Dr. Sawyer."

This game is slower than the last. I miss my next two shots in a row—can't seem to keep my stick straight. I go refill my cup again, and Webster keeps on ignoring me when I get back, even though he seems more interested in chalking the pool stick than actually playing at this point.

Finally I bump my shoulder against his. He's so warm, standing this close. "Having a good time?"

"A blast."

I scratch my cheek and glance at Caitlin as she lines up another shot. Then I turn back to Webster. "You mad at me or something?"

"Why would I be mad?"

"I don't know." My voice grows tense. "That's why I'm asking."

"Well, no worries. I'm not angry." His tone implies he's not anything—not affected by my presence at all.

Every time. Every single time I let myself get sucked in, I start to care—always more than he does. Always to the point where I get hurt and he gets the last laugh. I'm sick of it.

"Thank god for that."

Across the table, Holland tries to get my attention. I'm about to go over to him, but Webster rests his weight against the pool stick and says, "Do I detect sarcasm?"

"Nope." I curl my lips in to keep myself from saying anything I might regret.

"Oh, my mistake. You probably want to save all that fire for Holland, huh?"

My mind flashes to the other night, when Holland and I were alone in my room. What happened after Holland left. My skin goes hot. "Stop."

His forehead pinches. "Stop what, exactly?"

"You're just—you're so immature. I know Holland wants us to get along, but I don't even know why I try anymore."

Webster huffs a humorless laugh. His mouth twists into a tight-lipped smirk. "Me, either."

I slowly become aware of Holland standing at my side. I glance up to find both him and Caitlin watching us. And seeing the crease between Holland's brow, wondering how much he heard—it's like two fists closing around my stomach and twisting in opposite directions.

Caitlin holds out the pool stick. "It's your turn, Aubrey."

I take the stick from her and glance once more at Holland. He's examining the blue chalk now, wearing an expression like he very much wants to escape this moment.

Which makes two of us.

Only the eight ball remains at this point. How is Caitlin so *good* at everything? Meanwhile I keep seeing three balls instead of one. I close one eye and squint. And miss the cue ball completely.

I'm bent over the table now and I can't stop laughing. Holland walks around to me and pulls me upright. "Okay, I think you've had enough."

"No. You don't get to decide everything." I lift my chin and stare at him with as much defiance as I can muster. "S'your turn."

Holland plucks the pool stick away from me. He gets the eight ball in a corner pocket on his first try. Game over.

He tosses the stick onto the table and brings all that intensity right back over to me. I grab what's left of my beer before he has the chance and take a sip.

"Aubrey, come on."

"Come on, what?"

He steps closer and I instinctively stumble back a step. "You don't need any more—you'll feel sick. Can you please give that to me?"

I bring the cup close to my chest. "Get your own."

He heaves a frustrated sigh. "Aubrey…"

"I'm *fine*. You just don't get it, okay?"

I'm vaguely aware of how loud my voice has gotten. But Holland is always better than me, so he doesn't yell back.

"What don't I get?" he asks calmly.

"You're all like, *oh, it's gonna work out.* 'Cause everything always has an upside, right? And no problem's too big. But it's so stupid. Like, *yeah, we'll just become vets and work in the same clinic and stay together forever.* You think it's so simple."

The line between his brows relaxes, the confusion slowly melting off his face. His expression is blank now. Detached. He stares at me for a long moment. "That's stupid, huh?"

"Just…" I shake my head. Lose my train of thought and end up looking beside us instead. At Caitlin, who seems embarrassed for some reason. Then Webster, who won't even meet my eye.

"Come on, I'm taking you home," Holland says. "Give me the cup."

"No."

He steps forward. I twist away as he reaches for the cup. "Let *go*—"

I yank my arm back, out of his grip. The beer splashes everywhere. But mostly on Caitlin.

She yelps and looks down at her soaked shirt. Webster puts himself between us a beat too late. "What the hell, Aubrey?"

I get a flash of meeting Holland on New Year's Eve and fumble for an apology. "That was—accident. I didn't mean… Caitlin, I'm so sorry."

"It's okay," she says without looking at me.

"Here, follow me." Webster takes her hand and starts leading her across the basement, toward the laundry room.

I stumble after them. We pass Reese—who seems to know something is wrong with just one look. She catches up with us as Webster is unrolling some paper towel and handing it to Caitlin. "What happened?"

"Just a little spill," Caitlin explains at the same time Webster growls, "Ask Aubrey."

"I'm sorry," I say again. I try to get a better look at the damage done and stumble to the side.

"Shit, how much did you drink?" Reese asks me.

I run my hand over my face. I'm starting to not feel great. "Like. A few?"

She glances over her shoulder. "Where's Holland?"

"I can't drive home in this shirt," Caitlin says to Webster. "If I get pulled over, I'm screwed."

"You can have my shirt," I blurt out.

She avoids looking at me, and I get the sense they'd both rather pretend I wasn't here. Then again, Webster is good at that. "Thanks, but…I think I'm gonna go see if Megan has something I can borrow."

"I just saw her a second ago," Reese says, and motions for Caitlin to follow her.

Webster keeps messing with the roll of paper towel, like if he doesn't have something to do with his hands, he'll snap.

"I didn't mean to," I say quietly. My body sways. I concentrate on standing still.

He tosses the paper towel on top of the dryer and laughs bitterly. "Yeah. I know. Just a side effect of being close to you."

My teeth clench. "What's that mean?"

Webster finally looks at me. "Just, you don't seem too concerned with who you hurt."

My gaze wanders outside the room. I can see Holland talking to Reese, his arms crossed. My legs aren't so stable right now. The floor keeps shifting under my feet. I stumble over and prop myself up against the washing machine.

I frown up at Webster. "That's not true."

"No? You literally just said you only talk to me because

of Holland. Remember that? Had a pretty familiar ring to it, actually."

"I didn't mean it like *that*—"

"You know, it doesn't even matter. Because you were right—we're not actually friends, you and I. Who knows? After graduation, we might not ever have to see each other again."

His words swirl around in my head and I want to fight back, tell him—he's the one who acts better than me, like I'm not good enough for Holland, like I'm pathetic for even trying to have a boyfriend, and none of our history matters, not now, because we're nothing and the only relationships he should worry about are his own. But my tongue is heavy and the room is spinning and I'm clinging to cold metal, sliding down to the floor. My face is hot, neck sweaty. My vision blurs harder and my next breath comes out sounding like a sob. "I fucking—" I'm not sure he's still there, can even hear me over the *thump thump thump* of the music. My arms curl over my head. "I fucking hate you."

Someone is pulling on my arm. It falls limp at my side and I open my eyes to see Reese crouched in front of me. Her voice is soft and soothing. "Hey, girly. We're gonna get you home, okay?"

I tilt my head back. It hits the washer door with a *thunk*. Webster is standing across the room, his face paler than before. Kevin's hand is on his shoulder, like he's expecting to have to hold Webster back. Reese shifts to my side. "Kevin, can you give me a hand?"

"I got her." Holland comes into my line of sight, kneels down and drapes my arm around his neck, then stands, hoisting me with him. I fall against his side but his arm is secure around my waist. He dips his head. "Okay?"

I lift my other arm to his neck and lean my weight entirely against him. His arms envelop me and I mumble against his chest, *I'm sorry I'm sorry I'm sorry.*

"I know." He pulls back and wipes my cheeks with the pads of his fingers. I blink the room into focus. Webster is gone. "You ready to walk?"

I nod and Holland half carries me toward the door. Reese leads the way, clearing our path and opening the sliding door. When we make it to his car, she climbs into the back seat first. Holland helps me inside, and my head rests against Reese's shoulder.

"I think she should stay at my house tonight," Reese tells him. "I'll text her mom."

No one talks for the whole drive, except for Reese giving occasional directions to her house. When we get there, I spill out of the car and falter, reaching for Holland's arm through his open window. "Thank you."

"Yep."

"No, but I mean…" I grip his arm tighter. "You're so good to me."

His hands twist around the steering wheel. His head is turned toward mine, but he's not looking at me. Not really. I step forward, lean in to kiss him and his head tilts away, shifts so he's staring out the front. "Remember to drink water," is the last thing he says before pulling out of the driveway.

24

I WAKE UP in Reese's bed, and it takes me a minute to remember how I got there.

"Hey," she says in a soft voice. She's curled on her side, facing me. "How are you feeling?"

Even her whisper is enough to bring my splitting headache into sharp focus. "Ow."

"I thought that might be the case." She rolls away from me and grabs something off her nightstand, then turns back to me and props herself up on her elbow. "Here."

She hands me a glass of water, and I take a sip. Even that small amount of liquid makes my stomach feel sloshy and heavy.

"Bet we can get my mom to make us pancakes." She has her Cartoon Princess Face on. Which is how I know last night was exactly as bad as I remember.

I hand her the water and sink back into the pillow. "Just need a minute."

"Okay." She sets the glass down, and I can feel her watching as I squeeze my eyes shut and press the heel of my palm hard against my brow bone, trying to relieve some of the pressure inside my skull. After a long pause, she says, "I'm sorry. I know I kind of disappeared these last few weeks. That was shitty of me, to bail when you're having such a hard time."

My eyes shoot open and I roll my head to look at her. "No. I mean—it's not your fault. I was such an asshole to you. That stupid list... I'm so sorry."

"It's okay," Reese says. "I know you didn't mean it. I was just really blindsided, you know? Especially since you'd helped Kevin with that anniversary dessert, I guess I thought you were coming around to him."

"I was—I like Kevin. It wasn't about him at all. And I wanted to apologize sooner, but I wasn't sure what to say, or if you even wanted me around."

"Of course I do. Oh my god, I've missed you so much you have no idea," she says with a thick laugh. She runs two fingers over her eyebrow, and I notice how thin they've gotten. "I just feel...I've *been* feeling really lost."

"Lost how?"

Reese sits up, pulls her knees to her chest. "My whole life in high school was mapped out for me. I just did everything Rachel did. I joined cheer because of her, and I wore her clothes, and now I'm graduating and I have no idea what I want, or what I even *like*..." She rubs her shins. "Even Becca already has her shit together. But you were right, I have no idea who I am or what I'm going to do when I get to college. The only things I'm sure about are you and Kevin." Her eyes swell up. "But sometimes even you guys don't feel certain."

"I really am sorry for what I wrote about you and Kevin."
I roll onto my side and reach for her hand, lace our fingers
together. These past couple weeks have underscored how differently Reese and I view the future. And how impossible it is
to know the inside of someone's relationship from what you
see on the outside. "It's like you've always said, I'm a cynic.
But what you and Kevin have seems kind of rare. I didn't really get it before, but I do now."

"Thanks." She wipes under her eyes.

I lift onto my elbow. "You love him, don't you?"

She sniffs and gives a resigned sort of shrug. "Yeah."

"What's that like?"

She looks at me for a long moment. "It's kind of the best.
I wake up happy every morning because I know as soon as I
get to school, I'll see him. And it just feels like…" She touches
her fingertips to her sternum. "I get this thrill every time he
wraps his arms around me, but then at the same time I'm so
calm, because I know I can count on him. I know he'll be
there when I need help, and he'll listen when I just want to
talk about random shit, and if we don't have anything to talk
about, that's fine, too. And I feel like myself around him. Even
if I'm not sure who that is—I don't feel like I have to pretend
to be someone else. Basically, it's like you and me, except I
also want to jump his bones."

I can't help matching her grin. "Well, that does sound like
the best."

"And also the worst, because I think about him all the
time. Way more than is probably healthy." She slips her hands
under the covers. "It's kind of scary, sometimes. Like…there

are moments when I wonder if I'm feeling more than he is. But I think that's part of the package, you know?"

"Not really," I say with a smile. "But I'm happy for you." She deserves this kind of all-consuming love. "So have you guys…?"

"Not yet. I decided to wait a bit longer." She tilts her head and examines me. "What about you and Holland? Do you think you might love him?"

Here's the question I keep coming back to: If you've never been in love before, how are you supposed to know when it's happening? When you're falling in a good way, instead of tumbling straight toward a bitter end? People don't generally see that conclusion coming, otherwise they'd call it off before hearts got broken.

I still don't understand how much of a successful relationship is mutual attraction. How much is having perfectly compatible personalities, versus finding that person who will push you, who drives you crazy half the time, but also makes you feel alive.

"I really like him." I stare up at the ceiling for a beat and try to figure out if it's ever been more than that. "But…I guess the thing that gets me is that when I think about going to MSU, I'm not heartbroken over being farther away from him. Like, I'm way more upset about being far from you next year."

Reese cups her chin in her palm and offers me a sad smile.

I picture the way Holland looked at me when he dropped us off last night and wince. "Not sure it matters how I feel, anyway. He was so mad last night."

"I mean…he wasn't happy."

"He tried to get me to stop drinking. Guess I should've listened."

She hesitates. "Mm-hmm."

I swallow against the wave of nausea that sweeps up my throat. "What does mm-hmm mean?"

"Well, I'm sure the drinking was part of it. But also…you and Webster were a little…"

"What?"

"Intense."

Everything he said in the laundry room comes rushing back. No wonder Holland was angry—I probably embarrassed him. I made a total scene. "Yeah, well, I should have known better than to engage with Webster. Bad idea given how much we hate each other."

"It didn't really look like hate to me…" she says softly. "And I don't think it looked that way to Holland, either."

I twist the duvet between my fingers and say, "There's some stuff I haven't told you."

I summarize everything that happened with Webster while Reese and I were fighting, from Webster coming to my defense over the school dress code to our study date and the almost-kiss, then thinking about him when I should have been thinking about Holland, and all the mixed-up emotions I was dealing with last night.

It feels horrible to admit my feelings out loud. Even as Reese's eyes widen and she has to smash her lips together to keep from smiling. Because I'm with Holland. And sure, nothing technically happened with Webster, but last night would've had a way better ending if I'd kept myself in check.

I fold forward and groan into the covers. "I'm a bad person."

"No, you're not!" Reese waits for me to lift my gaze again. "You just…can't logic your way out of this one. You have to—"

"If you say 'follow your heart,' I might vomit all over your bed."

"I mean…that's not exactly what I was going to say…" Reese flashes a smile.

"I do like Holland," I say again. "A lot. But it's not like you and Kevin. I never got to that point of feeling like…"

"Like he's your best friend?"

I look at her and nod. "And that's probably my fault. Maybe I've been using the whole Bayes' rule thing as an excuse to keep from getting closer to him."

"That is a distinct possibility," Reese says in a measured voice.

"I know, I may have overthought it for a minute." I cover my face, then drop my hands back down to my lap. "I needed some way to stay in control. That was the point of the list you saw. I figured if I could map out all the ways people fall out of love, I might be able to predict which one we'd fit into and know what pitfalls to avoid. Or I'd be able to orchestrate it so it happened in the least painful way."

"Oh man. That's some impressive overanalyzing, even by your standards. Though after your parents and everything… It makes total sense that you'd want to find some sort of loophole. But you saw how long my list of exes was," she says wryly. "Take it from someone who's tried multiple times— you can't force it. Relationships are hard sometimes, but they shouldn't constantly feel like work, you know?"

"Yeah." My mouth scrunches to the side.

After a beat she asks, "So what are you going to do?"

I sigh and think back to our conversation on the snow day. When Reese first told me I had to let myself feel my feelings.

I get that her point is actually extremely valid. The problem is, my feelings are still all over the place.

"Holland has been a great boyfriend." That's what makes this so hard. Even if I was to utilize Bayes' rule to evaluate our relationship—properly this time—Holland hasn't done any one thing wrong that led to this point. He's patient and accommodating and aside from last night, we don't really fight.

But no matter how much time passes, our lives still seem so…separate. And it never seems to bother Holland—and maybe it shouldn't, because it's not like we don't have some shared interests, so maybe it's fine if we enjoy totally different music and activities—but to me it just seems like something is missing. "I guess at the end of the day, when I think about who I'd want to be with when disaster strikes and the world is falling apart around me, it's just…not him."

Reese bites her lip. "And Webster?"

His voice echoes in my head: *you can't help who you fall for.* And yes, fine, I feel *something* for Webster. But I'm not sure Webster is available. And even if he *is*, the idea of us getting involved is sort of scary. Despite clearing up the whole homecoming fiasco, we still can't stop ourselves from fighting. It's too close to the kind of dynamic my parents have. Exactly what I've been trying to avoid all this time.

I meet Reese's eye and simply shake my head.

She draws in a deep breath and nods once. "Well, hey, maybe they have another cousin."

"Oh my god," I groan, and pull the covers over my head.

For the next two hours, Reese plies me with pancakes and coffee and we lounge in bed watching episodes of *GBBO* on her laptop. We talk about Kevin and a little about my parents—

what it's been like since my dad moved out, and how I blew up at my mom last night over *David from work*—but mostly we don't talk, which is kind of what I need right now.

I finally force myself to go home, and I'm surprised to find a note from my mom saying she's out for coffee with Mrs. Casey. I realize that, as much as I was dreading coming home, part of me was hoping she'd be here, that she might even ground me for last night so I'd have an excuse to avoid Holland a little bit longer. But after I've showered and changed my clothes, I can't handle being home alone anymore, so I get in the car and head to Holland's house.

When I pull up to the curb in front of Holland's, I sit for a moment with the engine turned off. Close my eyes and listen to the heavy silence in the empty car. My stomach knots like a necklace forgotten at the bottom of my jewelry box. I should have practiced what I was going to say. Because right now, I have no idea. And I don't have any time to figure it out, because there he is, opening the door and shuffling onto the porch. Hands in pockets, patiently waiting.

My head is still throbbing and, despite scrubbing my tongue until I gagged before coming over here, there's this taste in the back of my throat that's vaguely reminiscent of rotten fruit. Yum.

Deep breath. I click off my seat belt and climb out of the car. The walk up his driveway feels like miles. He doesn't move, doesn't meet me partway. By the time I reach him, I feel firmly on his turf.

I no longer know what to do with my arms. Crossing them feels cold, the wrong kind of body language. I step up to him and there's this moment of hesitation as we look into each other's eyes. I'm not sure if I should move closer, make the first move. I'm not sure he wants to be touched by me anymore.

"Hi."

He sits down on the porch steps. "Hey."

I sit beside him. "So…I'm really sorry about last night."

"Which part are you apologizing for?"

I eye him, all of my organs rebelling against this moment. I can't decide if I'm hungry or about to throw up. "Well, I'm sorry for drinking too much. Acting like an immature ass-hole. That's a big one. And I know you tried to tell me to slow down…"

"It's not like I've never gotten drunk."

"Okay…" I'm not sure what point he's trying to make. If he's telling me he accepts my apology or if he's saying I'm still not apologizing for the right things. "Well, so, I just wanted you to know that I appreciate you driving us."

He laughs in a frustrated way, fingers picking at a hangnail on his thumb. "I'm not your Uber driver. You don't need to thank me for that."

My hands slide over my face, pushing stray hairs off my forehead.

Holland seems to soften, leaning forward to rest his fore-arms on his knees. His long legs reach a step lower than mine. He turns his face toward me. "You know, in the three months we've been together, this is only the third time you've been to my house?"

It sounds an awful lot like a criticism. But it's not like he's invited me over here a bunch. And we live so far apart. It just makes sense that we've met halfway between us. Only…we haven't, have we? More often than not, Holland's driven all the way to my area. Gone to parties with my friends. And I've told myself it made sense, because he got to see his cousin at the same time, but if we're being honest, it had more to do with not being willing to make the same effort. And he knows it.

"I told you I'm not good at this," I say quietly.

"At what?"

"Being someone's girlfriend."

Holland looks at me for a long time. "Yeah. Guess you were right."

It's hand sanitizer rubbed into a paper cut. Stinging all the way down my chest. It shouldn't come as a shock—after all, he's only agreeing with me. But it makes me feel like he regrets getting involved in the first place, like he wasted his time.

"Look, I'm sorry," I offer again. "I didn't mean for things to be so...uneven."

Holland lifts a brow. "Uneven. That's a good word for our relationship, isn't it?"

"Holland..."

"I tell you I love you, and you just...never respond. Guess I shouldn't be surprised we ended up here."

"That's not fair. Holland—you know I care about you." I'm appalled by the fact my voice has started to waver. I turn my face away and try to get myself back under control. "And you know what my parents are like. I've spent the past year trying to figure out if I even believe in the concept of love. Last night when I said you didn't get it—this is what I mean. I'm not like you. I'm not an optimist. Good things happen and I just...look for all the ways they could turn bad. And I've been trying to work on that, but...you have to understand, growing up with two people who are at each other's throats all the time doesn't exactly make love the most appealing prospect."

Holland frowns at the step below us. "So why didn't you ever talk to me about this stuff? I've asked you about your parents—you didn't even want me to meet your dad."

"That's not true! I just—I wanted to keep you separate from that part of my life. And…"

"And what?"

"And you're not always the easiest person to talk to about serious things." I shift so I'm facing him. "Look, I love that you're such a positive person. But you have a tendency to try to find a silver lining in everything, and sometimes it comes off as kind of dismissive. Sometimes things are just shitty, and I just needed you to *listen* and say 'that sucks.'"

Holland's jaw knots. "At least I never lied to you."

We're both too quiet for a moment. My skin feels flushed. "What does that mean?"

"It means, let's talk about the real reason you're here." He looks at me, and I don't know what to say, because I thought that was what we *were* doing. "Last night you made it pretty clear you don't see a future for us. And you made it pretty clear why."

I'm trapped under Holland's ice-blue stare, palms tingling and heart beating fast. I watch his Adam's apple slide in his throat as he swallows. Then:

"You have a thing for Webster. Don't you?"

All of my interactions with Webster this semester flash through my mind, all of his snide comments at the start of my relationship with Holland, and the things he said last night. My lips part and I want to deny it. I can hear in Holland's voice how badly he still wants me to answer no. And suddenly I wish more than anything I could say the three words that would put Holland's doubts to rest and make this right. But I can't.

So I say three that will break us. "I don't know."

He holds my gaze for a long moment—long enough for me to see the hurt and betrayal tightening his eyes. And part of me resents the fact that he's pinning this entirely on me, making it all about my shortcomings. When the truth is, we both could have tried harder, and it wouldn't have made a difference, we still would have ended up right here. With Holland looking heartbroken—because of me—and…so I guess it is partly my fault. But that doesn't mean I'm not disappointed, too. I'm sick to my stomach, a tiny voice in the back of my head asking if I'm making a massive mistake, losing a great guy like Holland. But deep down, I know this is how it has to be.

Finally, he looks away. "Honestly, it doesn't even matter." He sounds more resigned than angry now. He wipes his mouth and mumbles, "I should've seen this coming, anyway."

My mouth opens and I press it shut again. Swallow hard. All I can think to say is, "Right. I wasn't exactly nice to you on New Year's Eve."

A half-hearted smile tugs at his lips, like this is still an inside joke between us. "Exactly. Ever since then, you've been so nice."

First of all, I'm not entirely convinced that's accurate. And second, since when is that a bad thing? I've been worried about how shitty I've treated him, and now he's saying I'm too nice?

I drag my palms along my shins and shrug my shoulders up

to my ears. It's over. I know that it is. But one of us still has to say the words. "I'm sorry this didn't work out."

Holland nods, still not looking at me. "Me too."

I wish there was more to say. A way to make sure he believes me—that I'm sorry, that I never wanted to hurt him, that I know I'm partly to blame and hate myself a little for it. That he'll be better off with someone else. That we both will be.

After another moment, I grip the railing and pull myself up. I can't be here anymore. Holland climbs to his feet and looks at the space between us, wincing a little. "I guess I'll be seeing you around."

It's a nice lie. Pretending we'll remain friends, even though we were never friends in the first place. I guess that's the silver lining here. I won't actually have to see him at all.

I rock forward and wrap my arms around his neck, lifting onto my tiptoes as I breathe in his fresh-laundry-and-boy smell for the last time. "Take care of yourself, Holland," I say against his shoulder.

"You too, Aubrey."

I pull back and move quickly down the steps. Holland watches as I retreat to my car. By the time I turn the key, he has already disappeared back inside the house.

As I drive away, tears flood my eyes. And I can't stop wondering—if it hurts this much to lose someone you haven't handed your heart to, how does anyone survive losing the one you have?

FIVE:

The Fine Line Between Love and Hate

WEBSTER...AGAIN.

25

ON MY WAY to Life Skills on Monday, I try to nurse my resentment back to health. It would be so much easier to sit next to Webster every day if I could just hate him as much as I did at that party. But my resolve keeps crumbling.

As I pull out the seat next to his, Webster drags his elbows off the countertop and straightens. He flicks a glance my way. "Hey."

I dissect that syllable for signs of pity. I try to hear an *I told you so*, or at the very least an *I haven't forgotten what a bitch you were on Friday*. But I don't hear any hint of disdain in his voice. He watches me out of the corner of his eye, as though I'm a solar eclipse. Like he's afraid if he looks directly at me, I'll hurt him.

Which only exacerbates my problem. It's hard to stay angry at someone who already looks like they've been to hell and back. And here I thought the circles under my own eyes were bad.

"Hey," I reply, just as Miss Holloway starts class and we're forced to face forward again.

We're working on an accounting overview this week, which means I actually need to take notes. I flip my notebook open to a fresh page and reach for one of the handouts Miss Holloway is passing around. She starts talking us through it, but Webster doesn't seem to pay any attention. He can't sit still. Keeps sending me sidelong glances.

When Miss Holloway tells us to work through the first problem set, Webster leans closer. "Are you…" He seems to be choosing his words carefully. "How are you feeling about things?"

"Depends what things you're referring to," I say without looking up from my worksheet. "But on the whole it was a pretty shitty weekend, Webster."

This seems to catch him off guard. "Yeah, you could say that."

I finish the first problem before asking, "What made it shitty for you?"

"Well, Caitlin dropping me didn't help."

"Oh." …*Oh.* I'd kind of assumed he was in rough shape because of our fight. Which…seems embarrassingly narcissistic now. "Sorry to hear that."

"Yeah, well…" He shrugs. "Probably the right call."

I don't know what to say to that, so I just nod.

He's fiddling with his pen, tapping it against the edge of the table. "I feel like we should talk about the other night."

I jot down the answer to the next question. I'm pretty sure

I got it wrong, but I'm having all kinds of trouble caring. "I'm not sure there's anything left to say."

He watches me awhile longer before he finally picks up his worksheet for the first time and chews on the cap of his pen while he reads it. But as soon as class lets out, he follows me into the hall.

"You have lunch now, right?" Webster asks. "I'll walk you."

I start toward the cafeteria without responding.

"Look, I'm sorry. Especially if I caused any problems… with you and Holland."

I cough a laugh and step around him. "Yeah, sure."

We turn the corner into the crowded main hallway, and weave through bodies in silence. The warning bell rings as I reach the line for food. "You're going to be late for class."

Webster tugs a hand through his hair and then drops it to the metal railing that divides the lunch lines. Finally he takes a big step back, right as the line moves forward. I get my food, pay, and then go to sit with Reese and Veronica—whom I invited to join our table when I passed her in the hall this morning—inside the cafeteria. But when I reach the entrance, Webster steps in front of me again.

I tilt my head back and blink at the fluorescent lights above us. "What do you want, Webster?"

"I want you to listen to me."

I lower my gaze, scan the tables behind him. Maybe if I can catch Reese's attention, she'll rescue me.

"And look at me," Webster amends.

I meet his eye. "My mashed potatoes are getting cold."

"I want to tell you I'm sorry—"

"You said that already."

He catches my arm, gently pulls me to the side of the cafeteria doors. "Aubrey, please…" His hand falls away and he lets out a deep breath. "Look, in the interest of avoiding a repeat of what happened last year, I'm just going to be upfront with you. I didn't mean what I said at Megan's party. I was frustrated, I took things too far, and I didn't mean any of it. Okay?"

My grip on my lunch tray tightens. "Okay," I say.

He hugs his notebook to his chest like a shield. "So then can we talk? After school?"

I shift my weight from one foot to the other. "I guess."

Webster nods once, visibly relieved. "Great. Okay, so, since we're both dealing with recent breakups, I was thinking we could get some pie? Susie's bakery, maybe?"

I balance my tray against my hip and squint at him. "Pie."

"A tried-and-true bad-week cure." Hands in his pockets and notebook tucked under one arm, he curls his shoulders in and bends his knees so we're closer to the same height. "Couldn't hurt, right?"

My heartbeat is in my ears. Suddenly this proposition seems bigger than what I originally agreed to. But he looks so desperate, I can't bring myself to say anything other than: "Okay."

"Great. I'll meet you at your locker after sixth period."

He leaves before I get the chance to back out. Which…I am immediately tempted to do.

We're just going to talk, I keep telling myself over and over ad nauseam on my way to my table. But it only takes about ten seconds for Reese to pick up on my weird vibe.

"What's with your leg?" she asks.

I lean back so I can look under the table. "What about it?"

Veronica rotates her foot an inch so that her toes land on top of mine. I realize I've been bouncing my heel nonstop since I sat down.

"Oh. I dunno, just kind of anxious today, I guess."

She looks at me carefully. "What's wrong? Are you upset about your parents? Holland?"

"No, it's…" I twist my fork around in my mashed potatoes. "I'm fine. I had coffee this morning. It's making me all…" I pop a bite into my mouth and shrug my shoulders to my ears.

"Okay… Well, maybe lay off the caffeine for a little while."

"Ha, yeah." I swallow another forkful of mashed potato, then tuck my hands under the table. "So, also, in addition to the coffee thing, Webster asked me to get pie with him after school and I have no idea if it's a date or not and I need you to tell me what to do."

Reese just took a huge bite of salad, so she freezes with chipmunk cheeks. She meets Veronica's eye across the table, then covers her mouth and in a muffled voice asks, *"What?"*

"Yeah, he said because we'd both gone through breakups, we should get pie. And I said okay. And I need you to tell me not to go and also think of an excuse I can give him."

Veronica laughs and tucks back into her lunch, apparently feeling compelled to stay out of this. Reese, on the other hand, drops her fork and abandons her salad. "I can't tell you not to go."

"Why not?"

"Because I think you do want to go."

I don't say anything.

"Don't you?" she asks.

"I…am not sure. Because. On the one hand, yes. But then

I think about what it's been like between us lately and how every time I let my guard down with him it backfires, but maybe all of that was circumstantial, and maybe now we have a chance to be really honest with each other."

Reese nods gravely. "They do say honesty is the best policy."

"Can you be serious for a second? I am in crisis."

She grins. "I can see that."

"Look at it this way," Veronica cuts in. "If you get there, and you're not comfortable, then you can leave."

Somehow I expected Veronica to pull through and be the one to talk me out of this. "What happened to your whole, *sometimes you're better off going it alone* philosophy. I mean, you wouldn't randomly meet up with Sam to talk things out, would you?"

"Actually, I'd love to do that. I've tried a hundred times to get her to talk to me." Veronica sends me a look that says, *Ball's in your court.*

I chew on my bottom lip. Smoosh my potatoes with my fork.

"If you want, one of us can call you twenty minutes in and we can do one of those really transparent 'I have an emergency!' bailouts," she offers.

"I guess…"

Reese pulls her salad closer again, grinning like she knows I've already made up my mind. "You and Webster Casey. Who could have *possibly* predicted this outcome?"

I shoot her an annoyed look. "So, what, you've converted to Team Webster?"

She bites down on her fork and wiggles her eyebrows.

I manage to force a change in subject for the rest of lunch, and once we're all finished eating, I walk with Veronica to class. She's been quiet for a while now, so when the first warning bell rings, I blurt out the thought that's been circling since her comment about Sam: "It still bothers you, doesn't it?"

Veronica looks at me. "What does?"

"Whatever happened with you and Sam."

Veronica chews her bottom lip. She glances around the hall, but everyone is wrapped up in their own conversations. "What if I told you everything you heard about me was true? I hooked up with Andy Zomeski while he and Sam were... well. Not technically together, but close enough."

I try to find something nonjudgmental to say. "It wouldn't be the first time two best friends liked the same guy..."

"I didn't like him."

"Then...why?"

Veronica sighs. "Sam and I had been friends a long time. But we come from very different families. She has one of those perfect situations. Parents who are always there for her, and who she actually enjoys spending time with. They're great."

I'm not sure how this relates to what happened, so I just say, "And your parents...?"

"It's just me and my mom. And...yeah. We're not like that. But when I started high school, my mom tried. Except the only way she knew how to get closer to me was to act like my friend. So she let me have all these parties. And one time, Andy showed up early, and we started drinking..." She cuts a look my way. "I wish I had a better excuse. I wish I could say Sam screwed me over first, or that Andy and I were soul mates. But really I just wanted to know what it was like to be her. And maybe...I guess part of me was angry, because when we got to high school, she made other friends and had all these guys interested in her, and I felt...kind of abandoned. Not that I was thinking about any of that in the moment. But years of replaying that night have helped me figure a few things out."

"Did you ever talk to her about it? Try to explain?"

Veronica shrugs. "She didn't really give me the chance. Sam had already made hating me her religion. Made it her mission to spread the good word that I was a slut." She picks at some chipped polish on her fingernail. "You don't come back from that."

26

WEBSTER IS ALREADY standing in front of our lockers when I get there after class. I wait for a few people to pass before I can cross the hall to him. As I spin the dial on my locker, Webster pretends to need something out of his, too, even though he seriously has not used it all year. It's amazing he even remembers his combination. Meanwhile, my fingers are clumsy, and I can't get mine to open. On my second failed attempt, I smack the heel of my palm against the door.

Webster turns and watches me with an amused smile, which is not helpful.

Slowly, and with so much concentration you'd think I was defusing a bomb, I spin the combination lock once more. Finally, it opens. My foot automatically perches against the bottom of the door, blocking it in case Webster tries to shut it before I'm ready, the way he used to last year.

He's still watching me.

"You don't actually have anything in your locker, do you?"

He turns his head to glance inside. "Some old papers. And a library book I should probably return at some point."

He shuts the door and I stifle a grin, press down the curling edge of the photo I have taped to the inside of my locker door. One of me and Reese in her car from last year.

I finish swapping out the books I'll need for homework, and then shut my locker and turn to face him. "Ready when you are."

We turn and walk down the hall together. Somehow I expect people to notice, to stare. No one does.

We move with the masses, everyone flooding down the main staircase and down the long hallway where the art and music classes are held. Out the door to the student parking lot. Webster digs his keys from his pocket and gestures to where his car is parked. "So I figured we could carpool over to Susie's?"

I glance down the row of cars toward my own. Carpooling means forgoing my escape plan. But now that he's mentioned it, *not* driving together seems sort of silly. "Sure."

Susie's is only a few miles down the road, tucked in one of the older shopping strips. In a matter of minutes we're sitting at a table for two, surrounded by the smell of powdered sugar and freshly brewed coffee. The space is small, and the decor is sort of shabby-chic, with a bud vase on every table and drinks served in vintage teacups. I order a hot chocolate before I've even decided on what kind of pie I want, because I need all the comfort food I can get.

Webster doesn't even look over the menu, because apparently he already knows exactly what he wants. So when the waitress comes back with our drinks, I try to make my mind up fast. They have over a dozen varieties of pie, and I settle on lemon meringue. As soon as we've ordered and I no longer have a menu to hide behind, the awkwardness of this situation sinks in.

After a few beats of silence, Webster rests his forearms on the table and leans closer. "So. I feel like we should address the elephant in the room."

My hands slide under my thighs and I lock my elbows. "Okay…"

His eyes narrow. "I know you were the one who messed with my car last year."

My shoulders relax away from my ears, a smile tugging at the corner of my mouth. "Oh. That." I make a face. "Yeah, it was definitely me… Sorry."

"I guess I can get over it. Seeing as I sort of had it coming."

"You *absolutely* had it coming."

The waitress comes back and sets the slices in front of us, then freshens Webster's coffee. He grins at me, and we both try bites of our pie.

"While we're on the subject of elephants," I say after I've swallowed, "I didn't mean what I said the other night, either. Obviously I don't hate you."

"Not always obvious," Webster counters, but he's smiling again, a bit more relaxed now. "But I think we were both dealing with things that night. And maybe we're still a little too used to turning each other into targets. I don't want it to be that way, though."

"I don't, either. I definitely prefer when we're both playing nice." I offer a crooked smile, then press the back of my fork into a crumb.

"Good. Glad we got that cleared up." Webster shifts and hooks his ankles around the legs of the chair. "So, on to the next painful subject. How are things at home? You been holding up okay?"

His expression is even. Calm. I try to make mine match, even though so far this isn't at all how I expected this talk to go. Though to be fair, I had no idea *what* to expect. I seldom do, when it comes to Webster. "Yeah, I'm fine."

"Well, I'm convinced," he deadpans. His gaze is trained on my face, waiting for me to crack.

I take a bite of pie to buy some time. After the meltdown he witnessed at the party the other day, it's probably pretty obvious I'm a few steps removed from *fine*.

"It's been kind of weird," I admit after a moment. "I guess I have a hard time understanding how you can spend years with someone, build a life together, and then realize it's not the life you want? Why would anyone want to get themselves in that situation, you know?"

Webster's grip on his fork tightens. He scrapes the prongs against his pie. "I think…at least in my parents' case, they went into it thinking the other person would change."

I'm not sure if that's true of my parents or not. But I ask, "Would you take that risk?"

He glances at me, then back at his plate. Slowly, he shakes his head. "I wouldn't want to change a thing."

The way he says it makes me think he's talking about someone in particular. Like he could be talking about *me*, even though I'm sure he isn't. But there is *something* between us; I know I'm not imagining that much. Holland saw it, too. Which—shit. Webster knew we broke up, so they obviously talked, except I have no idea what was said, and what if Holland told Webster I have a thing for him?

My cheeks flush, and I sip my hot chocolate. I grimace when the flavor mixes with the lemon meringue left on my tongue.

"Did you burn your tongue?" Webster asks.

"No." I shake my head fast, reach for my napkin. Butterfly wings flutter in my stomach and I can't look him in the eye right now. "It's just the lemon and chocolate... I didn't really think this flavor combination through."

"You want to try mine?"

I glance across the table at Webster's plate. I didn't even pay attention to what Webster ordered, but now that I see it involves several layers of chocolate, I realize he has excellent taste. "No, that's okay."

He pushes the plate toward the middle of the table. When I still don't touch it, he nudges it even closer to me.

I relent, slice off a sliver with the end of my fork and then flip it onto my tongue. So chocolatey. *"Uhhhmygod."*

He picks up his fork again. "Good, right?"

"Mm-hmm." I keep the fork flipped on my tongue, sucking off any last sugar molecules. I glance back down at my stupid slice. Lemon meringue. What was I thinking?

"You like mine better, don't you?"

I finally pull the fork out of my mouth and press my lips together. "No."

He snickers and swaps our plates.

"Oh. What? No, you don't have to—"

"It's fine, really," he says with a grin. "I'm pretty equal opportunity when it comes to pie."

Webster might put up a fight when it comes to pizza toppings, but it's true he'll eat pretty much any baked good you put in front of him. It's infuriating how I can feel like I know him so well, yet never actually know where I stand with him. Even now, after talking things out, I'm back in the same, uncertain holding pattern I spent most of our first summer in. Like that night right before junior year, sitting on his living room floor with pizza crusts scattered on plates, with his hand inching closer to mine, wondering if he might kiss me...

God. Kissing Webster is at the top of the list of things I shouldn't be thinking about right this second.

He's quiet for a long moment. Then he sets down his fork and says, "I have another confession to make."

I raise an eyebrow and scoop a bit of whipped cream off the top of my pie, my heart still beating way faster than this moment probably warrants. "What's that?"

"You remember when you asked why I sat next to you the first day of spring semester? I told you I was looking out for Holland, but that wasn't the entire reason. I also just...missed you. And I don't think I even consciously realized it at the time? But I'd seen you around the past year, seen how you were with Reese and your other friends, and I could never shake the feeling that something didn't add up with what happened between us. So I figured if we were stuck together for the semester, I might get some answers."

"Wait, you knew we'd be partnered up all semester?"

Webster's cheeks go faintly pink. "I have some friends who took the class in the fall. Miss Holloway did the same thing to them."

I swallow hard, silently screaming at myself, *Do not read too much into this!* But Holland, Reese—they were right. I have a thing for Webster. A huge thing.

"I know the feeling," I say quietly. "And…I missed you, too."

"And look, I know we already talked about that, but I just want to say again that I'm really sorry for how things went down with homecoming, and how I treated you after. You were right, I should have just asked you about what I heard. I should have known better than to think you weren't my friend."

As much as I appreciate him apologizing, suddenly all of that feels so long ago. I'd much rather focus on the future. "How about we just agree not to be assholes to each other anymore?"

"Deal," Webster says quickly.

A small smile tugs at his lips as he picks up his fork again. We finish the rest of our pie, and after we pay, we head back out to his car.

He pauses by the driver's side door and says, "If you promise not to mess with my tires, I can give you a ride to school tomorrow."

I'm struck with how ridiculous it is that I left early for school every day for a year in order to avoid Webster. That we both put so much energy into trying to hate each other, when we never had any reason to. No wonder it didn't stick. I pop open the passenger side door and pause before getting in. "Deal."

27

WHEN I GET home from the bakery, I find my mom home early from work, crying on the phone. She hangs up after I walk in and pulls herself together pretty quickly, immediately focusing on what we're going to eat for dinner—making it clear she doesn't want to burden me with whatever that phone call was about.

But it doesn't take much to guess.

It also doesn't come as much of a surprise when my parents sit me down again a few days later to tell me they've decided to file for divorce.

"We want you to know that we both tried really hard to make this work," my father says from his favorite chair in the living room. "But after a lot of talking and thinking, we've decided this is what's best for our family."

"Sounds about right," I say.

They share a look and Mom turns back to me. "I'm sorry?"

I shrug and glance between them. "It makes sense. You guys don't get along. You tried to make it work, but…you shouldn't be married."

They're both quiet for a moment. Then Mom says, "We want you to know how sorry we are to have put you in the middle of all this. None of it is your fault."

That part is a little harder to believe. I'm not positive Mom told Dad about *David from work*. But it was only a week ago I forced her hand—and now here we are.

My eyes well up and Mom moves to sit next to me. She holds my hand between hers and that just makes it even harder to breathe evenly. "I'm sorry, honey," she says in a soothing voice. "I know the past couple of months have been hard on you—"

"The past couple of *months*?" I lift my free hand to wipe my cheek. "This has been going on for years. You get that, right? I mean, you say you're sorry for putting me in the middle. But that's what you both have done, over and over again, for as long as I can remember. I've *wished* for you guys to get divorced more times than I can count. And I feel bad about that, but I just—I can't do it anymore." I pull my hand away and look at both of them. "I mean it, I'm not going to be your middleman. I'm not going to be your therapist."

"No," Mom says. "Of course not. We don't want to put you in that position."

Dad's eyes are red-rimmed, his forehead creased. He runs a hand along his five-o'clock shadow. "Your mother and I have both made mistakes in the past. With each other, and with you. But we never meant to hurt you."

My chest is clawed out, each breath scraping against raw

lungs. But at the same time, I'm lighter than I've been in a long time, because I feel like they've finally *heard* me. They understand how much their relationship has affected me.

We talk for a long time, my parents outlining the logistics and answering my questions—even though some things don't have answers yet. And I realize I'm just going to have to be okay with not knowing exactly how the future will unfold.

The next couple weeks are an adjustment, while Dad officially moves out and Mom and I both get used to navigating the house now that his stuff is gone—the empty space in the living room where the reclining chair he took with him used to sit, the tools that cluttered the garage my entire life now cleared away.

And through all of it, Webster is there.

After our trip to Susie's, Webster and I started driving to school together every day. And it wasn't long before we started hanging out after school, too. Some afternoons it almost feels like the past year of drama never happened. Spending time with Webster is just…easy. He's always willing to listen when I relay any divorce-related drama, or commiserate when I just feel crappy about it all. It's easy to talk to him about that sort of thing, because he's been through it before. He knows exactly how it feels the first time you see your dad's side of the closet completely empty.

Usually we drive around for a bit or grab some food before heading home. Last week he brought me to the movie theater where he works and got us into a matinee for free—though that guy Henry he went out with was working, which was slightly awkward (though possibly only for me). But even when we just head back to one of our houses to do our homework or bake together, it's never boring. No matter what we're doing, I'm just happy to be near him. Happier than when I'm on my own.

Today we still haven't discussed any plans as we head out to the student parking lot. This was one of the rare mornings Webster managed to get his shit together before me, so we took his car. His Cadillac is old, ancient actually, and doesn't have an automatic lock. He stops on the passenger side and unlocks my door first. He holds it open for me, and I slide my backpack off one shoulder and pull it around to my front as I sink into the low seat. Webster gently shuts the door after me, and I track him as he lopes around the front of the car, flipping the keys back and forth over his knuckles. When he angles himself into the car and turns over the engine, Taylor Swift's latest album blasts from the speakers, and he lunges for the volume knob.

This is something I've had to get used to, the days we take Webster's car. Another piece of information I folded up and tucked into the Webster file in my head. *Webster listens to Taylor Swift at top volume in the morning.* I reach for my seat belt and click it into place.

For the first time maybe ever, the traffic lights heading home are all timed perfectly. We hit every green. Beside me, Webster seems perfectly relaxed, slouched a bit in the driver's seat with one hand on the wheel. Meanwhile I can't stop touching things—flipping through his preset radio stations, pulling the visor down and then pushing it back up. When I start fiddling with the latch on the center console, Webster can't hold it in anymore.

"Why are you so fidgety?"

"Sorry." I slide my hands under my thighs. I'm not sure why I can't sit still today. It's not like today is different from any other day the past few weeks. But sometimes, when we're in close quarters like this and I can smell his grapefruit shampoo, I suddenly find myself daydreaming about holding his hand or leaning in against him and then something swells inside my chest and it becomes impossible to ignore the fact that I like one of my best friends as *more* than a friend.

I keep telling myself it will pass. Either that, or he'll give me some kind of sign—confirm he feels the same way—only he hasn't. And that's probably smart, because we're still rebuilding our friendship after all, and I should just cool it and enjoy spending time with him, but *oh my god* he looks good in that shade of green.

We finally catch a red light, right outside our subdivision. Webster slides his hands off the wheel and turns his head toward me. "Are you hungry?"

"A little." My stomach is in knots, actually, but if I tell him that he'll ask why, so I keep my mouth shut.

"What do you want?"

It's a valid question. One I've been asking myself a lot lately. And honestly, I'm not sure I know what I want. I know how I *feel*, but if I tell him, and if he feels the same way… What we have right now is so good. I'm not sure I want to change things, risk ruining it again.

"I'm kind of craving a Slurpee," he says.

"*Yes*. Slurpee. That does sound good." I shift in my seat. "Wait. Does this mean you're finally going to let me eat in your car?"

This is another thing I've learned—Webster keeps his car impeccably clean and has a strict no-food policy.

The light turns green and he side-eyes me as he accelerates. "Depends on what you get."

"What are the rules, exactly?"

"Nothing sticky that isn't contained with a lid. So, no ice cream. No fried food, either, unless it's warm enough to keep the windows down."

"That is very specific."

"I don't want Klaus to smell like French fries forever."

I hold my hand up. "Klaus?"

"Yes." He looks at me, straight-faced. "He's German."

"Sure. Of course he is. So do you ever make exceptions to these rules, or…?"

He shoots me an amused look. "You mean for you? Who do you think you are, anyway?"

Heat floods my cheeks because I know exactly who I am. I'm the girl riding in Webster's car, the girl who can't seem to get enough time alone with him lately.

I turn my gaze out the window until we pull up to the 7-Eleven. Webster holds the door for me as we walk in, and we head straight for the Slurpee machines. Both of us reach for large cups. I opt for the cherry flavor, while Webster manages to fit all eight varieties into his cup.

"See, the trick is to start with the one you like the least," he says as he moves to the last machine, "and then finish it off with your favorite. So that's the last one you drink."

"Why don't you just fill the whole thing with your favorite?"

He grins. "I'm sensing a lot of judgment from you right now, and I'm going to have to ask you to check your tone."

"But like…by the time you get to the end, it's all melted and the flavors have run together. If you're gonna layer, you should *start* with your favorite."

"This is my process," he says with a shrug as we head to the register. "You don't have to understand it, Aubrey. You just have to respect it."

I roll my eyes behind his back. At the register, he reaches for his wallet and I swat his hand away. "I got this. Besides, I still owe you that celebratory drink for getting into MSU."

He smiles in a way that doesn't seem all that authentic. "Right. Thanks."

"Did I tell you I finally sent in my deposit?"

"No—that's great, though."

"Yeah," I say, and take my first sip of Slurpee. "I just realized it's where I always wanted to go, and none of the benefits of the other schools really topped it." I sigh happily. "I can't wait to find out who I'm rooming with. And sign up for classes."

We walk back to his car and while putting my seat belt on, I demonstrate how very careful I will be not to spill.

"You want to find somewhere to park to drink these?" I ask.

Webster chews on his straw the same way he does the cap of his pen. "I should get home."

"Oh. Okay."

Something is definitely off with him. He fiddles with his phone, which is hooked up to the stereo through a series of adapters. Once he's finally satisfied with his music selection, he puts the car into Reverse and backs out of the spot.

I suck down another sip, and ice-cold cherry flavor coats my tongue. I stir my Slurpee around with the straw and watch the way his throat moves when he swallows. He catches me staring as he pulls out of the parking lot.

"What?" he asks, automatically wiping his mouth like he's got food on it.

"Nothing."

He doesn't say anything for miles. When we're nearing our subdivision again, I finally call him out. "You're just kind of quiet."

He checks his blind spot and changes lanes. "Sorry. You can put on different music if you want."

I shake my head. That's not even close to what I want. I take a drink and try not to overanalyze things, but Webster hasn't interacted with anyone else in the last five minutes, so this shift in his mood must be because of me.

We're turning onto our block when he finally looks at me again. "Can I ask you something?"

"Sure."

"If you had ended up at NC State instead, do you think you'd ever get back together with Holland?"

Hearing Holland's name come out of Webster's mouth is like hitting my hand on a hot oven rack. I flinch back, pull my hair over one shoulder. I look out the window and jab my straw into my drink.

"Or what about if you'd met him later. In college. Would things have turned out differently?"

"No? I mean…" An exasperated noise crawls up my throat. "I don't know. Why are you asking me this?"

"Because that's your type, right? Future doctors. Guys who are good at Scrabble."

"I hate Scrabble, actually..."

"Crossword puzzles, then. Whatever." He pulls into my driveway and throws the car into Park. Keeps his gaze on the gearshift. He seems annoyed with me, and I wish for once he'd stop talking in code and just tell me what's really going on inside his head.

I can't keep the edge out of my voice. "If I recall, you were the one who kept pointing out all the ways Holland and I weren't right for each other."

"Yeah. Well. What do I know, right?"

I stare at him for a long moment. Give him the chance to say something to make me stay. To prove I haven't been imagining our connection all this time, prove the past couple weeks have meant anything to him at all.

His hand moves to his plastic cup, bending the chewed-up straw. His mouth stays in a straight line.

"Apparently less than I thought," I say as I throw the door open. I grab my bag from the floor and slam the door behind me. I don't make it five steps before Webster is out of the car.

"Aubrey—"

"What?" I whip around—Webster is much closer than I expected, so close the toes of our shoes touch. All the harsh words I had locked and loaded get lodged in my throat when he catches my waist. Time stills. His free hand reaches up, tucks my hair behind my ear. My backpack slips off my shoulder. It dangles in the crook of my elbow for a second, then drops to the ground as he leans in and I lift onto my toes to meet him halfway.

He kisses me with a gentle kind of intensity. Like this is something he's wanted for a long time, but he's afraid of taking what I don't want to give. My hand wraps around the back of his neck, pulls him closer. We're both breathing heavy and fast, his grip tightening on my waist when I part his lips with mine.

The tingle that runs through my whole body when our tongues first touch, his hips pressing hard against mine—already this is a feeling I don't ever want to live without. And I'm almost angry with myself, because maybe if I hadn't said that stupid thing to Reese when we were juniors, I could have had this a year ago.

Webster's hand shifts down to my neck. He slows our kiss and pulls back, though only far enough to look at me. "So is now a good time to mention I like you?"

I laugh and grip the front of his shirt. "I kind of picked up on that." I tilt my face up toward his again. "It's a little bit mutual."

"Oh, good, then I don't have to avoid you for the next few weeks."

"Please don't."

He smiles and dips his head to give me another quick kiss. Then he reaches down to pick up my forgotten backpack. "I should probably go. From the weight of this backpack, I can only assume you were planning to spend the rest of your day studying, and I wouldn't want to interrupt that."

I snatch the bag from him and hoist it over one shoulder. "You are supremely annoying."

"Yeah." He grins broadly and starts walking backward to his car. "But you like it."

He's right. God help me.

★ ★ ★

Reese crouches by my bedroom window, peering through the blinds at Web's house like a total creeper.

"Would you stop that?"

She sits back on her heels and looks at me. "Okay, I need way more details. What kind of kisser is he?"

"What kind of question is that?"

"Come on. Describe it to me."

The fact that we've already been over every detail of my encounter with Webster is apparently irrelevant. I called Reese as soon as Webster backed out of my driveway, so she already asked a million questions on the phone. But for once, I'm okay with her unwavering enthusiasm and intrusive questioning about my love life. Especially since I can't seem to stop reliving the kiss anyway.

"Was it, like, slow, soft, and lingering?" she asks. "Or hot, heavy, and full of tongue?"

"It was definitely hot…but not full of tongue. It sort of started out soft and slow and then built up to more. But we were standing in my driveway, so we stopped before it got too intense."

"So school got out at two thirty, and then you went to the 7-Eleven. How long do you think you spent there?"

"Um…I dunno, like ten minutes?"

"And what time was it when you got back inside?"

"I have no idea."

"Didn't you look at a clock?" She seems personally offended when I shake my head. Then she pulls out her phone. "Well, you called me at three nineteen. So factor in driving time…"

My eyes narrow. "Are you trying to figure out how long our kiss lasted?"

She grins broadly and nods.

"Stop."

"Okay," she says without dimming her smile even a little.

"I'm serious."

"I can see that." She bites her thumbnail. "But does approximately nine minutes of kissing sound right?"

"That seems…long. But I guess time flies when you're having fun?"

Reese rocks all the way onto her butt and crosses her legs. She cups her chin in her palm and looks at me with this pinch at the corners of her mouth like she knows something I don't.

"What?"

"You *loooove* him."

"You can see yourself out."

She hops up and onto my bed. The mattress bounces under her weight and I bury my face in my furry throw pillow.

"Hey." She waits for me to lower the pillow before saying, "Have I mentioned I'm really happy for you?"

I cover my cheeks with my hands, then spring off the bed. I have too much energy to sit still. "Let's not get ahead of ourselves. It was just a kiss."

"A kiss and a declaration of *loooove*." Reese wiggles her shoulders and makes a heart with her hands.

"Not love. No one said love." I stop pacing and look at her. "I feel like I'm still bracing for him to take it back. Like…" I think back to the conversation Webster and I had at Susie's. "Maybe this is too big a risk."

I've wondered lately if my parents think it was worth it. If their good years outweigh everything they're going through now. All of that compromising and investing so much of yourself into someone else, only to have your plans fall apart. Maybe they would have separated sooner, if it wasn't so hard to untangle themselves from the life they built together.

Reese relaxes her posture and gives me a small smile. "You know what they say. The bigger the risk, the bigger the reward."

My mom calls up the stairs to let us know she brought dinner home. And as we leave my room, I glance once more toward the window that faces Webster's house. "I hope you're right."

28

MY MOM KNOCKS on the bathroom door while I'm brushing my teeth the next morning.

"Webster's here," she calls. "He's waiting out front."

I check the time on my phone. He's way earlier than usual. I fling the door open, my toothbrush still in my mouth. "What?"

Mom smiles softly and runs a lock of my hair through her fingers. She's been getting a bit sentimental lately, probably because she still isn't used to boys coming around. I'm not entirely used to it yet, either. And I have to admit, I've felt sort of awkward since yesterday. It's weird to be this happy about something when my mom is so sad.

She takes a big breath and raises her eyebrows, her smile becoming more mischievous—like she's in on a secret. "Better hurry up."

"Okay…" I race through the rest of my routine and grab

my backpack from where I left it in the living room. I sweep my hair—which, as of this week, has *finally* reached shoulder length again—out from under the straps, then dart out through the garage door, barely registering Mom calling after me when I realize Webster's car isn't in the driveway.

"Aubrey!" My mom is leaning out the door to the kitchen.

"What?"

"I said, Webster is around front." She waves for me to come back inside, but from here, it's faster to just cut through the front lawn.

I round the corner and spot Webster standing on our porch. "Hey!"

He spins around. "Why are you coming from that way?"

"Because...that's the door I always use?" I shoot him a confused look and raise my hand like, *What's your deal?*

Webster tugs his hand through his hair and glances at the porch behind him, and when I follow his gaze, I find out what the issue actually is. Behind him, at least two dozen cupcakes are arranged on the ground. I tilt my head and realize they spell out *PROM?* Of course, from here, the word is upside down. Because I was supposed to come out the front door.

We're standing next to each other at this point. I curl my lips in and turn to Webster. "Do you want me to go back inside and come out this way?"

He sighs. I can see my mother peeking out at us through the front window. Webster's ears are a violent shade of red.

"Okay, I know prom is still a few weeks away," he says, turning to me. "But...I spent all night thinking about you. I spend *most* nights thinking about you, actually. I really like spending time with you, Aubrey. And the more I thought about what happened junior year…I just really wanted a do-over." He glances down at the cupcakes, then back to me. "I think we owe it to our past selves to go to a dance together." He smiles nervously at his own joke. "So…what do you say?"

My throat swells and I have to swallow hard to relieve the pressure. I bend down to pick up one of the cupcakes. Swipe my finger in the frosting and lick it off. Webster watches with a pained look on his face. "German chocolate, huh?"

"I made sure not to eat any of the coconut this time."

I grin. "Webster, I would love to go to prom with you."

He breaks into a huge smile, one that even makes his eyes crinkle. He leans in and gives me a chaste kiss on the cheek that tells me he's well aware my mom is still watching us. We start gathering the cupcakes to take them inside and he says, "I'm really glad you said yes. For all the obvious reasons, but also because my car battery is dead and I need a ride to school."

"I see. Well, it's a good thing I like you. 'Cause that would've been an awkward drive."

Webster laughs and carefully steps toward the front door.

My mom helps us carry the cupcakes into the kitchen. "I'll get all of these put away," she says. "You two get to school."

She waves us off, and Webster carries my backpack for me out to the car. I feel like we're in a movie set in the 1950s, and he's going to offer me his letter jacket next.

When we get to school, he walks with me all the way to my locker. The warning bell rings, and he grabs the strap of my backpack and tugs me closer. He leans in like he's going to kiss me goodbye, but just as I start to tip my face up to meet him, he changes course and kisses my neck instead.

When he straightens again, he's wearing a wide grin. "You had a little bit of frosting there."

I try and fail to suppress my smile. "Oh really?"

"Yeah, but don't worry. I took care of it." Then he lets go of my backpack and walks away, looking over his shoulder just once, with a gleam in his eye like he knows kissing him is literally all I will be thinking about for the next two to three hours.

Across the hall, I lock eyes with Veronica, who witnessed the whole thing from her locker. And from the way she cocks one eyebrow, I'm guessing it's completely obvious how flustered I am right now. All she says is, "Girl."

I let out a long sigh. "I know."

My mom comes home from work early again that day. I've just gotten home from an after-school detour to Gilbert Lake with Webster a few minutes before she walks in the door and sets her purse down on the kitchen table. Her hands clasp together, and her voice takes on an excited pitch as she says, "Prom!"

"Yeah," I say, trying and failing to muster the same level of excitement. "It'll be fun."

"We need to get you a dress."

I wave the pen I was using to mark up my planner. "I'll probably just borrow something from Reese."

Her shoulders visibly sink. "Oh. All right, then."

As much as I was worried my new relationship would be salt in the wound, my mother actually seems more upset about me not wanting to shop. And I realize that, even though the dress isn't something I care about that much, it's still a nice thing she wants to do for me. It's something that would make her happy, and it'll take very little effort on my part.

"On second thought, a new dress could make it a little more special."

She practically lunges for her keys. We go to the mall and head straight for the food court, because my mother says there's nothing worse than shopping on an empty stomach.

Well. What she *actually* says is that she doesn't want to shop with me when I'm hangry. But…same thing.

Anyway, I happily accept my cinnamon-sugar soft pretzel and then we walk to the nearest department store.

"So, did you have any ideas of cut? Or color?"

"Um…long?" Lord knows how Mr. Davis is going to police prom dresses. Though he'd probably be writing literally every girl up if he stuck to the dress code on prom night.

My mom pinches her lips. "Okay. Okay, that's a good place to start."

Clearly she expected me to come more prepared than this. But I'm honestly just relieved that she's prioritizing finding something I actually like. The main reason I've always dreaded shopping with my mother is that she has a tendency to take over and pick out all kinds of stuff for me to try on, regardless of how I feel about it.

"And maybe green…?" I add.

"Green is a lovely color on you." She dives right in, pulling an armful of floor-length dresses off the nearest rack. She holds one of them up. "This one isn't green, but if you're open to purple, I think it could be a nice option."

"Sure. I can try it."

She unloads the dresses onto my bent arm, and I check out

the price tag on one. It's over two hundred dollars. It seems stupidly expensive for a dress I'm only going to wear for a few hours. To an event that wasn't even on my radar until Webster asked me. And I know her job pays decently and that she probably hasn't gotten this far in life without learning to budget, but I still feel like she shouldn't be spending this kind of money on me. Especially with the divorce, and when I have college coming up, and will need her help much more then.

"Maybe we should look at the sales rack," I offer.

"Sure, just try these on first."

She hands me a few more and leads me to the dressing rooms. They're pretty much empty, except for one woman with a stroller who is occupying the largest room. We pick one near the front, where there's an armchair for my mom to sit in while she waits.

"Before you know it we'll be shopping for your wedding dress," she says as she settles in.

I freeze with one hanger clutched in my fist. "I don't know about that…"

"Well, I don't mean tomorrow. But you're reaching so many milestones lately…graduating, first boyfriend—"

"Webster isn't really my boyfriend. I mean…we haven't really talked about it yet."

My mom gives me a funny look. "Honey, I meant Holland."

"Oh. Right." …*Awkward.* I close the door to the changing room and make a face in the mirror. How did I forget about Holland this quickly?

"How are things with Webster, by the way?"

"They're good. We have a lot of fun together."

"You two were joined at the hip the summer they moved in across the street. Carol and I could never figure out why you two stopped hanging out after homecoming. Anyway, I'm glad there hasn't been any tension between you, after the breakup with Holland."

"No tension about that. Not for me, anyway. I'm not totally sure how things have been between the two of them…"

"Well, it's all pretty recent. Give it some time, and I'm sure they'll smooth things out." Mom sighs again, her mention of time seemingly enough to set off her nostalgia once more. "Soon you'll be at college. You're just growing up so fast."

I start to undress. "To be fair, you said the same thing when I left elementary school, so."

"It's all been fast."

I pull the purple dress overhead—it's tight enough that I have to wiggle it down over my shoulders, and suddenly I'm super glad I didn't wear makeup today because it would be smeared all over the lining by now. I zip it into place and run a hand over my hair to get rid of some of the static.

"Well, you can relax, because I'm not even sure I want to get married." I open the door and hold my arms out, ready for my mother's inspection. But she barely seems to register the dress. Her eyebrows are knit together, her expression still caught in processing the last thing I said.

"What makes you say that?"

I shrug. "I just think people grow up with this expectation that it's what they're supposed to do. Get married, buy a house, have kids. But that's not the right choice for everyone. It doesn't always work out."

My whole deep dive into Bayes' theorem did at least get

me to move past my original theory on the subject. I don't really believe love always fails anymore, or that marriage *can't* work. Reese's parents are proof happy marriages do exist. Just, sometimes you can care about someone, and be good together for a while, but not forever. And a million things can happen in life to complicate even loving relationships—especially the ones that span years.

Her lips purse. "Honey, I know everything that's happening between your father and me is confusing, and it's not easy... but I hope you realize I don't regret the choices I made."

I know she's not thinking about *David from work* right now, but I am. I'm thinking about how I've put so much blame on Mom for that incident, even though I knew it was a side effect of my parents' problems, not the root cause. And while I still think she should have told my dad back when it happened, after my close call with Webster when I was still with Holland, it's not so difficult anymore to understand why she tried to bury it in the past.

I cross my arms. They're blasting the AC in here—all the muscles in my shoulders have gone stiff from the chill. "So even knowing what you know now...you'd do it again?"

"Absolutely. Those choices led to you. And we had so many good years. I wouldn't trade those for anything." She stands up and puts her hands on my arms. "What I'm trying to say is, there's a difference between giving up and knowing when it's the right time to let go. You don't have to decide if you want to get married or have a family right now. And whatever you do decide will be the right choice for you. But I don't want you to hold back when you still have your whole life ahead of you."

I relax my arms and smile at her so she knows the message got through. Then, because I can't help myself, I add, "But didn't you just say my life was going by fast?"

She steps back and lets out an exasperated sigh. Her gaze travels down the front of me and she makes a face. "Oh, no, that dress is all wrong. Go try on one of the green ones."

I grin and step back inside the dressing room, ready to try again.

29

SENIOR SKIP DAY comes the following week, when the entirety of the senior class pretends they have permission to bail on school. Mike Chen throws a pool party at his apartment complex, and Reese and Webster tag team in their efforts to get me to go.

Webster drives, because he knows where Mike lives and possibly also because he's afraid I'll bolt if I have my own mode of transportation. He is not wrong. I'm weirdly nervous, even though I've known most of these people since middle school. But this is the first time Webster and I have shown up somewhere *together* since we started seeing each other—it makes everything feel so public. I fidget the whole way over, until Webster reaches over and holds my hand.

When he parks by the pool, I pivot in my seat and rest my elbows on the center console. "You sure you want to go to this? Because we could just stay here and make out."

He answers by tracing his knuckles across my jaw, up to my ear. My pulse kicks it up a notch, and I move in for more. But Webster pulls back, a smile tugging at the corners of his lips.

"Come on," he says, and opens his door. "What would Bayes do?"

"You think you're so clever, don't you?" I say, as I follow him up the sidewalk.

He turns around and waits for me with a shit-eating grin on his face. "Gotta keep you on your toes, Cash."

It looks like the entire varsity basketball team is in attendance, everyone either in the pool or milling around it, music from someone's Bluetooth speaker pumping bass into the air, though it's mostly drowned out by all the splashing. Reese and Kevin beat us here, so for the next hour I mostly stick by Reese's side. It's hot enough already that we hit the water right away, and it's not long before Sam and Mike challenge Reese and Kevin to a game of chicken. Reese is the first to topple, and after she surfaces, I watch the sweet way Kevin pushes the wet hair out her face, the easy way she clings to him.

Sam asks if I want to go up against them next, but she's kind of fierce, and I would rather not get dunked—plus I feel slightly weird about getting any friendlier with her, because even though I still don't know much about what went down between them, I'm loyal to Veronica by default—so I pass, and one of the girls from the cheerleading squad volunteers.

Webster swims closer, and my arms automatically cross around his neck. He spins me around in the water, and it isn't until I look over and see Kevin doing the same thing to Reese that I realize—we're becoming like them. A real couple. The kind that has a certain way of looking at each other, a specific way of touching. A few months ago—weeks ago, even—seeing myself act this way probably would have sent me spiraling. But being with Webster—I wake up excited to see him every morning, and I'm not constantly worrying about the status of our relationship anymore. Instead I'm just…happy I get to spend so much time with my best friend.

Which isn't to say I'm completely cured of my commitment phobia. Feeling this strongly about someone is definitely still a bit scary. But I'm done trying to turn my life into a science experiment. I just want to enjoy the summer. And I'll admit, knowing Webster and I will be at MSU together makes me feel a lot better about things. We'll have time to let our relationship evolve naturally, to find out if we're built to last.

Of course, there's *also* the probability Webster will be just as popular in college as he is here. We'll go to school together, but then he'll be surrounded by new friends, just like the start of junior year.

I swim to the edge of the pool and lift myself up onto the ledge to sit with my legs dipped in the water. Webster follows me over and plants his hands on either side of my thighs. He hoists himself up to give me a chlorine-laced kiss, then slips back into the water.

While he volleys a beach ball back and forth with Mike, Sam swims over and pulls herself up next to me. "Hey, Aubrey."

I look sideways at her. "Hey. Having fun?"

She stretches her legs out long in front of her, toes painted a pretty shade of pink that's a bit distorted under the water. "Yeah, definitely." She pauses and then meets my gaze. "So…

Reese mentioned you've gotten pretty close with Veronica lately?"

This again. My back straightens and I nod cautiously. "Yeah, I guess so. We're lab partners, and we hang out. Mostly at school."

Sam nods thoughtfully.

"Was there...anything else you wanted to ask?"

"No." Sam's cheeks are a bit pink, though it's possible that's just from too much sun. "Well—I guess I was just curious what she's like now."

"Um..." I glance around the pool, searching for an out, because I have no idea how to respond to that. What Veronica would *want* me to say. "Yeah, she's...nice. She's been a good friend."

"Good." Sam nods again and braces her arms on either side of her hips. "That's good."

While Sam's line of questioning is a bit weird, there's nothing malicious in her responses. I more get the sense she's just been thinking about Veronica lately, the same way I know Veronica has been thinking about her.

"Yeah, I didn't really know her before this year," I add, hoping I'm not making it too obvious what I know about their history. "But she's definitely worth knowing now."

"I think it's time to get the grill going," Mike says as he hauls himself out of the pool as well. "Who's hungry?"

"Me," Sam calls out, followed by echoes from Kevin and Reese. She shoots me one last smile, then pushes to her feet and paces over to the grill.

Webster helps Mike get the food ready, and when the burgers are cooked, we all head over to a group of lounge chairs.

I put on my cover-up, and Webster hands me my plate. We sit side by side while we eat, and as soon as the others are finished, they jump back in the pool. Webster takes my empty plate and stacks it on top of his. He sets them both on the ground, then shifts in the lounge so he's sitting forward, one leg on each side. He lies back and tugs the fabric of my cover-up gently. "Come here."

I swing my legs up and lean back against his chest. He takes my hand and laces our fingers together over my stomach.

"I could get used to this," he says, his eyes drifting closed as I peek back at him.

"Hopefully we'll end up in the same dorm next year. Lots of naps between classes," I murmur.

For a moment, neither of us says anything, lost in our own daydreams. Then he squeezes my fingers and says, "I wanted—"

His phone buzzes, and he sighs and lets go of my hand to grab his phone from the towel where he left it. He reads the text he just got and types out a quick response, then meets my gaze again as he sets the phone back on the towel. "Holland."

"Oh." I nod and we lie in silence for a few more seconds. "So…have you guys talked much about us?"

"He knows we're hanging out."

"Right. And…he's cool with it?"

Webster nods. "Seems to be." He shifts so one arm is behind his neck. With his other hand he twirls my ponytail around his finger. "You want to tell me what's on your mind?"

"What makes you think something's on my mind?"

"You mean aside from the fact that a dog walked by while we were eating and you didn't say anything?" He traces his fingers over my collarbone. "I can just tell."

I swallow hard and fix my gaze on the oak tree just outside the gate of the pool area, its leaves rustling in the breeze.
I twist my fingers through the slats of the lounge chair, and I
know I'm probably being silly, worrying about Webster making all kinds of new friends. Meeting people who are more
interesting than me. I tell myself to let it go. But my mouth
doesn't get the memo, and I blurt out, "Hey, how many people have you been involved with?"

Webster cranes his neck to look at me. I think I've given
him whiplash. After a beat he lowers his head again and says,
"Um...well. There was someone back in Chicago. He was
sort of my first noncelebrity crush on a guy. But, you know.
We were pretty young, and he was still figuring things out—
we both were, I guess—so it never got too serious. Then a
few girls from school. It sort of depends what you mean by
involved? Like, I've only really *dated* three people. Four if you
count Henry, but we only went out twice before deciding
we were better as friends."

"Okay."

Neither of us says anything for a long moment. The breeze
has stopped, the courtyard drenched in a stillness that makes
me hyperaware of the rise and fall of Webster's chest, coming faster now than before.

"That's what was bothering you before?" he finally asks.

"No," I say quickly. I shift so I can look at him properly. "I
was just curious, I guess. About your dating history."

"Okay," he says with a wary smile. "Any particular reason?"

My gaze drifts back to Reese and Kevin. It makes more
sense to me now, why Reese is so confident they could stay
together. They just sort of *work*. And even if I'm not quite

at the point of believing that yet about me and Webster, we have come a long way since last year. So maybe I am starting to get my hopes up, just a little.

"I guess I just want us to know each other really well. Especially with college next year—people change in college. And you'll meet a ton of new people. You could meet someone else—"

"So could you," he says, his voice taking on an edge. "Look, being bi doesn't make me any more likely to be into someone else than you are. Okay?"

"No—I know that. God, I'm sorry, that's not what I meant at all."

"What did you mean?" He doesn't sound angry. More like…cautious. "Because first you ask about my past relationships and then say I might meet someone else, and honestly, I'm not sure where you're going with all this."

I drag a hand over my face, embarrassed that—however unintentionally—I said something biphobic. And Webster's right—this conversation wasn't headed anywhere good. "I know I'm being weird. Just, we're getting so close to graduation, and I've been looking forward to it for so long, and I've worked so hard because I *wanted* things to change, but now… Reese and I were talking the other day about how people *find themselves* in college, and it's going to be really hard being away from her, but then I think about how even if she was going to MSU we'd still have all these separate, life-altering experiences, and…the same could be true for me and you. And things are good now. With us. So I want some things to stay the same, you know?"

"Yeah." Webster swallows, nods once. "I do know."

I take a deep breath and smile softly at him. "I like you. Like, a ridiculous amount."

He grins and pulls me closer. Then he kisses me, just long enough to make me want more.

"Do you want to go back to your house?" I ask, a little breathless.

His eyes flash to mine. "Yes. Let's do that."

It takes a few minutes for us to say goodbye to everyone and get our stuff. When we get back to his house, I follow him inside and toe my shoes off in the foyer. I nudge them so they're lined up next to his. The house is so quiet. It's like there's too much energy in the air, not enough bodies home to absorb it. The pads of my fingers tingle. I take out my ponytail, just so I can play with the hair tie.

A beat of heavy silence passes, and I move past Webster, down the basement stairs. He follows two steps behind me. I head straight for his bed. Sit down on the end and lean back on my palms.

He eases himself down next to me, his body angled so it's facing mine. His phone buzzes with another text, but this time he ignores it. Already I'm breathing heavy as he leans in and presses a sweet kiss against my lips.

We kiss soft and slow like that for a while, until his hand slides into my hair and I slowly lower onto my back. Webster rolls more of his weight onto me and teases my tongue with his. Our kisses grow deeper, and then Webster slips his arm around my lower back and in one swift motion slides me up the bed, placing my head on his pillow. He pulls his arm out from under me and grabs the hem of my cover-up instead. I pull his shirt overhead, wanting more of his warm skin against mine, to feel the flat planes of his stomach that I spent all day admiring.

He pulls back, lifting onto hands and knees and staring down at me in a way that makes me feel shy. His gaze flickers over my face, my shoulders, my hair—like he's memorizing every detail. Like he wants to save this image of me in his bed.

Both my hands lift to pull his face back down to mine. He laughs softly against my mouth and then shakes his head. "You have no idea how many times I've thought about this."

"I'm not ready to have sex," I blurt out.

His expression turns serious. "That's not what I meant. I never expected—"

"No, I know. I just…thought I should make myself clear."

He tips his forehead against mine and nods. "I understand."

We start kissing again, and a few minutes later his hand migrates back to my bikini bottoms. His thumb hooks under the side tie. "Is this okay?" he whispers.

I nod and lift my hips so he can pull them down. Somehow it isn't until he tugs the fabric off my ankles and I'm left bottomless that it finally hits me. *Hey, hi, you're basically naked in Webster Casey's bed.*

My cover-up is balled up around my waist, and I gasp when Webster touches me, my head tilting back. His fingers move in slow circles that make it so hard to keep from panting. His kiss moves under my jaw, then down my throat, across my collarbone. He looks up at me. "Can I try something else?"

He's lower down my body than before, and after a moment I understand what he's asking.

"You want to?"

"Only if you do…"

I nod. "Okay."

He shifts lower on the bed and kneels between my legs. The instant his tongue touches me my jaw drops. I suck in a breath and press my lips together to keep the sounds I'm making muffled. My fingers twist around his sheets, then move to his shoulder, nails digging into his skin.

"Oh my god," I say in a raspy voice I barely recognize. A guy has never made me feel like *this* before.

One of Webster's hands wraps around my thigh, and he somehow manages to increase the pressure of his mouth against me. My legs are trembling, my whole body flushed and hot and my eyes squeezed shut as I focus on the wave swelling inside me. My back arches as I finish, and Webster plants a soft kiss against the sensitive skin on my inner leg. He moves back up the bed. I'm still trembling, but the second I've caught my breath I reach for the waistband of his swim trunks. He catches my hand. Shakes his head.

"Not right now, okay?"

I can see that he's turned on, and I don't understand why he's stopping. "But I want it to be fun for you."

He gives me a crooked smile. "That was fun for me. Watching you...yeah. I definitely enjoyed that."

"You sure?"

He laughs and shifts so that he's spooning me. "Yes."

His arm wraps around my midsection and I turn to plant a kiss on the inside of his arm. He tucks his chin over my shoulder. "Aubrey—"

"Oh man!" The familiar jingle of an ice-cream truck filters in from outside. "You know what sounds so good right now?"

Webster nestles in closer to my neck. "Hmm?"

"One of those ice-cream sandwiches that's like two cook-ies with ice cream in the middle? And they give you a sugar headache but it's totally worth it?"

Webster lifts onto one elbow and looks down at me. He tucks a lock of hair behind my ear and then kisses my temple before leaping out of bed. "Okay."

"Okay, what?" I pull the sheets with me as I sit up, alarmed. "What's happening right now?"

Webster does a funny hop, adjusting his…area under his swim trunks. He reaches for his T-shirt. "I'm getting you ice cream."

"Oh my god, no. That was a hypothetical." I hold out my arm. "Come back."

He flashes me a smile and then takes the stairs two at a time. "Webster!"

This is ridiculous. And I can't even chase after him, because I still have no bottoms on. If he was leaving for any reason other than to run an absurd errand for me, I'd probably be offended at how easy it was for him to walk out while I was half-naked in his bed.

I hear the front door slam shut above me, and the silence that follows is heavy and creepy. About five minutes in, I pretty much lose my mind. I seriously cannot believe he ran out of the house like that. I was totally kidding. Mostly. But I can't even hear the truck anymore. There's no way he could have caught up to it.

Which is confirmed when I hear the door open again a moment later. I sit up in the bed, then freeze as a voice that does not belong to Webster comes from upstairs.

30

HIGH HEELS CLACK across the kitchen floor. Webster's mom is home.

I scramble to locate my bikini bottoms, my breath sharp and fast. I can't find them. My cover-up is short and entirely see-through, and *I can't find my fucking bathing suit*. This isn't happening right now. Where the fuck is Webster?

I shake out the sheet and finally see a flash of pink. I yank my bottoms on underneath the comforter just as two more voices filter down from upstairs, followed by the quick clattering sound of a dog racing across the hardwood floor. I launch off the bed and straighten my cover-up, which got twisted around my waist at some point.

The basement door opens and footsteps thud down. "Hey, Web, you—"

Holland freezes halfway down the stairs. I lift my hand in a feeble hello.

"Aubrey."

"Hey, Holland…"

Lucy scurries down the stairs, skirting around Holland to get to me. I kneel to give her some pets and bury my face in her fur, because frankly, I need a moment to compose myself. When I look up again, Holland's eyes have shifted to Webster's unmade bed. They snap back to mine.

I wish I was wearing more fucking clothing.

Mrs. Casey appears behind Holland at the top of the stairs. Because what this situation was missing was a parent's involvement. "Did I hear Aubrey's name?"

"Yeah, hi, Mrs. Casey. Webster actually just ran outside… He was trying to catch the ice-cream truck," I say with a laugh that sounds fake, even to me.

"Oh. Okay…" She smiles, but she seems to be looking past me. Assessing the situation through her narrowed field of vision at the top of the stairs. "Well, my sister and I were just about to make some coffee. Can I get you anything?"

Her sister's here. Holland's mother. That's fantastic. "No, thanks. I actually need to get home."

I give Lucy one more scratch behind the ears and step toward the stairs. Holland shifts to the side to let me pass. I run my hand over the back of my hair and climb up. A moment later he follows.

Mrs. Casey has moved to the living room. I smile as I walk past, and Mrs. Sawyer catches my eye. I met her only once, a brief introduction the first time I went over to Holland's house, when we dropped Lucy off after going to the pet store. The look she gives me now isn't what I would call warm. Apparently she's not quite over the fact that Holland

and I broke up. Or, possibly, she thinks I'm kind of slutty for switching from one cousin to the other.

I remind myself I'm not slutty—that word is bullshit anyway, and it certainly wouldn't be used if a guy was in my situation. Besides, I have no way of knowing what Holland's mom is actually thinking. Her disapproving look could be about something else entirely...though right now, I'm having a hard time believing it.

As I reach the front door and dip to put on my shoes, Holland hovers over me. Despite the fact that I'm 95 percent sure the post-orgasm flush has worn off, I still feel like he can tell what Webster and I were doing. That he can see it on me. My hair is hot on the back of my neck. I pull it around my shoulder as I straighten.

Holland's arms are crossed tight against his chest. Maybe I should have asked Webster more questions earlier, about how Holland took it when he told him about us. Maybe I'm supposed to say something, apologize. Except, I didn't mean for any of this to happen. I didn't do anything wrong.

I open my mouth to ask how he's been, at least, but Holland beats me to the punch.

"You and Webster, huh? That didn't take long." His expression has a raw quality to it, a hurt he can't quite hide. Not the look of someone who has had time to process this information.

I pull at the hem of my cover-up, try to make it longer. "He said he talked to you..."

He gives one tiny shake of his head.

My jaw shifts. I can hear his mom talking to Webster's in the other room, a conversation filled with long silences because they're probably more interested in eavesdropping on us. A sweat has broken out across my back, and I fold my arms tighter. I'm pretty sure nothing I say will make this better.

I pull open the door and step onto the front porch. Holland follows, closes the door behind him.

"I know it looks bad," I start, and then I can't *stop* talking, the words tumbling out of me. "But Webster and I have this whole history, and we're still figuring things out, but we'll be at Michigan State together next year—"

Holland laughs coldly. "Wow. Okay."

The sound makes my whole body clench. "What?"

He looks at me for a long moment. Eventually, his hard gaze softens just slightly. "Webster's not going to MSU. He committed to a school in Boston." His mouth twists into a smirk. "Guess he's been leaving us both out of the loop lately."

Holland keeps talking, something about a basketball scholarship, but I can't hear anything except the blood pumping through my ears. *He lied.* Webster lied to me, about something so *huge*, and I don't know why he'd do that. How he could go so long without telling me.

"Sorry, I need...should go." I turn and there's Webster, just reaching the bottom of the driveway. He stalls when he sees us, then climbs up the lawn.

When he gets closer, he looks from me to Holland, and I catch a flicker of panic in his eyes. Though presumably it's because he's worried his cousin just found me naked in his bed. "Hey, man. What are you doing here?"

"Texted you earlier. My mom and I ran into Aunt Carol while we were running errands after school."

"Oh. Cool." Webster makes it all the way over to me and

holds out the ice-cream sandwich. "I haven't run that much since basketball season ended, but I got it." He's breathless, but clearly trying to keep his voice light.

I take it, then stare at it in my palm. I can't look at him, even when I feel his searching gaze on my face. "Thanks."

My voice comes out too quiet and Webster notices. He fidgets at my side. "You're welcome..." He clears his throat. "So...what were you guys talking about?"

"Oh, I was just telling Aubrey about how excited we all are for you to play ball out East next year."

Webster is frozen. Hands laced behind his neck, gaze fixed on some spot near the welcome mat. Then he turns his wary eyes on me again and it's like splashing icy water on my face. I have never been so alert. So ready for a fight.

Holland reaches for the door. Suddenly he seems much more relaxed. "Well, I should see if my mom's ready to get going. Nice catching up, Aubrey."

I can't respond. Can't do anything except stare at Webster, wait for him to say something that makes all of this seem better. He doesn't.

I turn on my heel and jump off the porch. I'm halfway down his lawn before he catches up to me. He's running his hands through his hair, then he's reaching for my arm. I shrug him off, step onto the street.

"Aubrey, hang on."

I keep walking, across our street and up my driveway. "Why did you tell me you were going to MSU?"

"I didn't."

My eyebrows ratchet up. "Excuse me? Did I imagine our whole conversation when you got in?"

"No, I just—" He pushes the heel of his palm against his eye. "I never said I was for sure going there. You just assumed. And for a while, it looked like that's where I'd end up anyway, but then I got offered a scholarship to play at a D1 school. And…you seemed so happy about us both going to State—"

"*Ohh*, so this is my fault." I gesture to myself and realize I'm still holding the stupid ice-cream sandwich. I shove it back at Webster.

"That's not what I'm saying. I'm trying to explain…it got complicated."

"It's really not, though. Is the thing." My lips curl in and I squeeze them hard between my teeth. "You didn't actually tell Holland about us, either, did you?"

He hesitates—not that I actually need him to give an answer at this point. Then he reaches for me, still wearing a nervous smile, like he thinks we can laugh about this. I'm not laughing. In fact, my eyes are stinging, and my hands are shaking, and I don't want him touching me. I pull my wrist away from his grasp and stumble back a step.

"Do you have any fucking clue how humiliating that was for me?" I glance back across the street. We're still in the line of sight from his living room window. I turn and keep walking up my driveway. "You should have seen the way your aunt looked at me. And Holland…"

"I know, I'm sorry. I tried to tell him—"

"Just stop. You didn't fucking try. How do you *try* to tell someone something without actually telling them?"

"Can you let me explain?" He's losing his temper now. Getting desperate. And I am so not here for it.

"Yeah, why don't you explain the real reason you didn't

tell Holland. Or why you didn't tell me that you'll be half-way across the country next year. Was it because you didn't think we'd last long enough for it to matter?"

"*No.*" He wipes his mouth. "Oh my god, Aubrey, this is all so—"

"You know what? I can't do this right now. I have to go." I put another step between us. Fold my arms tight across my stomach.

For once, the *why* doesn't matter. All that matters is how this feels. And it feels just like last year. Like I'm a fucking idiot for thinking Webster was done playing games.

"Aubrey..." He steps closer again.

"I don't want to hear it." All the anger has drained from my voice. My eyes tighten and I turn away as a tear slips out, my mind racing with everything we've been through the past few months...the past few *hours*, even. I stare at cracks snaking across the blacktop, the tiny patch of grass growing inside one of the gaps. "I really don't."

I opened up to Webster, talked to him about my anxiety, all the insecurities I have over being far away from Reese, and it turns out he'll be even farther. He had every opportunity to tell me the truth, and he still didn't. He still let me kiss him and get undressed in front of him and all that time, I thought we were something else.

I trusted him. I thought I could let go of Bayes' rule and just let my life unfold. I thought I was safe from Webster hurting me again.

I was wrong.

31

WEBSTER IS WAITING in my driveway when I walk outside the next morning. He scrambles off the hood of his car.

"Hey."

His car is blocking in mine. I slow my pace as I get closer, stopping between our bumpers. "Hi."

"I was wondering if I could give you a ride to school?"

I've never seen him look so desperate. I think he might not move his car until I agree.

One ride. I can handle that. I'll just ask Reese to drive me home after school. "Fine."

I pocket my keys and walk around to the passenger side door. Webster beats me there, holds the door open for me, and closes it gently once I'm settled in. I watch as he walks around the front of the car. Watch him shake out his hands.

When he climbs in, he starts the car right away and fiddles

with the heating controls. Holds his palm in front of the vent. "This okay for you?"

"Yep." I look out the window. Already this is excruciating. I wish he'd just say whatever it is he has to say.

But no. Instead we drive the whole way to school in silence. Every red light lasts a lifetime. I steal a glance at him. His expression is pained, his knuckles white from his death grip on the steering wheel.

We pull into the student lot and I click off my seat belt before he even has the car in Park. "Well, thanks for the ride—"

"Wait." He scrunches his eyes closed for a moment, then turns to look at me. "I know I made a mistake. Two mistakes. I should have told Holland how serious it had gotten between us, and told you about MSU sooner. But I really never meant to lie to you. It just…got away from me, and I know that's not really an excuse, but I swear—I swear to god I will never lie to you again."

He sounds sincere enough. And deep inside my chest, I feel that familiar tug, the twinge in my heart tempting me to trust him. But.

How is this any different from the ups and downs my parents went through at the end? Things between them were getting better, and they might have been able to work it out if they'd been completely honest with each other all along. Webster lied to me—*twice*—about things he knew were important to me… What are the odds it won't happen again?

"We were starting over, Webster. I don't understand why you didn't just talk to me about this stuff. I mean…the Holland thing…that's awkward, I get it. But you could have just said you needed more time. And then with school…you let me go on and on about how we'd be together, you didn't say a *word*—"

"It was stupid. So stupid." He swallows hard. "I know how worried you are about next year, and I'm so sorry that I made it worse by not telling you the truth about Boston. I don't know why I didn't say something when we first got together… But you were wrong yesterday, when you said I didn't tell you because I wasn't sure we'd last. If anything it was the opposite—being with you feels so right, and I kept hoping we'd reach a point when it would get easier to tell you, but the closer we became the harder it was to even think about, and the last thing I wanted was to hurt you again, or lose you again, so I kept putting it off."

Trust—that's what Reese says is the most important thing for successful long-distance relationships. How can I trust Webster when he's all the way on the East Coast and it's that much easier for him to avoid telling me awkward truths?

I'm staring straight ahead. Because if I look him in the eye, I know I'll think about the tender way he touched me yesterday. How it felt to lie next to him, my head on his chest, his heartbeat in my ear. I'll give in, and I'm not sure that's the best thing for me.

"Aubrey, please. I know I'm asking you to take a leap of faith, but I promise I won't lie to you again. I want to be with you. We still have all summer, and after that…we can figure it out together."

"You made me feel like…" *A fool.* I let myself buy into this imaginary, safe future he dangled in front of me. I actually believed we could be different, that we'd already gotten all the screwups out of our system junior year. I let myself dive headfirst into this, was more open with him than I've ever been, and where did it get me?

We've become the exact situation I wanted to avoid. And now I keep thinking I should have been more careful, I should have taken things slower, shouldn't have been so trusting, and I *hate* that I'm back here. That *we* are.

He seems to know I'm at a loss for words. He wipes his mouth and shifts in his seat.

"Do you still…" He pauses, wipes away a smudge on the dashboard with his thumb. Then he looks at me, head tilted like he's deciding which way he wants to take the end of that sentence. "Have you thought at all about prom? Like…if you still want to go together?"

Sure, I've thought about it. I thought about it yesterday when my mom came home with a new pair of shoes to go with my dress. Thought about it when she pulled out a pair of diamond earrings she wanted me to borrow, because in her words, *You only get one senior prom. Might as well make it really special.* And I thought about telling her I wasn't going, but I didn't, because she was excited, and I didn't want to get into the whole explanation. And because part of me does still want to go.

"I can't."

He stares sidelong at me. Unblinking. Until finally he faces forward again, hands gripping the steering wheel as he nods.

His dejection is palpable. And I don't know how to fix it—I can't give him the answer he wants, but my brain conjures the image of him dancing with someone else and my chest squeezes painfully.

"It's just, prom night has turned into this whole cliché, you know?" I say in a rush. "All this pressure. Like New Year's Eve times a million, because you only get one shot at your senior prom. And I think it's better if we don't have that kind of pressure. Right now. Like maybe we should just take a step back, take some time as friends. Can we do that?"

Webster freezes. Just for a second, with his eyes locked on something through the windshield. Then he snaps out of it, eyebrows raised as he nods. He forces a smile, one that makes his lips look tight and chapped and doesn't come close to reaching his eyes. "If that's what you want."

My hand finds the door handle. I grip it hard so I'm not tempted to reach across the car and touch him. "Great. So. We'll talk more later."

Webster nods—the only response he seems capable of giving anymore—and I open the car door. He lifts his fingers off the steering wheel to say goodbye, doesn't walk with me into the building. As I slide between two cars on my way to the front doors, I check over my shoulder. Just in time to see Webster pull out of his spot and speed toward the exit.

32

IT TURNS OUT being friends with Webster is not like riding a bike. Don't get me wrong—he's friend-*ly*. We are both so freaking neighborly and amicable over the next few days. Which of course translates to totally stiff and overly polite conversations all through Life Skills.

I just wanted to slow things down, not bring them to a screeching halt. But now he's not driving me to school anymore, and he hasn't asked me to hang out after school, either, and it doesn't take long for other people to pick up on the weirdness between us. For Anna Simmons to see an opening.

Anna has been glancing in our direction since the start of class, trying to get Webster's attention. He's either oblivious or ignoring her, so the first chance she gets, she comes over, clutching her yearbook.

"Hey, Web. Will you sign for me?" She holds the book out with this arch in her brow, like it was expected he'd sign anyway. Like she expects him to write something flirty and adorable.

He scrubs his eyebrow with the heel of his palm, then smiles and reaches for the book. "Yeah, of course."

He scribbles out a quick note and tries to pass the book back. But Anna pushes it toward me next. "I'm trying to get everyone in our class. Do you mind, Aubrey?"

I manage a flimsy smile and take the book. The cover pages are already mostly full—I can't find Webster's note, and I can't sit here reading all of them right in front of Anna and Webster.

My pen hovers over a blank space near the bottom. I can't think of anything original to say. So I default to: *You're such a sweet girl, hope we stay in touch!* Which is pretty much exactly why I hate signing yearbooks. They're filled with these kinds of clichés. *Keep in touch! Don't ever change! Friends forever!!!*

Because when you've never gone more than a summer without seeing someone, forever doesn't feel so long.

I pass the yearbook back, and Webster's gaze flickers to me for just a moment before shifting back to Anna. They talk about the all-night party planned for seniors in a couple weeks, and since I'm not included in the conversation, I fold my arms on top of the table and put my head down, doing my best to ignore them.

Which works, until Anna corners me after class, just as I'm reaching my locker.

"Hey, Aubrey." She leans against Webster's locker—he stopped using it again.

I focus on my combination. "Hey. What's up?"

"I was wondering...did Webster ask you to prom?"

I tuck my hair behind my ear. "Yeah. He did. But we're actually not going together."

Anna tilts her head. "Oh, okay. *Soo*, does that mean you guys aren't dating anymore?"

My hand tightens on the lock and I yank the door open. "We're just friends," I say to the inside of my locker.

"Got it." She hesitates, exhales a nervous laugh. "So you'd be cool with me asking him, then?"

My throat is dry. I find my water bottle in my bag and take a sip, then choke on it and start coughing. I look for somewhere to set my bottle down but the lid is off and the only flat surface around is the floor, so I just keep holding it. Anna stands there wincing while I try to breathe like a normal person.

"Sorry. Wrong pipe," I finally say. I clear my throat and screw the cap back on. "Anyway. Yes. Of course it's okay."

"You're sure?" Her eyes narrow. She lightly touches my arm with cool fingers. "Because I don't want to go for it if it's going to cause any problems."

I smooth my lips together. What does she want, a written fucking contract spelling out how cool with it I am? "Yeah, you're totally free to ask him. I mean, I appreciate you checking in and everything, but…you don't really need my permission to talk to Webster."

"Okay." She smiles. "Thanks, Aubrey."

She walks away and I turn back to my locker. Realize I'm holding the door open with my foot. I step back and slam it closed.

"What are you doing?"

I look over my shoulder. Veronica is watching from her locker across the hall. "Nothing."

We fall into step and head toward the cafeteria. She waits to resume her train of thought until we make it to our table, where Reese is already seated.

"You could have played that so much better."

"Played what better?" Reese asks.

Veronica raises an eyebrow at me, and I sigh before launching into an explanation. "Anna Simmons asked me if it was cool if she asked Webster to prom, so I told her to go for it."

Reese stares blankly at me, her fork hovering a few inches off her plate. "You didn't."

"She did," Veronica says as she bites into her sandwich.

"*Why* would you do that? Wait—please tell me you haven't reverted back to using Bayes' rule to orchestrate your love life."

Veronica scrunches her forehead and turns to me. "What?"

I side-eye her and shake my head as I turn back to Reese. "No, it's not—look, I already told Webster I wouldn't go with him. And he's barely spoken to me since then. So. If he wants to go with Anna instead...that's his prerogative." And frankly, he'd probably have more fun with someone else anyway.

"But...it's *prom!*" Reese says. "You have to go!"

"I never said I wasn't going," I tell her, surprising even myself. I'm actually not sure when I made this decision, or why it even feels so important to me, but I'm not okay with sitting at home with my mother while everyone else is at prom. I'm going. By myself... Or maybe with Veronica, if I can convince her to be my date.

Reese claps her hands, and before she can even string a sentence together, I'm out of my seat.

"Be right back."

I cut through the caf to the table student council has set up outside and buy two tickets. When I sit down next to Veronica again a few minutes later, I slide one of the tickets over to her.

She eyes the piece of paper, frozen with a mouthful of her sandwich tucked into her cheek. Finally she blinks, chews. She swallows and cuts her gaze up to me.

"No."

"Please? We don't have to stay the whole time. Just like, a couple dances."

Across the table, Reese lets go of her fork and spreads her fingers wide. She looks dangerously close to doing jazz hands. "You're seriously coming?"

"Yep." If I was having any lingering doubts about prom, picturing myself watching *GBBO* reruns while Webster dances with Anna pretty much sealed the deal. "I'm not going to miss out on anything I'm even remotely interested in because of Webster Casey. I spent a year avoiding him, and I'm not doing it for another second."

"Yes!" Reese sucks in a huge breath, lets it out with a squeal. We both look at Veronica.

"This is peer pressure," she says.

"Is that a yes?"

She groans and tilts her head. "I don't have anything to wear."

"I've got you covered," Reese says. "Seriously, between me and my sisters we have like, a dozen dresses you can choose from."

Veronica picks at the crust of her sandwich. "It'd be a while before I could pay you back for the ticket."

"No way. You're doing me a favor, and I totally sprang this on you, so the ticket's on me."

She wrinkles her nose, but a resigned smile takes over. "Okay. I'm in."

This earns another excited screech from Reese. I grin and tuck my own ticket away. For the rest of lunch we talk logistics, deciding Veronica will meet at my house (despite my warnings that my mother will make us pose for no less than fifty pictures), and that we'll both be putting minimum effort into hair and makeup. Reese arranges for Veronica to come over and pick out a dress after school, and then tries to convince us to join their limo group since the spots reserved for me and Webster are now up for grabs. But since I'm not sure Veronica and I will want to stay for as long as Reese's group, I tell her Webster can take the spots.

We part ways with Veronica as we exit the cafeteria, and it isn't until then that Reese's giddiness fades and she says, "I really am glad you decided to come."

"Me too. I really think there's a solid seventy-five percent chance I'll have a good time."

She tilts her head and gives me a goofy grin. "Eighty percent, easy." She softens and adds, "Seriously though, I know you're still hurting after what happened with Webster—"

"I'm over it."

Reese just stares at me. "Oh, okay."

"I am. Mostly. Besides, I should've seen it coming. Remember when I said it wasn't a family I should get involved with?"

"And yet, you got so very involved…" She curls her lips in and dips her chin.

"Ha ha." I grip the strap of my backpack and say, "The point is…I've worked too hard to let this drama be the only thing I remember about my senior year."

I'm not sure anymore if I'm better off alone, but I do know I'm not defined by who I'm dating. And I don't need a *date*-date to have fun at prom. Veronica and I are going to prove it.

Reese nods. "You're right. Which is why I'm gonna go ahead and say it—ninety-five percent chance of fun on prom night."

"Gotta love your optimism."

I manage to stay excited about our new plan until the next morning, when I walk past Anna and Webster talking outside our Life Skills class. I pretend to be searching for something in my bag as I pass them, but once I'm in my seat, I hunker over my notebook and peek out the door. I slide my chair all the way to the end of our counter so Webster's in my line of sight.

Anna tosses her hair and rests her hand on Web's arm. She says something that makes him scratch his neck and put on an apologetic face. But Anna just shrugs her shoulders and whatever she says next makes Webster's gaze cut to me. His eyebrows knit together, and I'm frozen in this moment that drags out forever, unable to look away from the question in Webster's eyes—until his jaw twitches and he turns his attention back to Anna.

Webster takes his seat right as the bell is ringing. He says nothing to me, doesn't even look at me again for the rest of class. And when the period is over, he and Anna walk out together.

33

A GOOD WAY to get over a breakup with your neighbor is to sleep with your window open, so you can actually hear your ex get home at midnight from the party you weren't invited to. This method is very effective, because it allows ample time to consider the fact that you are polar opposites who had nothing in common to begin with and are probably both better off with other people.

I'm not a stalker or anything. It's just unseasonably hot out and we don't have air-conditioning.

To distract myself from the fact Webster and I have become totally awkward around each other again, I channel my frustration into writing a letter to the administration in reference to the sexist and outdated dress code. Then I clean my room, which leads to purging my closet of clothes I won't want to bring to college. Once I drop those off for donation, I decide I might as well continue preparing for college, and I submit my roommate application, look through the course book, and write up my dream schedule filled with all the courses that look most interesting.

And then, suddenly, it's the last week of school for seniors. Which is good, because I've finally become susceptible to senioritis. In Anatomy, I kept forgetting the names of all the arm bones. I thought Veronica was going to murder me when I filled out our final lab report incorrectly. And then I actually forgot about a homework assignment in AP History last week. I just didn't do it. Had nothing to turn in. Fortunately my grade is high enough that missing one assignment shouldn't really affect anything. But still. It was unsettling, to say the least.

Meanwhile Webster doesn't even show up to Life Skills anymore. Which means I don't talk to him for the entire last week of school, until that Friday, when I walk to the end of my driveway to get the mail just as Webster is taking his trash can to the curb.

We both pause and look at each other for a long moment, before I lift my hand in a wave and Webster makes his way over.

"So…" He sucks in a deep breath, then kind of shakes his head like he opened his mouth before he was actually sure what he wanted to say. "It's been a while."

"Yeah. You sort of disappeared."

Webster winces. "It seemed like you wanted space. I figured you'd reach out if you wanted to talk." His voice takes on a note of desperation when he adds, "But if you *do* want to talk, maybe we could catch up this weekend?"

We said we'd be friends. And no matter how many times

I told myself I was over him the past couple weeks…no matter how busy I've kept myself since that morning in Webster's car, I haven't been able to stop thinking about it. About him.

"Yeah. I'd like that. I mean, I'm sure I'll see you at prom tomorrow. But maybe Sunday we could do Susie's?"

His mouth hangs open. He seems not to have heard that last part. "Wait, you're going to prom?"

His voice comes out strange, strangled. Surprise and hurt mixed with something else—something like bitterness.

I nod and his expression turns sour. He's pissed I'm going without him, which is absurd, considering he's the one who got a new date about five seconds after our fight. Tension tightens like a fist around the base of my skull. My own voice takes on a mean edge as I ask, "Why wouldn't I be?"

He stares down at the crumbling asphalt at the end of my driveway and licks his lips. "I just thought…"

"You thought you'd be able to avoid me there, too?" I cross my arms, hugging our mail to my chest. "Well, don't worry, I won't interfere with your date."

"Oh, now you're mad because I'm going with Anna?" Webster's mouth presses into a flat line. "You were the one who pushed this, you told Anna you were totally fine with her asking me—"

"Yeah, *asking* you," I snap. Heat flushes my cheeks again and I lift my chin, stare over his shoulder. "And you said yes, so…clearly this is what you wanted."

Webster's exhale is heavy, like he has been kicked in the chest. "So, what, that was a test?"

I purse my lips and shake my head. "No. Just a choice."

My mom's car comes down the street and slows to a stop

in front of us. Webster and I shuffle out of the way while my mom rolls down her window and says hello to Webster, who offers a stiff smile in return. Then, once she pulls up the driveway and into the garage, I take a step away from him. "I should really get inside and help with dinner. I'll see you tomorrow, okay?"

"Yeah. See you." Both hands are jammed in his pockets as he trudges back across the street.

I meet my mom in the garage and help her carry groceries into the house. Mom's been trying out new recipes lately (with marginal success), so there are more bags than usual despite fewer people living in this house. While I unload them into the refrigerator, my mom arranges a bouquet of tulips in a vase.

Mom hasn't had fresh flowers in the house since my dad brought them home on their last anniversary. Almost a year ago now. And Holland was the last person to give me any—my corsage from the Snow Ball. This bouquet reminds me of a sunset, deep coral fading to bright yellow at the tips of the petals.

The vase is between us on the kitchen table when we sit down for dinner, and I keep catching Mom smiling at them. She's been doing better lately, the crying has cut way down the past couple weeks, but it's still nice to see her actively happy about something for a change.

And all because she got herself something she wanted, instead of waiting for someone else to give it to her.

She rakes spaghetti around her plate for a moment, then sets down her fork and asks, "How's Webster?"

I glance at the flowers once more and sigh. "I wouldn't really know."

Mom makes a sympathetic face. "When I saw you two talking, I thought maybe you had worked things out."

I shake my head and stab a meatball with my fork.

"I know I'm probably the last person you want to be taking relationship advice from right now," my mom says.

"Actually, yes."

She stares at me for a beat. *"But,"* she goes on, unfazed, "there is such a thing as a self-fulfilling prophecy." I open my mouth to protest and Mom holds her hand up. "I'm not saying it's your fault Webster lied to you. That's on him. But it seems to me you're so afraid of this relationship ending in a way that will hurt you, that you're hurting yourself by ending it before you've given it a real chance."

Huh. That doesn't seem completely off the mark. Still, I don't know how to change what's already done. Webster *has* hurt me.

"I just don't want to end up…" *Like you and Dad*, was the unspoken end of that sentence. And Mom seems to know what I meant without me having to say it. She nods and waits for me to go on. "I've been trying so hard to figure out what goes into a successful relationship, and what kinds of compromises you're supposed to make, and what kinds of things you're supposed to forgive."

"But relationships shouldn't be about what you're *supposed* to do. They're about what you feel comfortable giving another person, and what they offer you in return."

And really, that right there is why things didn't work out with Holland. Because he was never the one I wanted to share with. He wasn't the person I immediately wanted to call when something amazing happened, or the first person I'd turn to when I needed comfort.

But ever since a boy who started out as a stranger moved in across the street, I've known exactly who I wanted that person to be. Webster.

34

THE DOORBELL RINGS as I'm putting the finishing touches on my makeup. I run downstairs expecting to greet Veronica, but instead I find both my parents sitting on the living room sofa. I freeze on the stairs for a moment, my heart lodged in my throat, because seriously, no good ever comes from meetings around that couch. But they're both wearing relaxed smiles. Weird.

"This is trippy," I say, eyeing them as I hedge closer.

"Your father stopped by so the two of you could get a picture together."

"Really?"

"You've got so many big events happening over the next couple months, I don't want to miss any of them. Plus, I wanted to give you this," he says, and hands me a boxed corsage. "I brought one for your friend, too."

I pull out the corsage and smile at the yellow baby roses. "Thanks, Dad."

"You're welcome." He slides it onto my wrist and hugs me to his side. "You look beautiful, honey."

We take a couple pictures together before Veronica arrives. Then my mom takes a few dozen more when she does get here. Veronica opted for one of Reese's shorter dresses—probably because she's too tall for any of her floor-length ones. Paired with some three-inch heels, Veronica is over six feet.

"Um, you look amazing," I tell her.

"As do you."

"Both of you girls look great," my mom says before relocating us to the front yard for more pictures by her azalea bushes. By the time they let us leave, we're fashionably late. Which, given Veronica's hesitation about the night in general, she doesn't seem to mind.

"I thought you said your parents were divorced," she says as we climb into her car.

"They are. That's the most time they've spent together in weeks, actually." I glance back at the house, watch the way my father holds the front door open for my mom, the way she squeezes his shoulder like she knows him well enough to know he needs support today. And I realize there's still a lot of love there, even if it isn't the same kind they had before.

"Well, they're nice. Thank your dad again for the corsage, okay?"

We reach the reception hall across town where prom is being held, and both of us take a big breath before walking in. Then we look at each other and start laughing, because this isn't exactly a life-or-death situation. As we reach the ball-room decorated in black streamers and white balloons, I try not to scan the tables for familiar faces. But I do spot Reese at a table to my right and wave. Unfortunately, it's also the table Sam is sitting at, so Veronica and I head for a different table with some empty seats nearby.

This is the kind of venue where they host a different type of event every night. In a few hours, all of our school-colored streamers will be taken down and tomorrow this room will host a family reunion, or a wedding, or an anniversary party. I think I'm starting to understand what Reese has been feeling these past few months. Suddenly it feels like something big is about to end.

"The decorations were better at the Snow Ball," I say as we sit down.

Veronica smirks, but a moment later, her gaze shifts over to Reese's table. To Sam.

"Why don't you go talk to her?"

She shrugs and picks at a spot on the tablecloth. "Too late for that now."

I take a sip of water from the glass at my place setting. "I'm not convinced that's ever the case." I relate so hard to that feeling of distance and desperation, though. Of pushing someone away so at least, when you lose them, it won't come as a surprise. "I'm just saying, who we are now doesn't have to be who we are forever. People fuck up. It happens. But if you still miss her, I think you should tell her."

Veronica doesn't respond to this, but glances over there at least four more times while we eat. Dinner is already wrap-ping up, so we finish quickly and then join everyone flooding the dance floor. Which is when I finally catch a glimpse of Webster, right as Anna throws her arms around his neck. Hugs him closer. He's laughing, happier than I've seen him in days. Until he lifts his head and he sees me standing here, staring at them like the pathetic loser the old Webster always told me I was.

He straightens, his hands pressing her hips away, putting space between them. Clearly he feels guilty, but he shouldn't. Doesn't need to.

I fix my smile back into place and spin Veronica around. Reese and Kevin catch up with us a little while later, and for a string of fast-paced songs we all dance in the same group. Reese throws her arms around me, and for the length of a ballad we sway around the dance floor belting out lyrics and dissolving into laughter whenever one of us hits a particularly terrible note.

Time slips by and I stop worrying how I look, stop worrying what Webster is doing, and focus instead on how good it feels to just move, to laugh with my friends, to make a new memory.

The DJ announces there are only a few dances left, and Veronica slows to a stop after the song winds down. She chews the inside of her lip. I follow her gaze, which has predictably landed back on Sam again.

"I'll be right back, okay?"

I nod and watch as Veronica makes her way over, hands in loose fists at her sides.

The next song is moody and slow. Everyone around me couples off and I'm stranded, searching for an exit. Then my eyes lock with Webster's again. I don't know where Anna went, but now he's moving closer. Standing right in front of me.

"Hi."

I shift my weight from one heel to the other. "Hi."

"You want to dance?"

In his voice I hear a note of vulnerability, and it softens the knot inside my chest. I nod and step closer, slide my hands over his shoulders. His palm finds the small of my back, pressing me against him. My breath hitches.

I listen to the song playing overhead, but I can barely hear it over the sound of my heartbeat in my ears. I stare over Web's shoulder, eyes scanning the swaying couples around us, but in truth I can't see much. Everything's a blur. My senses are entirely tuned in to Webster—the smooth fabric of his dress shirt under my fingers, the warmth of his palm through the back of my dress, that citrus-and-earth scent of him coupled with a bit of dewy sweat.

After the first verse, Webster lowers his head, his mouth just beside my ear. "You look beautiful tonight, Aubrey."

I turn toward his neck, but don't pull back enough to see his face. I can't. If I'm able to see his eyes I'll read too much into them. Already I'm feeling too much. This growing pit in my stomach, this burning in my sinuses like I might need to cry. I squeeze my eyes shut and press my forehead against his jaw.

"That's probably the kind of thing I'm not supposed to say as your friend," he says lightly. I feel him swallow. "True, though. You're always beautiful."

I can't take it. I lean back and look him in the eye. Webster is wearing the saddest smile.

"Where's your date?"

He flinches. He tries to recover his smile but it's like a flashlight with a dying battery. Only a flicker comes through. "Around somewhere."

"I saw you guys earlier—seems like you're having a great time together."

He stares at me for a long moment, his jaw coiled tight. "What do you want me to say, Aubrey? I mean, is this your way of asking if something's going on between me and Anna?"

"No. I wasn't—" Heat flashes across my face and there's no way I'm not blushing. "That's none of my business."

"Not anymore."

A nonanswer. A blank for me to fill in. And I'm not usually the most creative person, but my mind takes this and runs with it, conjures all kinds of images that I'm pretty sure will be stuck behind my eyes forever. I blink at the floor. Focus on the scuff mark left behind by someone's black-soled shoe.

The song ends, and his hands pull away from my hips like two magnets with the same pole. They land in the pockets of his trousers. My hands slip off his shoulders, landing stiff and heavy at my sides.

"Yesterday, you said I got what I wanted," he says quietly. "But I told you what I wanted when I drove you to school that morning. You just didn't believe me."

His voice breaks and he looks away. When his gaze finally meets mine again, his expression is so defeated. "I messed up, I'm not trying to pretend I didn't. But you're the one who gave up on us. I never wanted that." He shrugs, his shoulders pausing at his ears for a moment before crashing down. "Enjoy your night, Aubrey."

With that, he steps around me, weaves quickly through

the crowd and grabs his jacket from the table he was sitting at before. He finds Anna at the edge of the room and walks into the foyer outside the ballroom with her. I'm stunned into stillness. His parting words echoing in my head—so similar to what he said to me at homecoming, yet so completely different at the same time.

Under my ribs, a dull ache I've carried all week starts to sharpen. A fragment of bone that has finally come loose, scraping against my lungs. My next breath stings so much that my eyes flood with tears.

Reese pulls me off the dance floor, then brings me over to her dinner table. I'm vaguely aware of Sam and Veronica talking in low whispers nearby, but Reese curves her arm around me, like she wants to shield me from the rest of the room. "You okay?"

I shake my head and feel the first tear fall down my cheek.

I'm not okay. And I'm not over it. Because Webster isn't just my neighbor, not just a boy I had a crush on when he first moved in across the street, and he's definitely not my enemy. He's the only person I've ever been able to imagine a future with. The only person besides Reese who makes me feel *more* like myself, like I never have to filter what I say or pretend to like something I don't. He's the person I want to turn to when I'm sad or angry, who I can trust to be there for me without trying to fix things that aren't his to fix.

Reese wipes a tear off my cheek and runs the pad of her finger under my lower lashes to catch my mascara. "You have a tendency to do this, you know."

"Do what?"

She stops fussing with my makeup and looks me in the eye.

"Convince yourself you're the only one who gets scared. But we all do. The way I see it, if you're not a little bit scared of what it would mean to lose someone…then they probably aren't your person."

The bigger the risk, the bigger the reward.

I look toward the doors Webster disappeared through. "I have to…"

Reese nods. "Yeah. Go."

I move quickly into the foyer, but he's not there. The automatic doors whoosh open as I walk outside. But half the dance has emptied into the parking lot now, on their way to one of many after-parties. Webster is nowhere to be seen.

Veronica appears at my side with both of our purses. "You ready to get out of here?"

I nod and we head to her car. We skip the after-parties in favor of hitting up a pizza joint in a strip mall near school for some slices. While we eat, Veronica tells me about her conversation with Sam—they still have a lot of ground to cover, but tonight set them in the right direction. But as happy as I am that it went well for her, the whole time she's talking, I'm distracted, replaying what Webster said to me. Picturing what he and Anna might be doing right now—in a spare bedroom at some house party. I don't even know which after-party they were going to, but I'm debating asking Veronica to drive around to all of them. And then I get a better idea.

I place another order at the counter, and when it's ready, Veronica and I head back to my neighborhood with the to-go box warm in my lap. We pull up to my house, and I smile at Veronica as I click off my seat belt. "Thanks for being a great date."

She nods. "Right back at you."

When she pulls out of my driveway, I don't go inside. Instead I carry my pizza box across the street to stand under Webster's basketball hoop.

It's so easy to fixate on the past. I could obsess about my mistakes forever, pick my memories apart and keep trying to use them to predict the future. But right now I have so much to look forward to—going to Michigan State, taking classes in a subject I love and pursuing my dream career—I don't need to know exactly how everything is going to turn out. I'm determined to enjoy *this* feeling instead. The excitement that comes with endless possibilities unspooling ahead of you.

Though a solid percentage of that excitement is replaced with nerves when headlights flash across the asphalt.

I turn around and blink in the sudden brightness. I start to panic, because if Anna is in Webster's car right now, I will absolutely die of mortification. But when he parks and cuts the lights, I can see that he's alone.

He gets out of the car and slowly walks around the front to me. "What are you doing here?"

"I thought you might be hungry." I close a little more of the distance between us and open the pizza box, lips caught between my teeth while I watch for his reaction.

"You hate olives."

"Well, that's why I only got them on half." I lower the lid and say, "I was sort of hoping you might share with me."

Webster's mouth slowly tips into a smile. He takes the box and sets it on the hood of his car, then turns back to me. "That sounds really good."

I haven't reached a point where I'd consider myself an optimist. I don't expect a long-distance relationship to be easy, and I know it's still a risk. I know we might fall out of love one day. But trying to control for that outcome hasn't exactly worked out. I couldn't stand the thought of losing him when I wouldn't see it coming, so I made sure that didn't happen. And in the end...losing him that way hurt just as much.

"It sucks that you lied to me, Web. And you better not do it again. Like, ever. But..." My voice wavers and Webster leans even closer. "I think I'm ready to take that leap of faith."

Webster slides his arms around my waist and holds me like we're back on the dance floor. "I missed you."

My eyes are still stinging, but I break into a grin. "Yeah?"

"Little bit." He reaches up and gently brushes a tear off my cheek. "Nothing happened with Anna. Nothing was ever going to happen there."

I shake my head—that doesn't matter now. I trust him.

A thick laugh catches in my throat. "So much for our do-over, huh?"

He tilts his head and grins. "At least we didn't wait a year to talk it out this time."

My arms fold around his neck, and for a moment, we just grin at each other. And as his lips meet mine, I'm certain this is worth the risk. Because I'll always want another day with Webster. And then another, for as long as forever lasts.

★ ★ ★ ★ ★

ACKNOWLEDGMENTS

If you're the sort of person who reads acknowledgments, you're probably well aware that creating a book is a group effort.

This book simply would not exist without my amazing agent, Lara Perkins. For a long time I was stuck on a different story, one that was sucking all the fun out of writing for me, but that I just couldn't seem to let go of. I made Lara read that manuscript approximately eighty-seven times before deciding to shelve it, but each time Lara gave me the most encouraging, insightful feedback. When I finally had a shiny new idea I was excited about, she read my messy early draft and immediately found the heart of the story. I'm forever grateful she understands my writing and the stories I want to tell (often better than I do!), and that she's such a constant source of support and inspiration. Also, she comes up with the best titles.

It has been such a joy working with my editor, Tashya Wilson. It's possible she loves my characters as much as I do, and she pushed me to dig deeper into their interior lives, which was ridiculously fun. Thanks to Tashya's thoughtful edits, I also fell down the rabbit hole of Bayes' theorem applications and now have a decent understanding of it...I think.

The team at Inkyard Press and HarperCollins made this journey a delight, especially Bess Braswell, Brittany Mitchell, Laura Gianino, Gigi Lau, Mary Luna, Peter Cronsberry, Nancy Fischer, Heather Foy, Andrea Pappenheimer, and the Harper Children's sales team.

There have been a fair amount of ups and downs since publishing my debut, and I don't know where I'd be without my critique partners, Laurie Flynn, Victoria Lee, RuthAnne Snow, and Mackenzi Lee. These excellent humans brainstorm with the best of them, have stopped me from quitting more times than I can count, and always offer invaluable feedback (and on more than one occasion, a thorough explanation of Bayes' theorem—thanks, V!). In short, they make me a better writer.

Special shout-out to Ashley, my high school anatomy lab partner. I may not remember the names of every muscle in the body anymore, but our inside jokes live on.

Always and forever thankful for my husband and best friend, Jim. He makes following my dreams possible, and I fall more in love with him every day.